Cardinal Red

by

Ross Tarry

Copyright © 2011 by
Ross Tarry
Printed by Minuteman Press
All rights reserved.
No part of this book may be
reproduced without
the written permission of the Publisher.
This is a work of fiction.
Names, characters, places and incidents
are used fictitiously. Any resemblance
to actual persons, events
or locales is entirely coincidental.

Cover design and format
by Genny Kieley

ISBN # 978-098-322-6659

Books by Ross Tarry

Cardinal Red

Eye of the Serpent

Last Cry of the Whipoorwill

Of Mourning Doves & Heroes

Dedication

Cardinal Red is dedicated to
Bunnie, my wife,
and to the
Night Writers
at the Maple Grove Art Center.
With a special thank you to
my daughter, Angela
for the awesome job of
copy editing
the manuscript

-1-

Tuesday Afternoon
August 30th
88 degrees, Humidity 92%

It was Tuesday, the end of August and muggier than hell. Everything steamed. I had taken my gun from the holster on my right hip and put it in the top right drawer of my desk, and rocked back in my swivel chair daydreaming, my fingers laced behind my head, my stockinged feet propped on the sill of my office window. The louvered blinds, the narrow, ivory colored plastic kind, were up. A broken yardstick held the bottom sash open, allowing in the street sounds and the stale smells of late summer. It was the kind of August day Mo would have loved. She would be in shorts, halter-top and floppy cotton hat, weeding her garden, or maybe pruning her roses, her tanned skin glistening with perspiration.

She's been gone nearly two years. Actually, one year and ten months to the day. Seems impossible. The deep-throated rise and fall of a siren of a fire apparatus came lethargically through the window on the heavy, damp air, growing louder with blasts of air horn as it crossed Division, then faded down Seventh Avenue.

When you're young, it seems the days, months, years just crawl by. For some time now, it seems the days flash past so fast that every evening I have to stop and think, where the hell did the day go? If I'd broached this with Mo, she'd have said it was because I hadn't created any memorable memories. She was probably right. She was all about living life.

I sat quietly in the sound of the street traffic and the fading siren, with Mo as heavy in my thoughts as the sodden air. One would think I'd remember her last words, or at least the last conversation we'd had before she died. There had been words, but as hard as I try I can't seem to bring them to mind. Maybe it's a coping mechanism. I can see her though. As emaciated and dwindling as she was, she was still beautiful. But it's those damn other words I remember. I can't seem to get them out of my mind.

It was a late June evening. We were in the hospice atrium watching the sunset on one of her better days, when she was exceptionally lucid, between the morphine drips and the pain. "Law enforcement can't be a reason for being, Darling, find it and live it," she had said.

We'd had conversations like this before. She understood these things. I didn't know anything else. I'd been a cop for thirty-two years. I needed more straight-forward concepts. But the words still haunt me.

The soft whir of the fan on the corner of the bookcase behind me blew warm air at the back of my neck, but it didn't help all that much. I still felt clammy. 'So Vic,' I thought to myself for the umpteenth time, does this fit into my search for purpose? Victor Pittaro Investigations? Doesn't seem like reason enough for being to me. Maybe something will come of it.

"I just wish I knew." I said aloud.

My office is on the first floor of the Division Street Office Complex. An old yellow brick building built in the fifties as a school and rebuilt ten years ago into office suites. There are five offices off of the central lobby. There's Cummings Real-Estate, a mobile home salesman, an insurance agency, a travel agency named "Time to Travel," and mine.

For six-hundred a month I get two-hundred and twenty square feet of space, a mail drop, and limited secretarial services. The restrooms are located off the lobby. My office is second-hand store furnished. There's a gun-metal gray steel desk with two drawers on each side. There's a bookcase against the right wall, and a coat stand where my gray herringbone sport coat and blue nylon windbreaker hang. On the left wall, stands a steel, cream colored four-drawer file cabinet. Next to the file cabinet is the small square maple table that I picked up at a yard sale. On the table sets the Mr. Coffee, the brown-stained carafe half full of this morning's brew. On the top of the file cabinet is a can of coffee and another can with packets of sugar and faux cream. There's two mismatched cups and a short, heavy glass. The office door with its pebbled glass is open, propped against the wall with a rubber wedge. There's no sign on the door.

The call of a male cardinal caught my attention, now that I can hear. I squinted into the smoldering daylight toward the back of the Liggett Park band shell across Division Street. The band shell is set on a grass knoll in a grove of mostly old growth Oak and Maple. Finally, I spotted the dot of brilliant red in a tall Poplar. Always look for the cardinal at the top of the tallest tree around, my father used to say.

Too far away to see the bird clearly, I imagined the red fringe of the crown, the brilliant crimson feathers, the posturing of the proud bird as he sent out his call for a mate. Suddenly, I missed Mo more than

I had in a long time. Cardinals have always reminded me of her, colorful and vibrant, and some would say assertive. I had had that redhead in my life for twenty-eight years and seven months. I was lucky in love, I guess, though not so lucky in the procreation field. I wonder sometimes, what different directions my life might have taken if we would have had had a son or daughter.

On the corner of my desk, the screen-saver blasted brilliant stars. Was Tamara right? Was I becoming sorry I had succumbed to the 'work-hard-save-money-retire-early' propaganda, like she'd said? She was right about one thing. I seem to be floating listlessly these past months.

Across the street, three boys had dumped their bikes and were horsing around on the grass. I could hear their shouts but couldn't make out the words. The hum of the fan seemed to fade in and out, obscuring outside noise. In the early years, hearing protection wasn't required on the firing range. Those were years when nothing could traumatize youth.

I scratched at the back of my head. It was damp with sweat. What the hell am I going to do? Private Investigator had seemed a good idea at the time. I sat for a time, letting that thought fade into nothing. Then sat some more. Sometimes that can be a good thing.

What the hell was that woman's name? I turned away from the window, found my reading glasses, hung them on my nose and rummaged through the scraps of paper and mail on my desk. Telephone bill. Insurance premium notice. A phone message in Kitty's hand reminding me of my appointment with Doctor Preston. A check would be nice someday. Ahh, yes. AARP. Seems like I get something from them at least every other day.

Here it is. Barbara Mann. Can't place her. Should have said no right off, with the Jennings trial coming up and this damn Clyde Adams thing. That old goat should have known that leaving everything to a young wife would set his boys off. Jamie Adams has always been a spoiled, self-centered ass as far back as I can remember. Nothing can split a family quicker or surer than a ten million-dollar estate. My job had been to look into Janice Rue's past, her name prior to marrying Clyde, so that there were no surprises for the defense table. I did, and other than an uncontested divorce, there wasn't anything. Now all that was left to do was testify at the hearing, which at this time seems to be hanging in the wind. It'll feel good to give Jamie Adams a little poke in the eye. Vic Pittaro, Private Eye.

There is a silly retirement gift on my desk. It's a toy paddy wagon made out of a piece of oak with a clock set in the side. The brass plate below the clock face reads: 'Lieutenant Victor Pittaro - Monroe County Sheriff Department - Retired.' The clock read 4:45.

From the reception area I heard a file drawer slam close. "Kitty!"

"Yes, Mr. Pittaro?"

Katharine Hynen serves the suite of five, small, box-like offices from the semi-circular reception desk in the lobby. My office is the second from her left. I can just see the corner of her desk from my chair. Katharine is Spencer's youngest daughter who's just graduated from high school. I've known her since the day she was born. Spence was my best man when Mo and I were married all those years ago.

"Kitty, I'm expecting a client shortly. Leave the door unlocked when you leave."

"Yes, Mr. Pittaro," she squeaked back. Kitty's presence is a daily reminder that time doesn't stand still.

Minutes later I was alone in the steamy quiet. I keep a bottle of Myers Rum and a small glass in the top right-hand drawer of my desk, along with my gun, a 9mm Glock. I could never sit at a desk with a gun jabbing me in the kidneys. I opened the drawer, got the bottle out, poured two fingers of the dark rum into the glass, capped it and put it back.

At exactly 5:15, I heard the chime that signaled the door to the suite of offices. I swallowed the last few drops and stashed the empty glass back in the drawer.

A young woman stopped beside the lobby desk. She looked around, then came to my door. There was something inconsistent about her. Something that didn't look right. She was tall, lithe and blond, and from her complexion, spent as little time in the sun as possible. Her white, long sleeve silk blouse clung tightly, accentuating full, round breasts. Her short red skirt was slit nearly to the indecent line revealing an extremely long, well sculpted alabaster leg. She wore red leather sandals with spiked heels. Her toes and fingernails matched her shoes. A black leather purse was slung from her shoulder on a long strap. At first glance she looked as if she was the proprietress of the corner of Collins Avenue and Vine. The classier part of what Berring Harbor considered The Strip. Don't get me wrong, I'm not a prude. In fact, like that country song says, "I like my women a little on the trashy side."

She hesitated just outside the doorway. I straightened, stuffed my feet into my shoes.

"Are you Mr. Pittaro?"

Her voice was my first clue. It had a hint of finishing school. "Come in. Ms. Mann, isn't it?"

"Barbara Mann, Mr. Pittaro."

I stood. It seemed the right thing to do. "I'm sorry, Ms. Mann. Please, have a seat."

She chose the blue vinyl chair next to the coffee pot instead of the brown one directly in front of my desk, pulled it away from the wall and sat. She crossed her legs, revealing so much thigh I had to force myself to look away. "What can I do for you, Ms. Mann?"

It's funny, with some women it's the ankle or leg, other women it might be her complexion, or eyes, or mouth, the way she walks. For Ms. Mann here, it was her hands. With all that thigh showing, it was her hands that really caught my attention. Her hands were slim. Her fingers were long artist's fingers, the skin smooth and unblemished, perfect nails. The only jewelry she wore was a thin, gold chain around her right wrist.

She turned her head toward the open door. "I leave it open for circulation Ms. Mann," I said. "Plus, we're the only ones in the building."

She hesitated for another minute before answering. Finally she said, "Tamara Phillips suggested I talk to you."

She pronounced Tamara's name correctly, with the stress between the first and second syllable.

"So, you're friends with Tamara?" I had never heard Tamara mention a Barbara Mann, but then I hadn't spent as much time with Tamara as I would have liked.

"We grew to be," she replied in a guarded voice.

I watched her. It seemed like she still wasn't sure yet, so I tried to set the atmosphere. I rocked back in my chair, and smiled. "If you have Tamara for a friend, Ms. Mann, you must be pretty special. She's choosy about her friends."

She smiled back. And for the first time, I thought I saw a bit of fear. "So what is it that I can help you with?"

"Two things. First, I think someone is stalking me and my husband."

"Tell me about it," I said.

"At first I didn't pay any attention but then I noticed what seemed to be the same car around all the time."

"Can you describe the car?"

"A gray sedan. But I can't tell one make from another."

"Me either, most of the time. How about anything else? Letters, notes, strange phone calls?"

"No," she said.

I let my chair come forward. "Okay. When did you first notice this car?"

"About a week ago."

"Did your husband notice this car as well?"

She looked down at her hands. "He's been preoccupied lately. More irritable actually, than I've ever seen him."

"And that's the second thing?"

"Part of it, yes," she said.

"Okay. We'll get back to the stalker later. What about your husband?"

"I don't know. He's just surlier with people than usual. Not with me, though. Never with me. With me, he's like a big doting bear."

"You feel you or he is in danger?"

"I don't know. But he's a strong man, and nothing much scares him."

"And you've talked about this with Tamara?"

"Yes."

"Then she should have advised you as I will. If you think you're being stalked, and you feel you or your husband are in danger, go to the police."

Barbara Mann's face hardened. She moved to leave. "I'm wasting your time." She stood and slung her purse over her arm.

I took a deep breath. "Okay! Please. Sit. Tell me about it."

She hesitated, facing the door.

"Please sit. For now, we'll call it listening to a friend of a friend."

She did. John Mann was half of Mann Brother's Construction in Bayfield. The other half was Cookton County Commissioner Robert Mann. Bayfield is a small community in the southeast corner of Cookton County and is fast becoming a city due to the new Highway 101 loop. Mann Brother's, she said, had a big part of that state contract. Her husband's grandfather, Jonathan Mann started the business by building houses for GI's returning from Europe in 1946. His son Franklin took over the business in the mid-sixties. When Franklin died in 1981, his two sons, John and Robert inherited the business.

"You think his pre-occupation has something to do with the business?"

"Mann Brother's Construction is my husband's life, Mr. Pittaro," she said. "He regards it as such. If a business could be an heirloom, my husband would consider it such. But---"

She tipped her head, smoothed her skirt over her crossed leg then looked up. She spoke with a quietness in her voice. "Two months ago I discovered he had cashed in some securities. Quite a large sum."

"How much is a large sum?"

"Ten thousand dollars," she said.

I nodded. "What was his response when you asked about it? Or, didn't you ask?"

"Of course I asked," she blurted. "You seem to be under the impression I'm some kind of an airhead, Mr. Pittaro. Don't let the hair fool you, John wouldn't countenance stupidity."

I believed her. Sometimes a cop puts too much stock in first impressions. "Mrs. Mann, I'm---"

"John and I were married six years ago," she interrupted. "He's twenty-two years my senior. There are some in Bayfield who think ill of me, think I'm a gold digger. Some, I think, would go so far as to wish me harm. But I will tell you this, John is the best thing that ever happened to me. Do you believe there is such a thing as a grand passion, Mr. Pittaro?"

"Well--- I---" Mo popped into my head. "Yes. Yes I do, Ms. Mann. Listen, I'm sorry for the way this has started out. Please, accept my apology. I offer no excuse for my behavior. It's been a bad day, I guess."

She stared past me, out through the open window toward the park across the street. I couldn't tell if she was going to go on with her story or leave. Finally, she took a deep breath and said, "He said it was business, and it may have been. Three weeks ago last Thursday he was gone before daylight. I don't know when he left. He didn't come back until late evening. That's unusual. He always calls when he's going to be late. He got mad when I asked. I can't remember us ever having a serious argument."

"Where is he now?"

"Afternoons he's either at the new highway site with his brother Robert or at Pine River Estates south of Bayfield. Pine River is a housing development he's trying to get started."

"And you have no idea where he went that Thursday?"

"No," she said. "And there is something else."

She opened her purse, and handed me a ballpoint pen. It was from a chain hotel in Jefferson City. She must have read my face because she said, "Don't even think it." And somehow I knew she was right.

I rocked back in my chair turning the pen in my fingers. "Okay," I said, finally. "Let's assume you're right, even though there could be many reasons for any of these actions. Ten thousand dollars is a substantial amount to be secretive about. Could it have anything to do with the business?"

"That's the only thing I can think of, but it would be unusual. Though they're partners, John runs the business. His brother is the financial officer."

The cop in me thought blackmail? "Do you know of anything in your husband's past that could be troubling if it surfaced?"

"I couldn't imagine what it could be. John is very open and direct. He has told me everything about his life before we met, and I to him."

"We all have things in our past that if revealed could embarrass us." I saw her flinch. "I apologize for asking this Ms. Mann, but is there anything in your past that he would try to protect?"

She was examining the polish on her right thumb. "Last April Robert and Janet-"

"Janet being…?"

"Janet is his brother, Robert's wife." She put her hands in her lap and looked at me.

"Last April, at the Cookton County Cultural Center, Robert and Janet hosted a fundraiser for the Center. There was a man there that I knew in Los Angeles."

She was watching me closely, as if she was defying me to judge her.

"Before you knew your husband?"

She nodded.

I waited. Through the window the thump, thump, thump of heavy bass speakers rose until the vibration rattled the window glass, then faded as the car passed down Division.

"I was a dancer. Clubs, mostly. The man's name is Bobby Rico. He was my agent for a while."

"And your husband didn't know about your time in Los Angeles?"

Her eyes seemed to flash. "As I said Mr. Pittaro, we held no secrets from each other but for no particular reason I never mentioned this man."

A trickle of sweat tickled down the side of my neck. It didn't seem like the heat bothered Barbara Mann.

"I know Mr. Rico," she said. "I overheard part of a conversation between a man I don't know and Mr. Rico. The man, younger than Mr. Rico, was talking excitedly about what he called an acquisition. That it would be just the thing. That the Manley Athletic Club was just the beginning."

"And the club being…"

"I don't know."

I nodded. "That in itself doesn't mean anything. You don't know the younger man?"

"No," She said. "But I know Bobby Rico."

"You think this stalking, your husband's problems, and this man Rico are somehow connected?"

"I don't know. It could be a big coincidence."

"Could be that," I said. "But I don't believe in coincidences."

She uncrossed her legs and crossed them the other way. "This man, Rico," I said. "Tell me about him."

The lobby chime rang. Through the open door behind Barbara Mann, I watched a maintenance man stop at the corner of the reception desk. I leaned forward to hand the pen back. I saw the gun as the man turned and took a step toward my door. I reached for my desk drawer. There were three shots, very fast and a fourth. The computer monitor shattered over me as I dove for the floor. I had my gun in my hand. I kicked my chair aside, met his eyes for an instant and I shot him. He took a step backward, dropped his gun, went down on his knees and fell over on his back, his legs bent back under him.

I looked up at Barbara Mann. Her head was tipped down, there was an expression of wonder on her face, her arms hung slack over the arms of the chair and blood dripped from the corner of her mouth. It took a moment before I saw the red spreading through her silk blouse above her left breast. I got to my feet, shifted my gun to my left hand and felt under her ear for a pulse. It was weak and then it was gone. I tipped her head back. A thin line of blood ran from the corner of her mouth. One of the bullets had struck her in the back of the neck below the right ear taking out much of her throat as it exited. She let go a gurgle that bubbled blood from the raw wound. I let her head fall gently forward, shifted my gun back to my right hand and went out into the lobby. With a soft tap of my shoe I slid the shooter's gun out of reach, sat on my heels beside the body and felt at his neck. There was no pulse. He looked to be in his late twenties, crew cut, and square face. He wore green coveralls and work boots.

Still holding my gun I stood and went back to my office. I was aware of my heart pounding and my breathing seemed constrained. I got the bottle of Myers from the drawer and poured an inch of the dark rum into the glass. I took in a deep breath, let it out through narrowed lips, then took the rum down in one swallow. I set the glass down on my desk and leaned forward, my hands flat on the desktop, my eyes closed tight, and waited for my breathing to come to a semblance of normal. When I opened my eyes nothing had changed. Barbara Mann was still dead and her killer lie dead just outside my office door. I poured another drink, then dialed 911.

I set the phone down easy. "Shit," I said aloud. What else was there to say? There was a stink of body fluid in the heavy air. There was blood all over the place and two dead bodies in my office. The shattered debris from my computer monitor crunched under my feet. I holstered my gun and went to the window. Out on the street, traffic moved along unaware. My cheek stung. I wiped at it and checked my fingers. There was blood, but it didn't seem much. I could hear a distant siren. Across Division, a woman in sweatpants with a large Setter on a leash was looking toward the trees and the band shell where some kids were playing. The dog was barking and pulling against the leash. She was having trouble holding him.

I went back to Barbara Mann. Her head had tilted to one side. Blood was soaking into her skirt and was spattered over the back of the chair and dripping onto the carpet. She was dead I knew, but I pressed my finger to the side of her neck again anyway, then went back to the window as a Berring Harbor cruiser pulled to the curb. The woman and the dog were gone.

***

Doctor Hanley sat at my desk, writing in a tablet and talking with City Patrolman, Charley Daniels. The two EMT's from the ambulance stood at the window talking, occasionally turning to look back at Barbara Mann's body. I sat on the corner of Kitty's desk in the lobby, my hand on the phone, the dead shooter at my feet in a pool of blood. A big Sheriff Deputy I didn't know stood at my office door. It was 5:47 by my watch. The door chimed and Lieutenant Steve Tesch came through the lobby doors, his head tipped to one side as he lit a cigar. He was wearing his tie loose, his shirt open, his gold Sheriff badge pinned to his belt in the way of the big city detectives. Tesch is a stubby man. A good ten inches shorter than I. Bald and stocky, sort of DeVito-ish. He's also an ornery ass, and can sometimes have a big ego, but he's a professional. He had worked for me as Monroe County's only homicide detective for over eight years and was promoted to my position when I left. I can't remember one friendly word between us that was not police business.

"Lieutenant, the coroner wants to know if you want the body removed," Charley Daniels said coming from my office. Patrolman Daniels was Tesch's new son-in-law.

Tesch finished lighting the cigar, took it from his mouth with one hand and wiped his glistening forehead and dome with a stained handkerchief with the other. "For Christ's sake, I just got here, Daniels," he said. Cigar smoke wafted toward the ceiling as he turned taking in the room. "I'll tell Hanley what he can do and when he can do it."

"Right, Lieutenant." Charley Daniels cast a fleeting glance at me and turned to walk away.

"And, Daniels!" Tesch said, pointing the cigar at the Patrolman. "This is County jurisdiction."

"Right, Lieutenant. The Chief says to lend whatever assistance we can."

The room began to smell like a dumpster fire, but hey, I'm not going to get off on the wrong foot and besides it clouded the stink of feces and blood. I stood. "How you doing, Steve?"

Tesch puffed on his cigar, took it from his mouth and pointed it toward my office. "Who's she?"

I looked through the doorway at the back of Barbara Mann's blond head. She might be thirty-five or so. She won't get any older. What could she have done in her life that would make someone want to kill her? "Name's Barbara Mann," I said.

"And this one's your doing?" He jammed the cigar back in his mouth and squatted at the head of the shooter, careful to avoid the pooled blood.

I nodded.

"Know him?"

"Never saw him before."

Tesch reached out and patted the man's pockets lightly, then looked up at the deputy standing at the office door. "Before they haul this guy out check his pockets for some ID."

"Yes, Sir," the deputy replied.

Tesch got to his feet and looked down at the shooter's gun lying on the floor. "A .22 caliber Ruger Target pistol," I said.

"Damned if it ain't," he mumbled, turning to the doorway to my office. He took enough hard pulls on the cigar to fill both rooms with blue smoke, and took in the whole scene. Barbara Mann, her chin slumped against her chest. The glass shards on the floor from the shattered monitor. "Tell me about it," he said.

"I saw him come in. Didn't think anything about it until I saw the gun. I hit the deck. He shot four times from the doorway. Three hit her. Two in the back probably hit her heart, and one in the throat. I think the fourth was meant for me."

"Computer saved you, looks like." Tesch said.

"Yeah."

Tesch turned and stared down at the shooter thoughtfully, the cigar between his fingers. "Four in the chest in a nice tight pattern. Good shooting. Any reason to think you might also have been a target?"

I shrugged.

"You working for her?"

We hadn't gotten that far, but --- maybe it's just my curiosity. I shrugged. "Yes." I said.

He wagged his finger at my face, pale eyes steady. "Vic, I'm gunna tell you this once." He looked around quickly. "This is Sheriff Department business, an' you're a civilian now. Don't forget that."

"I'm retired, Steve."

He harrumphed and stomped through the doorway into my office. I heard him tell Daniels to have the State Police Crime Lab called. I picked up the phone and dialed Tamara's number. After a dozen rings I hung up and followed Tesch into my office. He was looking out the window. A crowd of people, mostly young, milled around the police cruisers in the late afternoon sun. On the sidewalk, two girls had stopped to taunt a shirtless boy on a skateboard. The ambulance had been moved across the street to allow room for the black hearse, which was backed up to the sidewalk. I looked down at the body on the floor in front of my office door. If I stay in here any longer I'm going to take up cigar smoking.

Tesch had squatted beside Barbara Mann, careful to avoid the pool of blood under the chair. He held his cigar in one hand and with the other tilted her head up. He studied her as he would study any object, then let her head slump back down. I knew he would study the office the same way next. He would put himself behind my desk and imagine the unfolding of the shooting. He would study the lobby and the area around the dead shooter. I knew this because that's what I had done as a homicide detective, more times than I can count. And I knew if I didn't get out of here, I would over step. Tesch would see it as interference.

"Steve, I'm going to get some air. If you need me for anything, I'll be outside. If not, I'll stop by your office in the morning." If Tesch responded, I didn't see it. I hesitated for a moment, then left.

I went outside and leaned against the door-jam and watched the crowd. An old habit, watching faces. After a while the EMT's came out with her corpse loaded onto the gurney, slid it into the back of the hearse and closed the door. I felt sick.

-2-

Tuesday, August 30th, 6pm
The air; Stifling and Still

After they left, I went back to my place. I parked my "change-of-life-mobile", a metallic copper BMW X3 soft-top, in the carport. Mo would have smiled and shaken her head at my extravagance, but being subject to impulse herself, she would have understood.

Nisha, my aging black and white Akita, was lying in her usual spot, on the rug in front of the couch catching the cool, air-conditioned air from the register under the window. Her coat is gloss black except for a white belly and chest, a white muzzle and white spats on three legs. She opened one vigilant eye when I opened the door. Her act of nonchalance is an elaborate hoax.

"You want to go out, girl?" Her only response was a slight lifting of the tail and the movement of that one eye. No wasted energy is also part of her M.O. A year ago, when I made my decision to take the early retirement the county offered, I sold the bungalow Mo and I had shared until the cancer finally claimed her, and bought this townhouse. It's on the south end of town, just off the interstate in a new development named Winsome Terrace. There is a lot of green terraced lawn between units, which gives the sense of privacy, but its main selling point was the open land on the back side of the property. I went to the pantry and took the leash off the hook. At the jingle of the chain, Nisha pulled herself to her feet. Priorities.

The population of Berring Harbor is about forty-five thousand. Thirty years ago it was the center of manufacturing in this part of the state. Then, in the sixties, many of the unionized plants moved south where labor was cheaper, leaving an unemployment rate nearly twenty-five percent and a crime rate that rose proportionately. Only in the last ten years have the area's fortunes improved. Unfortunately, in some sections of the city and county, the crime rate has not. That's when Nisha arrived.

A dozen years ago, I was appointed the head of a task force to apprehend a serial rapist that had expanded his area of operation into some of the better neighborhoods both in and outside the city. That's the way politics work here, as in most communities. About that same time, Mo became acquainted with a couple in Jefferson City who raised Akitas. She fell in love with a two-year old female named, Nisha. I hadn't had a dog since I was a kid and had no reason to want one now. But Mo being Mo, using all means of persuasion, including her safety with a serial rapist on the loose, I relented. The truth is Nisha is the most gentle dog. Would she rise to protect her territory or her family in a crisis, I don't know. Of course now, I'm not sure she could. She has severe hip dysplasia in her hind quarters making it difficult to walk, get up, and lie down. However, the only way you can tell she's in pain is by watching her eyes.

I sat at the oak dinette in the kitchen and pulled off my boots. As I tied the laces of the canvas shoes I wear for our duty walks, Nisha jarred my arm with her nose. Cats are patient and studious and have that air of superiority over everything and everyone in their domain. Dogs are impatient and only focused on what concerns them at any given moment. Like people.

We went out the back door, down the three steps carefully, and across the brown lawn. There's a row of a dozen small pine trees along the property line.

Beyond, is an open field grown over with knee-high grass that had that pale, dusty hue of late summer. High voltage power lines sagged from tower to tower diagonally across the field.

Nisha never chooses the same tree. And what the criteria is, is a mystery to me. It may be one of the great mysteries of the world. After close visual examination and an even closer aromatic examination, the fifth pine from the right fit the bill today.

Back in the cool air-conditioning, Nisha returned to the rug in front of the couch. Before settling she sniffed the rug to make sure no other dog had used it while she was out, made three tight circles over it and very tenderly sat. The 'someone's been sleeping in my bed' syndrome, I'm sure.

It felt like the right time for another drink, so I got the bottle of Myers Rum from the cupboard. I poured the dark rum into a tumbler filled with ice. While the drink chilled I went to the bedroom, took off my slacks and tossed them over the stack of cardboard boxes in the corner. I really need to do something with all these books.

I took off my shirt. I inspected the shirt, finding slivers of glass and blood, and discovered the pen from the motel Barbara had showed me in the pocket. I remembered I had picked it up as I was waiting for the police. And I wondered why I had. I set it on top of the dresser with the change from my pocket.

The blood on the collar of the shirt was mine from the cut on my cheek I supposed, but I wasn't going to try and get it out. I tossed the shirt into the wastebasket. I went to the kitchen, got my drink and headed back to the bathroom. I took a long, hot shower, stuck one of those dime sized plastic bandages that you always wonder what the hell they could be used for, over the cut on my cheek and put on a dark blue short-sleeved shirt and gray slacks. It was 9:20 by my watch and I hadn't eaten since lunch. In the kitchen, I fixed a sandwich with thick sliced Genoa, the meat cutter at the market knows how I like it cut, and a slice of provolone and refreshed my drink to wash it down. I wondered if Tamara had heard about her friend, Barbara yet. I carried my sandwich and drink to the coffee table, sat on the end of the couch and picked up the phone. The purr, purr, purr, said there was a message waiting. It was Tamara. "Vic, please call me," she said in a hectic voice.

She answered on the third ring. "Oh my God, Vic. I heard about the shooting on the news. Barbara Mann. I can't believe it. Could you come over?"

"Of course. Are you sure you want me to?"

"Yes, Vic, I do." There was a catch in her voice. I remembered our parting over a month ago, how confused I was.

"Twenty minutes, then."

I hung up, surprised at the feelings that had come back so strongly. I remembered our last and what turned out to be our only real date. We had seen the latest Eastwood movie in Jefferson City and had come back toward Berring Harbor. It was a weekday evening, I remember, and we had finished our Seafood Supremo in the back booth at Geno's Italian Village. The quiet moments had turned a bit awkward, I guess, when I asked her. In fact, the moment turned so damned uncomfortable I decided I had been foolish to think this newfound relationship would go anywhere. She stared into the glass of Chianti finally saying, "I don't feel the same way you do, Vic. Can't we just be friends?"

I buried the rejection that blasted through me deep, I'd hoped, and smiled. "Of course we can." I fear my voice sounded choked. I raised two fingers to Geno who responded too quickly with a look that said he'd overheard at least part of our conversation. We hadn't seen each other since.

-3-

Tuesday Night
August 30th
Raining

Tamara lives on Tower Street, two blocks off of Main in a Cape Cod style house on a bluff over the river that she and Roger bought when they were first married. There's a wide concrete drive-way and a two-car garage on the right with a security light on the gable peak. Three years ago, on the first day of March, Roger was murdered. At the time, he was the Monroe County Attorney. Shot by Jimmie Keenin as he was getting into his car in the courthouse parking lot. Keenin is serving life in Jackson. Tamara stayed on at the house. Her daughter Samantha and her husband live in San Antonio.

It was 9:50 when I parked at the edge of the security light. I got out, set the car alarm out of habit and went up the walk and the three steps to the door. The air was thick and heavy, a light rain had started and it was threatening to become more serious. Inside, the lights were on. I could see into the living room through the lace curtains. I pushed the bell and heard the chime inside. The curtains moved and a moment later the porch light came on and I heard the lock tumble. She opened the door and held out her hands.

Tamara is a striking woman. A dark caramel complexion, strong face, prominent cheekbones, vivid dark green eyes, and dark hair worn in a short, tight afro. Tonight she looked drained. I clasped her hands. "I'm sorry, Tamara."

She pulled me into the cool foyer, closing the door behind me. "It's so terrible, Vic." In the light I could see her brown face was tear-stained.

"Did you know Barbara Mann well?"

"Yes, Vic. Come, let's sit."

She was barefooted and wore black Capris and what looked to be a men's blue work shirt, opened at the neck and un-tucked.

Still holding my hand she led me to the living room. The room was carpeted in light beige, and decorated in what I would call country/modern with blue accents. Table lamps lit the room. There was a brown brick fireplace on the far end in the corner, with an oak mantel lit with track lighting. An arrangement of dried flowers graced the coffee table. I could see the kitchen through the wide archway at the other end of the room and beyond that, French doors which probably led to a porch or deck.

Looking around, I got the feeling that the décor had changed since Roger's death. People deal with the loss of a spouse in different ways. Some feel comfort in leaving everything the same. Feeling the departed's spirit close, out of respect and love, they try to maintain things the way they were before, changing gradually, if at all. Others deal through change, reflecting a new direction in life. Me, I tried to out maneuver the loneliness by selling our home and moving into a townhouse.

I sat in a blue leather lounger facing the windows. Tamara curled onto the sofa and folded her legs up. I noticed her fingernails were painted the same deep red color as her toenails. *Stop with these details!* I said to myself. We settled this a month ago.

"Barbara Mann was my sister, Vic. Or rather, my half-sister."

She noticed my mild surprise. She tried to smile. "Yes, I know. She was white and I'm black. A few years ago I became interested in genealogy. I traced

Roger's family back to the 1700's in England. I think I was a bit afraid to tackle mine."

On the end table next to me was a 5x8 photo in a gold-leaf frame. I picked it up. The photo was of a young woman who looked a lot like Tamara, a dark skinned man, and a child. "Samantha and her family?"

"Yes. And my grandson, Darren. George, Sam's husband, is an investment banker."

I set the picture back on the end-table. My eyes drifted to the mantel where sculptures were displayed. Dolphins, a sounding whale and what was obviously a headless naked man leaning against a rock. "Roger liked Mexico," Tamara said. "Especially the Sea of Cortez."

I got out of my chair and crossed to the fireplace. There were six cast pieces. "You got these in Mexico?"

"No. They're my creations but they're indicative of that area. And he loved Dolphins and the sea."

They were easy to admire, and I did. "So you sculpted these?"

"Yes. They're not bronze. It's a plastic-clay medium, then tinted."

"You've got quite a gift."

"It's not that big a deal, but thank you. It's one of those things that one wishes one had started earlier in life. In fact, sometimes I wonder why I hadn't. Life can end so unexpectedly." She came up beside me, took my hand. "Come on, let's have a drink."

She led me into the kitchen. I could smell her perfume. A pleasant lavender fragrance that reminded me of the first time I laid eyes on her. It was at Jack Kelly's retirement party. Councilman George Procter had cornered me at the open bar. Soused as usual, he slopped his drink down the sleeve of my jacket. Tamara was passing behind me. I stepped back and we literally crashed into each other. I managed to turn and catch her before she tumbled to the floor. I can still envision her in my arms. Get a hold of yourself, old man, I thought. She set the boundaries and made them clear.

She snapped the kitchen light on, motioned toward a stool at the counter, then went around to a cabinet above the work area.

"What would you like? I have wine, some rum. Beer?"

The kitchen area was much larger than mine and it seemed homier. Mine is strictly functional stainless steel. A place to fix a meal to be eaten over the sink or in front of the TV in the living room. Here, you wanted to stay, sit, enjoy the warmth. So I did. I pulled the stool away from the counter and sat. Beside me, the French doors looked out on a black night. Raindrops spattered and ran down the glass.

I settled on rum and coke, which she fixed in a tall glass, then poured Chablis for herself. Her hand trembled as she set my drink in front of me. She sat across from me, reached out and brushed the bandage on my cheek with her fingertips.

"A shard of glass or piece of plastic from the computer screen. Just a small cut."

"I'm trying to sort through what I'm feeling, Vic. Could it have been you the killer was after?"

I sipped the drink and set the glass down. "Without going into details, I'd say no."

She stared at me, her face hard, her eyes still. "What details?"

"Well I ---." I could see I wasn't going to get by with that. I tasted my drink and put it down. "I saw the shooter for a split second before he fired. She definitely was his target. She was hit three times. Twice in the back just below the neck and once in the neck. The shot at me was an impulse shot. I don't think he expected me to shoot back."

She was quiet for quite a long time, her hand holding the wine glass. "I sent her to you, you know."

I nodded. "She said she and her husband were being stalked. She seemed very worried. She said she talked to you about it."

Tamara had put a hand to her face. "Yes," she said, her voice muffled. Her head shaking side to side.

I touched her arm and she looked up. "She said someone was watching her. She was scared. I told her she maybe should talk to the police."

"Did she give a reason why she didn't?"

Tamara shook her head. "She said if it turned out to be nothing, she would feel foolish."

"It was enough to scare her."

Tamara nodded. "Yes."

"Don't make sense," I said, mostly to myself. "So then you sent her to me."

Tamara nodded. "I thought of you."

I looked down at my drink sitting there in front of me. Thought of me. We sat quietly for a while, the only sound, the refrigerator ticking. Finally I said, "Tell me about Barbara Mann."

She looked thoughtfully into her drink, "I have to start earlier, Vic." She took a deep breath and sighed. "My grandfather came to New York from a place called Morant Bay in Jamaica in 1930. He was a musician. My grandmother was a white Jewish girl from Long Island. They were married in '32. You can imagine what an interracial marriage must have been like for them then. My father, who was dark like grandfather, was born and raised there. He served in the army during the Korean War as a cook. After the war he ended up in Chicago where he met my mother, a white Catholic girl from the north side. Opposites attract, I guess. At least in my family."

She looked past me, out into the rainy darkness beyond the French doors. She seemed so sure of herself, and I wondered if that was what attracted me so.

"He wasn't a very good provider, or father. When I was five, he moved my mother and me here to Berring Harbor. One evening a few months later he walked out the front door and never came back. My mother never spoke his name again. At least I never heard her. She only referred to him as he or him."

She turned back to me, "She must have found speaking his name too painful." She gave me a strained smile and reached a hand across to touch my wrist. "Am I boring you, Vic?"

"No! You're not boring me."

She patted my hand. "Thank you for coming over. Well, to make a long story shorter, I found my father a year ago. Or rather, I found his grave. He's buried in Hillview Cemetery in Jefferson City. Who I did find though, was Barbara Mann."

"He had re-married and had a daughter."

"Well, sort of. The Monroe County clerk had no record of a divorce between my mother and him, but the clerk at the Cookton County Hall of Records found six birth certificates that listed a 'George Hobbs' as father. It was possible I had at least one sibling."

I picked up my drink and took a swallow. "Quite an emotional task narrowing that down."

"Well, I had help. I hired an attorney, Jerry Whitfield. Maybe you know him? He worked for Roger when Roger was first appointed county attorney. He was fresh out of law school."

"A tall, red-haired man?"

"Yes. You can't imagine the anxiety, when Jerry called me. Vic, I had a sister. I had to meet her."

"You obviously did."

"This past February--- I called her and told her who I was and what I'd discovered. It took her by surprise, as I'm sure it would anybody. We met for lunch at Chino's in Bayfield on a Saturday afternoon. I'll spare you the details, but I liked her right off."

She paused. I could see her eyes glisten. "Excuse me a minute, Vic." She got up and went down the hall. I heard her blow her nose. When she came back she had a tissue in her hand. "I just found I have a sister and now she's dead, and it's horrible to think someone murdered her."

Her gaze seemed to search my face. "Will you look into it?"

"Tamara, I can't interfere with the police."

"I know Steve Tesch. He'll be in charge of the investigation, right?"

"Tesch is all right."

"Roger thought he was an SOB."

I watched the bubbles rise in my drink. "Yeah, I guess he can be." She leaned across the counter, those dark eyes, those lips, that face, half a yard from mine. Her scent was intoxicating. The scent of a woman. I have always felt that the movie didn't do the title justice.

Her voice was soft but direct. "What if I hire you to find out who killed her?"

"Tamara! I can't."

"Please, Vic. I'll pay whatever your rate is. She was the only family I had."

This is exactly the kind of situation I don't want to get into, I thought. With the county attorney claiming he'll need my testimony in the Jennings' trial for two days next week, and Clyde Adams' estate coming up short by several million. I looked into Tamara's face. Her dark eyes were ringed with red. But, oh well. One is for money, two is for show, and this one is for--- Be honest, now. Shit. I don't know. "I'll do what I can," I said. "But I can't interfere with Tesch's investigation."

Tamara sucked her bottom lip in and nodded slowly. I took my notebook from my inside jacket pocket, found a blank page and wrote:

George Hobbs- Father. Hillview Cem. Jefferson City.

Jerry Whitfield- BH for Berring Harbor.

Met in Bayfield. February. Chino's.

"You remember the date last February in Bayfield?"

"Is that important?"

I winced a smile. "I wouldn't know, Tamara. If I'm going to do this, then all I can do is learn all I can about her life. It's the only way I can know what's important and what's not."

"Yes." She said with a quick nod. "I'm sure I wrote a check. I'll look it up for you."

"Later," I said. I put the notebook back in my inside pocket. "What was Barbara like?"

Tamara sipped at her wine. "She wasn't the flighty person you might expect when you first meet her," she said. "I think she felt that people had certain expectations of her and didn't see her for the person she felt she was. She was very bright you know, but I don't think she had many close friends."

"Did you see a lot of each other?"

"That's a funny thing. After our first meeting in Bayfield I didn't hear from her. I felt that after I had insinuated myself in her life, I wouldn't push it. Though, I had to force myself not to call her. I worried that she didn't believe me, or what I had discovered. I worried that my being black was an issue. She obviously had her mother's coloring and I had our father's. That takes some explanation, you know. We had just met. I'm sure she had a lot to think about."

"I'm sure she did."

Tamara scratched at an invisible spot on the counter with her fingernail, then looked up. Her eyes glistened. "Around Easter she called me. I invited her for an afternoon." She looked at me. "After that, over the months, we became some semblance of sisters. When John would leave on business she would come and stay."

"How often did that happen?"

"Once a month or so. For a night or sometimes two. Usually over part of a weekend."

"Do you know where her husband would go?"

"Business things. I think he and Robert went to Vegas once to a contractor's convention. Chicago. Cleveland once. I remember the time he went to Cleveland because he was supposed to be gone for the week, but he came home early. Barbara and I had planned to go to a dinner theater in Jefferson City. Interesting thing, she was disappointed about the theater but she was glad when he called. Thinking back on it now, I think I envied her marriage relationship a little."

I watched Tamara's face, thinking I was learning more about her than I was about Barbara. "When was the last time you saw her?"

Tamara got quiet. "This past Friday." Her voice was soft when she spoke, as though in pain. "She sat where you're sitting. That's when she told me about this gray car. She said she'd first noticed it more than a week ago when she'd gone to Jefferson City to shop. Then all week she'd had a feeling she was being watched. I asked her if it could be John. And she said he'd been with her a couple of the times she'd seen it."

"I thought maybe John was in some kind of trouble, and I asked her."

"And she said?"

Cardinal Red 41

"She got defensive, said if there was she would know."

"I'm not so sure about that."

Tamara shrugged. "I know."

"And the police?"

"She thought that because of Roger, maybe I knew someone in the police department who could check it out. You know, unofficially. That's when I told her she should go see you."

"Did she seem afraid?"

"Not for herself, I think. For John."

"What's John Mann like?"

"He's an ass."

My brows went up. "Really? You know him?"

"I guess I shouldn't say that. I met him only once. Barbara had invited me to their home for lunch. Hmmm. The first of May, I think. Yes. May first. I remember because he was angry with someone on the phone. Something about a contract that wasn't done right or paid. Something. I don't recall. But it was the way he shouted at Barbara and the housekeeper that bothered me."

"Do you remember what it was about?"

"He chewed out the housekeeper when she spilled a drink. When Barbara tried to down play it, he pitched a fit and stormed out. You just don't do that sort of thing around company."

"In the few minutes I had talked with Barbara it sounded like their marriage was all bliss."

"It's a strange thing. She was dedicated to John. I couldn't see why. I don't think it's---" She paused. I watched her lip quiver. "I don't think it was money, or the country club, or anything like that. I just think she was in love with him."

"You know the first person the police will talk to will be John Mann, if they haven't already."

"And you're thinking you would like to talk to him."

"Don't get ahead of me, Tamara. I don't want to step on Tesch's toes. It's not a big department. If I stay in this business I have to work with Tesch and his touchy ego. I think I'll talk to him first. I'll tell him that you're Barbara's sister, and that you have hired me to look after Barbara's financial interests. He won't like it but that would be better than having him think I was butting into his open case."

Tamara reached out and touched the back of my hand. I let it rest there for as long as I could, until I feared she would hear my heart pounding, then I pulled my hand away slowly and reached for my notebook. "Would ah--- Do you have John Mann's address? If not, I'm sure I can find it."

"No! I mean yes, sure I have it. Just a minute." She slipped off her stool and disappeared down a hall off the kitchen. I got off my stool and went to the French doors and watched the rivulets of rain streak down the glass. It had been a lousy day. Barbara Mann sagging in her chair dripping blood. The shooter dead on the floor. The thick stink of death that I'd known before but always comes as a surprise.

When Tamara came back she had a slip of paper in her fingers and was thumbing through a check register. "Here," she said. "I copied the address and phone number down for you, and, yes, February seventh at Chino's in Bayfield."

"Thanks," I said. I took the note from her, slipped it into the pocket along with my note pad.

"You will let me know how things go," she said. It wasn't a question.

She glanced around. I looked at my watch, finished my drink and slipped off my stool. "I can't believe it's going on midnight."

She followed me to the front door. "I'm very glad you came over, Vic. And I'm also happy you're going to help me. I had a sister from February until August. That wasn't near long enough."

I put my hands on her shoulders, and then I can't believe what I did. I kissed her. On the lips. I realized instantly what a terrible mistake I'd just made. There's a fool in every man and I'd just proved I'm no exception. I dropped my hands, stepped back in such a rush of heat that I'm sure my face was flushed. "I --- I'm sorry," I stammered. "I think I've just made a big mistake." She stood there looking at me. Her eyes still, her face stone. I couldn't tell if the look on her face was disgust or shock. "I--- I don't know what came over me, Tamara. I'm sorry." The words stumbled out.

She turned the door latch. "I think I need to get some rest now, Vic."

"Sure. Sure. I'll call you when I get something."

I turned left at the stop sign at the end of the block, pulled to the curb and stopped and shut the lights off. The rain had stopped. What in the hell possessed me to do that! What a fool! I slapped the steering wheel. I haven't felt such rejection since I was fifteen! But I brought it on myself. Damn!

It was at least ten minutes before the anger at myself cooled. It ended with the old saw 'nothing ventured, nothing gained'. But, I knew better. I turned south, down Ogdon, the street shiny in the headlights. Past the high chain link fence surrounding the construction site of what will be the new wing of Saint Regents Hospital, past Chandler Park, past The Church of the Redeemer, a red stone building built in the thirties. The stores and businesses were dark. The traffic lights signaled empty streets. At Third Avenue, I turned left, then right at Gerard toward the water and turned into the parking lot of Pinkie's Lounge.

Inside, locals stood solemnly at the dim lit bar drinking, most smoking, some playing Horse for beer, some in conversation. Some just staring at who knows what. Maybe into the past, at mistakes, or the missed chances. Whatever it was that got them here on a barstool, on a wet, rainy night. I ordered rum over ice and carried it to a table under a faded oil painting of Venice, so greasy and smoke stained the black gondolas looked a fuzzy gray. I sat with my back to the wall and thought about Tamara, and about Mo, and about Barbara Mann.

It was nearly two when I got back to my place. Nisha was glad to see me. I sat on the back step in complete darkness while she made the rounds, then went in, stripped my clothes and took a long, cool shower while mumbling expletives to myself. I went into the kitchen in my underwear, got three aspirin and a tall glass of ice water, and went back and sat on the edge of my bed.

When you're depressed it's hard to find a bright spot anywhere. I missed Mo more than ever. And this infatuation with Tamara is all one-sided. I should have known better. Plus, there is something very unnerving about a woman being killed as she's sitting in your office. One minute she was alive and talking, the next instant she's dead. In my thirty years as a peace officer, I've seen a woman beaten so badly her face looked like raw meat. I've pulled floaters out of the harbor so bloated with gas they didn't look human. I've seen burned and beaten children, but I've never actually witnessed a person murdered. The strange thing now is how calm I am about it. And right in front of me.

-4-

Wednesday Morning,
August 31st
Steel Gray Sly, Humidity 92

I woke up at ten to eight feeling like someone had beaten me with a club. I think the thumping in my temples is what woke me. My mouth tasted like I'd eaten road kill and my whole body ached. I went out to the kitchen, found the aspirin bottle where I'd left it on the counter last night and swallowed three tablets. I filled the coffeemaker, added coffee grounds, then went back and sat on the edge of my bed with my head in my hands. I like the word pathetic. Seemed to fit me.

I sat, feeling sorry for myself until Nisha nudged me with her nose. "You're right, girl. It's another day."

I pulled a pair of jeans over my underwear and we went for our duty walk, Nisha and I. After she finished, we came back in. I poured a mug of coffee, showered again, mainly to wash the cobwebs from my head, shaved, brushed my teeth and between swallows of coffee, I dressed. When I came back into the kitchen I was looking as spiffy as I was going to this day in gray wool slacks, a pale blue Arrow shirt, open at the collar, and black socks. I refilled my mug, then got the makings of breakfast from the fridge and set it all out on the counter next to the stove. I wasn't sure eating was the thing to do right now, but damn it, I wasn't going to whimper and whine, no matter how bad I felt. I had things to do.

I scrambled four eggs with a dollop of skim milk, poured them in a margarined omelet pan, dropped two slices of whole wheat bread in the toaster, and while breakfast was cooking, got the News Herald from the front step. By then, the eggs were done. I scraped half of the eggs in Nisha's food bowl, put the bowl to cool, then dialed Spencer's number and left a message telling Kitty I thought it wise that she not come in. That I would talk with the management company and get back with her later in the day.

I fed Nisha, then sat at the counter with the paper and took my time with breakfast, testing my system. Nisha had no reason to be tentative, and wasn't.

The story was carried on the front page. The column heading read:

Two killed in shootout

The Monroe County Sheriff Department identified a woman who was shot and killed Tuesday afternoon in the Division Street Office Complex as Barbara Mann, wife of John Mann of Mann Brother's Construction in Bayport. The shooter, a white male in his mid-to-late thirties, as yet unidentified according to Chief of Detectives, Steve Tesch of the Sheriff's department, was shot and killed in the melee by retired Sheriff's Department Investigator, Victor Pittaro.

Shootout a4

I refilled my coffee and finished the article. There was a photo of Barbara Mann and her husband at some society event, and it went on to explain in depth about Mann Brother's Construction's involvement in the Cookton County Cultural Center and other civic projects. There wasn't any other mention of the victim herself. It made me wonder.

It was 9:40 when I left the house and I was still wondering when I got to my office, or rather to the Division Street Office Complex. The building was sealed off with yellow crime-scene tape and there was a county cruiser parked in front. I recognized the deputy, pulled in front of the cruiser and parked. As I got out, John Horton was walking toward me, adjusting his campaign hat.

"A fine morning, Johnny," I said. Thinking positive was the way I was going to get through the day. "This your assignment for the day?"

"Over with, Lieutenant. Just got a call from Erskine's office. Lab guys're not coming back. Gun'na pull the tape and get out of here."

At the door, he pulled the plastic tape loose and began balling it up in his hands. He stopped, turned to me. "Glad you're okay, Lieutenant."

"Thanks, Johnny. But not Lieutenant. Not any more. Just a civilian, now."

The deputy shook his head. "Yeah, I know," he said. He gestured toward the door with his thumb. "You going in? It's a mess in there."

"I know. Partly my doing."

Deputy Horton smiled. "Yes, sir," he said. Then saluted, turned and headed back to his cruiser.

***

Horton was right about the mess. The smell is the first thing that strikes you. I've never gotten used to it. I stood at the corner of Kitty's desk and looked at my office. Except for the blackening blood and chalk outline at my feet where the shooter's body had lain, the dark pool of blood under the client chair where Barbara Mann had died, and the shattered monitor, it was as I had left it. The cleaners had a job to do. I would go see Tesch.

-5-

Wednesday Morning
August 31st--87 degrees
Overcast, Still

It was 10:35 and the traffic was light. I had the windows up and the air on. It was going to be another day like yesterday. In ten minutes, I was at the county building; a red brick, two-story building on Perkins. The public entrance is street level, but street level is actually the second floor. There's an asphalt parking area on the East Side for public parking. In the far right corner of the public lot, a down ramp leads to the lower level and the parking area for employees and county vehicles. There is a stairway against the building leading up from the lower level and a sidewalk. Two black and whites were backed up to the sidewalk in front of the side door to the jail.

I turned in, found a spot between a Ford Explorer and a lemon-yellow sedan and got out. It must take something I don't have, to appreciate a vehicle in that color. The mums and the marigolds that lined the sidewalk to the entrance of the Monroe County Offices were in full bloom. The geraniums had that exhausted look they get this time of year. I pushed the door open. The Clerk, and Treasurer's offices, as well as other County Offices are to the right. The Sheriff's office and jail are to the left. The Coroner's Office and Records are down the stairway.

Rick Stein looked up from his desk when I walked in. "Hey! Lieutenant."

I shook my head. "It's not Lieutenant anymore, Sergeant. Is Lieutenant Tesch in?"

"Sure," he said. "Go on back."

I went down the hall to my old office. I could smell the stale cigar smoke when I opened the door. Tesch was on the phone behind a mammoth oak desk, his holstered gun on the desk next to the phone. He was wearing a white, short sleeved dress shirt with no tie. The top two buttons of the shirt were open, revealing a thick mat of black curls. The stub of a dead cigar was stuck in the corner of his mouth. He nodded toward two chairs and swiveled around, his back to me.

Things had changed, and I wondered how Tesch had managed it. New furniture, new carpet, a water cooler in the corner. There were Terry Redlin prints on the wall for God's sake. He must know Sheriff Jerry Erskine better than I thought. I couldn't get Erskine to come across for more than paperclips. Well, more power to him I guess.

Tesch swiveled back around, hung up the phone and deposited the cigar butt in the ashtray. His collar was dark with perspiration in spite of the air-conditioning. "Been expecting you, Vic," he said, rocking back in a big leather executive chair and lacing his fingers behind his head. There were dark, half-moon circles under his armpits.

"I swung by my office on my way here."

"The State Crime Lab people are going to come back this morning."

"Evidently they're done. Horton was wrapping up when I arrived."

Just to annoy him, I said, "Horton said Erskine called, said the State'es were done."

Tesch let his chair snap forward and leaned over his desk. "Jesus Christ. Nobody tells me shit." His voice had a hard edge filled with indignation.

I ignored his tantrum and went on as though I hadn't noticed. "Horton pulled the tape and left. You ID the shooter?"

He was looking at me, but I don't think he was seeing me. Finally, he sat up straight. "Sure. He had no ID on him so we ran his prints through NCIC." He shuffled papers around his desk, found the one he wanted. "Julius Santos," he said. "Detroit, Michigan. Two convictions for assault. He did two years in Jackson for his part in a robbery ring. Ever hear the name?"

"No."

He stared at me a moment. "You feel sure you couldn't have been the target?"

"Been thinking about that. If it were me, he would have shot me first. He didn't. He made sure he got her before he turned his attention to me. No, I was just there, a witness. You find any connection between this Santos and Barbara Mann?"

"Not yet."

"I'd be surprised if there was a connection."

Tesch's elbows rested on the leather arms of the chair, his hairy forearms raised, his sausage-like fingertips together to form a tent. I'd seen this contemplative pose many times before. "You think this was a professional hit," he said.

"Yes. Though I wouldn't have a clue why. Just a feeling. No identification on the shooter. And the .22 Target pistol is the tool of choice for some professionals."

"If it wasn't you the shooter was after, then why kill her in your office? I mean, shit, if you want someone dead why have her hit in a public place where there's a chance of a witness to the killing? That fact alone tells me that somehow her murder is connected to you. And that raises the questions that I have. What was your connection with the victim and what was she doing in your office?"

"I told you yesterday that she hadn't been there long. That she had said that she thought her husband was in some kind of trouble. That's as far as we had gotten in the conversation."

Tesch frowned, leaned forward and fiddled with a pencil. "So…" he said slowly. "The kind of trouble she'd take to you rather than going to the police?"

"That was her decision."

"Anything in your conversation with her that might be construed to be motive?"

"Not something that killing her would make sense. You come up with anything?"

"None that I would go into now. We've talked with the husband."

"John Mann."

Tesch shook his head. "Yeah. The friends and family we've talked to so far, all say she was a dedicated wife and loyal friend."

"Family, being the brother."

"You realize who Robert Mann is?"

I nodded. "Probably a friend of Erskine."

Tesch looked down and shook his head. "No doubt. Won't be long I'll be getting a phone call."

I asked. "There are no kids."

Tesch sighed, leaned back in his swivel chair and lashed his fingers together behind his head. He lowered his eyes for a moment, and smiled. "You're wrong about kids," he said. "There's a son by Mann's first wife. Jonathan Jr. a senior at UCLA."

"Any problem there?"

"Not that we know of," Tesch said. "We'll get into the husband's finances and all that. You know, life insurance, inheritance."

I had the feeling he knew more than he was telling, but I wondered if his reluctance was professional or personal. "Who you got on it?"

"Danny Khanh."

Danny had risen through the ranks and was the youngest detective in my department. Like me in '70 and John Coburn in '88, Danny Khanh had broken a barrier in the Monroe County Sheriff Department. A dago, a black, and a Vietnamese. When Saigon fell to the North Vietnamese in '75, his father, an officer in the South Vietnamese Army, was evacuated along with his young wife and eventually ended up in Jefferson City.

Danny had been an exemplary young Deputy and when the Detective bureau was expanded, I'd recommended him for the investigator exam. "Mind if I get together with him when the crime lab gets done and you get the ME report?"

Tesch was quiet for a moment. He was watching me close; Like he felt threatened. Finally he said, "I don't want you screwing around in this, Vic."

"I'm not going to step on your toes in any way, Steve. I have a client who has hired me to look after Barbara's interests. Seems Mrs. Barbara Mann had a sister. Actually, a half-sister. This sister has some reservations about John Mann."

"Jesus Christ! Who the hell is this sister? We asked John Mann about family. He never mentioned any fucking sister. Who is this woman?"

A family secret, given her heritage? I wondered. "Tamara Phillips. She lives here in Berring Harbor."

"You have an address?"

I gave him Tamara's address.

"The name sounds familiar," he said.

"She's Roger Phillips' widow."

"D.A. Phillips, sure." He looked pointedly at me. "She's a darke if I remember right. You getting some of that?"

I stared back, feeling a pressure build in my gut to the point I thought my eyes would pop.

"Sure," he said with a lecherous smile. "Can't blame you. A real looker for a coon if I remember correctly."

My trapezoids bunched. I pulled my bottom lip between my teeth and bit down. We looked at each other. Pulling him across that desk by that mat of chest hair and kicking his ass would only get me an enormous amount of satisfaction that I couldn't afford right now. I needed him more than he needed me. I sucked in what must have been nearly all the air in the room and, without breaking eye contact, let it out slowly.

Tesch blinked, then looked down to where he had written Tamara's address. "I'll tell Khanh it's okay to talk with you. In fact, I'll have him call you. No reason we can't cooperate."

"Cooperate."

-6-

Wednesday Noon
August 31st
91 Degrees, High Humidity

I walked to my car still seething. Tesch had baited me deliberately to let me know that he was the alpha dog now. The son-of-a-bitch. I got in my car, started the engine and sat, letting the AC cool me down. But it didn't. Finally, I backed out and left.

I drove down to the park along the river. There were people walking, people jogging, people sitting on benches eating their lunch from brown paper bags. Probably secretaries, mail clerks, title researchers, contract drafters, assistants to the executive assistant. The real movers, the people who made the deals and signed the contracts, were in the restaurants having martinis or old fashions and probably lobster salads.

I found a place in a turnout and parked. I got out and leaned against the left front fender and watched the river. A squirrel came headfirst down a nearby tree, stopped, watched me for a moment, turned and went back up.

Steve Tesch, who worked for me for three years, must have had a hell of a time keeping that asshole personality from showing. Why does that surprise me?

Two women, maybe in their mid-twenties, came by in a fast walk, forearms up, elbows swinging. One had loose-fitting blue shorts and an oversized T-shirt. The other wore the same shirt, but very tight, very short, white shorts. She also wasn't wearing an athletic bra. They both wore silver jogging shoes with a red stripe. Neither one looked my way.

I went back to watching the river flow. The Temperance River runs through the city of Berring Harbor. But along this stretch of the river, the bluff on the opposite side is wooded, concealing much of the city, leaving the impression of wilderness. I've come here often. A woman asked me once if I had felt the earth move. No, I'd said. Of course the setting was different. And I fear my answer had disappointed her. But here, among the quiet subtle sounds of nature, I could feel the calming movement of life.

Fuck Tesch. For now. I looked at my watch. It was 11:45. I hadn't eaten. What now? I could go to Bayfield and talk to John Mann. But since I'm not a cop any longer, and since the man just lost his wife, it might not be the right time. I got in my car and left. I headed down Seventh Avenue. I turned the corner onto Third, parked in front of Cathy's Kitchen, and shut the car off. My stomach grumbled. Damn, I don't know if I can stomach any more restaurant food. I went home.

In my kitchen, I put on a pot of coffee and went out the back door with Nisha. Back in, she settled on her rug in front of the air vent while I checked my messages. There were three messages. The first one was a hang-up, the second was the cleaners telling me my dry-cleaning was in, the third was from Felton Ridge, Janice Adams' attorney asking me to call. I called. His message said he was either away from the office or on the phone with a client, would I please leave a message and he would get back to me. I checked my watch and hung up. It was 12:35, I should know better. Ridge would be at the club having his martini lunch. That was good! Two pain in the asses in one morning were more than I wanted to deal with today.

I opened a can of asparagus tips and drained the water, put some butter in the electric skillet to melt, then went into the living room and snapped the TV on. A man in a gray suit and dark tie was saying that the unemployment rate was down one percent over the last quarter and if the trend continued, the recession would be over by the first quarter of next year. 'Whatever,' I thought. 'Bout right as often as the weatherman.'

When the butter was hot, I dumped in the asparagus. I put two slices of Chicago rye in the toaster. While the asparagus was sizzling, I cracked two eggs into a bowl, broke the yolks with a fork, added them to the skillet and seasoned them with salt and pepper.

Maybe I should let this Mann thing settle for a while. Tesch is working it. He may get it all settled quick. If he does, good. I dished up my lunch, broke two more eggs in the frying pan, scrambled them quickly and fed Nisha. This Jamie Adams thing will keep me busy, anyway. Besides the fat retainer, there'll be a nice check due to me when it's all settled. And right now, the money wouldn't hurt. In ten minutes, I was eating better than anything Cathy's Kitchen would make.

A voice from the living room was saying that a car bomb had exploded in London, killing six and injuring twenty-two. No group at this time had claimed responsibility. Instant World News from CNN. It's damn clear that technology has surpassed our humanity, I thought. The phone rang. I gulped a swallow of coffee.

"Vic, it's Danny Khanh."

"Damn, that didn't take long."

"Yeah. Lieutenant Tesch said I should contact you about the Mann murder."

"Anything from the ME yet, Danny?"

"Maybe later this afternoon. I'll call you."

-7-

Friday Afternoon,
September 2nd
71 degrees

I met Danny Khanh at Chick's Tap on the west side of town. Bar on the left, tables and booths on the right. The smell of fry grease nearly as thick as the odor of stale beer. The television mounted in the far corner over the beer cooler was playing a re-run of a NASCAR race. Danny was sitting at the bar. He had on his work clothes. Dark gray suit coat, light gray slacks, shiny black boots, and a white shirt with blue pin stripes. He'd removed his tie and unbuttoned his collar. I slid onto the stool beside him and nodded toward his drink. He was drinking a shot and a snit. The shot glass was empty. "Pretty harsh. Rough day?"

"No more that usual." His serene, Asian face masked what I knew to be a tough, by the book cop. "One of these and a glass of beer is my limit."

The bartender came over, set a draft in front of Danny. "Thanks Rick."

Rick laid a napkin on the bar in front of me. "Rum and coke," I said. He mixed my drink with a few quick practiced moves and set it on the napkin.

Danny sipped his beer, then turned on his stool toward me. "So, what is it you want to know?"

It was just past 4 o'clock. There were three women in a room full of men. The afternoon rush, with a mix of t-shirts and jeans, and dress shirts and slacks, was building. Chick's is in an older, mixed neighborhood of residential and mid-sized businesses. TungSteel Manufacturing is over on Grand and the new Candle Office Park is across the street. I looked at Danny, then over the bar room. Lights hung over the tables with colored plastic shades made to look like stained glass. There were pool tables and a bowling machine from the sixties against the far wall. I felt as ancient as that bowling machine. Then it dawned on me, I was at least twice as old as anyone in the bar; Including the bartender.

I picked up my drink and took a sip. "Well to start with, who hired the hit man?"

Danny nodded. "Yeah. That would help."

"Tesch said he talked to the husband."

"John Mann, yeah. We found him at a housing development south of Bayfield around 8:30 Wednesday night."

"Pine River Estates," I said.

"Yeah. That's the place."

"And?"

"He went to pieces. I thought for a minute he was going to have a heart attack. Ended up, one of his employees took him home." Danny took a sip of his beer and set it back on the napkin. "I'll interview him again after the funeral."

"You talk to the brother-in-law?"

"Commissioner Robert Mann? A politician? Too influential for me. I'm just a lowly detective. Tesch and I believe Erskine talked with him. What can I say? According to the lieutenant, Robert Mann says he was in Jefferson City at a meeting with some suppliers. My guess is, it'll check out. What's your take on this murder?"

"Someone wanted Barbara Mann dead and they wanted it done quickly. They didn't care where it happened or if there were witnesses."

Danny nodded his head. "Desperate."

"Very," I said. Through the mirror behind the bar, I watched a tall, intense man playing the bowling machine alone. Danny slowly turned his half empty glass wiping the sweat off of it with his fingers as he did. Without looking up he said, "It has to be connected with her reason to hire you."

"Probably," I said. "She thought someone was stalking her and her husband and wanted to hire me to look into it. Conversation never got any further than that."

"Tesch know this?" Danny was staring at me now, looking perplexed.

"Sure."

"Stalking her and her husband. Not just her?"

"Yup."

"Now if we just had the motive."

I wondered for a moment if I should mention her worries about her husband and the L.A. hood. Not yet, I decided. Tesch's people should be able to dig that up. "Yup," I said. "Motive is always the key."

Two women came through the front door. A dishwater blond, wearing a pink blouse, white shorts and sandals. The other, a brunette with a long ponytail, wore a red tube top and denim cutoffs. As the two made their way to the back booth, the room went silent for a moment. It was as if someone had turned the sound off. You could feel the testosterone level in the place rise.

"Someone around here has a connection," I said, trying to get my mind back into the real world. "You mind if I trail along behind you, Danny? I don't expect to find anything you missed, but maybe if we get together and compare notes, something might click."

"Be my guest. The Lieutenant said to cooperate, and besides I imagine I can still learn a thing or two from you."

We were quiet. People stood around the pool tables and bowling machine, sipping on bottles of beer, but it was the few women that were the center of attention. "You married yet, Danny?"

"Not quite. Sherry and I are closing in on a date soon. Probably sometime in October. Maybe we'll fly off to Vegas or something. The Lieutenant said you have a thing going with the Mann woman's sister."

My stomach clenched, I guess my face gave me away.

"Vic, I'm sorry if I'm out of line."

"Don't worry about it. It's not like he thinks."

Danny stared at me for a moment then nodded perceptibly. He picked up his beer and sipped a little then put the glass down. "I hear they put the funeral off until Monday morning to give the step-son time to fly in from Los Angeles."

"Yeah. You're going to the funeral, I assume?" I asked.

"I'll be there. For no other reason than to see who shows up."

We sat for a while. I nursed my drink. Danny Khanh was a good cop and I was sure he wouldn't miss anything. I didn't want to give the impression I was pushing. "I really appreciate you letting me trail along, Danny."

Danny drank the remainder of his beer and got up from his stool to leave. He put his hand on my shoulder. "Good to see you, Vic. You come up with anything, keep me in mind. I'll do the same."

He started for the door then stopped and turned. "Tesch never mentioned the stalking; to me anyway."

"Tesch likes to keep things close to his belt," I said.

"I guess," he said.

Now it was my turn to nod. After Danny left, one of the women came over and slipped between two of the stools on my right. It was Tube Top. She had put a lot of effort on her tan and smelled fresh, of soap and shampoo. The blessing of air-conditioning. From home to car, to Chick's Tap in 90 degree heat and not a drop of perspiration to offend. She...glanced sideways at me and smiled as she slid an empty beer bottle on the bar. Sure, I thought, tease the old guy. The bartender came over, took the empty and replaced it with another. As she picked up her change she smiled at me again, turned and walked away carrying her scent away with her. I turned and watched. She knew she looked good, and she knew that I thought so, too. No harm done, for either of us. Good legs, though. I caught the bartender's eye and ordered another rum and coke. It was too late to call Felton Ridge and I had nothing pressing.

I had been thinking of putting a small cedar deck on the back of my home where I could sit and watch the birds. You know, bird feeders, a stone birdbath, maybe a plant or two. And one of those Adirondack chairs. Where had I seen the one that rocked? It seemed appropriate in my advancing age. I turned and looked at the back booth. The two twenty-something's in work jeans and muscle shirts that had joined the blond and Tube Top had the two women laughing. I turned back to the bar and drank about half of my drink. "Probably a dirty joke," I said.

The bartender looked up from his glass washing. "What?"

"Oh, nothing. Just feeling my age."

-8-

Saturday, September 3rd
Late Morning 71 degrees
Blue Sky
High Cirrus Clouds.

I knew where County Road 7 crossed State Highway 29, just north of Bayfield. I guessed and turned north on 7, toward what I knew was the river. I checked the odometer and my watch. My watch said 2:10. I passed a farmhouse about every half mile or so, most were quiet with kind of an aged look, machinery at ease in the yards, weathered out buildings. Over a rise in the road and off to the right a combine, spewing a dust of chaff, ate its way through a field of wheat. I had gone 5.3 miles when I came to Greenhaven Way. I had guessed correctly.

Greenhaven Way was a series of 'S' curves through a conifer forest, with a house built on the inside of each bend. There were no mailboxes, only gold numbers affixed on a short wooden post at the edge of each driveway. I was a car length past 1620 before I saw the number. I backed up. I couldn't see the house from the road. I turned in. The river rock driveway curved through an oak and maple canopy for fifty yards where the rock changed to concrete. Pale yellow birch leaves fluttered across the drive. The first frost could be only weeks away.

The two-story brick house was the color of sandstone. There were low green shrubs along the front, and taller ones along the side of the house that I could see. A flagstone walk led up to the wide glass entryway. There was a granite fountain on the edge of the spacious lawn. A dark gray SUV with 'Mann Brother's Construction' stenciled in silver on the door, was parked in front of the attached three-car garage. The garage door nearest the house was open and inside was a silver Mercedes. I parked beside the SUV, got out, slipped on my gray sport-coat and walked up the walk. I punched the doorbell and could hear a chime from somewhere inside. I waited and checked my watch. I punched the doorbell again and looked around. The lawn needed cutting. The next time I punched the bell, the door opened.

At first glance, John Mann looked taller than he really was, but I had him by at least two inches. It was his build. Narrow waist. Thick and broad from the waist up like he had been a body builder at one time, though age had softened him a little around the stomach. His hair was the color of polished pewter and worn in a crew cut. He had a square, aged face and his coloring was a deep leathery brown, like a man who'd spent his life working outdoors. He wore dark slacks, slippers and a light blue short-sleeved shirt with sweat stains under the arms and around the open collar. He hadn't shaved too recently.

I introduced myself. He looked hard at me as if he was seeing something he didn't like, then turned away. I took it to mean I was free to enter, and did. The floor of the foyer was red field stone. There was an oak staircase with an oak railing in the center with a hallway on either side. To the left was a study; To the right was the living room. Straight down the hall was the dining room. I followed him into the study.

"If you hadn't phoned, Pittaro, I was going to call on you," he said. His face was puffy. He seemed nervous or maybe shaky, then I saw the tumbler of melting ice on the end table beside the recliner and the Jefferson City News with a photo of Barbara Mann and an article on the murder.

He picked up the glass and went to the bar. "Fix you a drink?"

"Sure."

"Brandy all right?"

"Sure." I looked around the room. There was a fireplace in one corner with photographs of him and Barbara Mann on the mantel and more pictures on the desk. To the right was a wall of nearly all windows and glass doors that looked out on a flower garden, and a tree line beyond. The study was a very light beige with a hardwood floor. There was an area rug with leather furniture the color of soft sandalwood, arranged around it. On the wall over the sofa was a painting, a winter scene with two wolves. There was a floor to ceiling bookcase and a computer desk. I checked out the bookcase. There was Hemmingway and Steinbeck. There was J.D. MacDonald and Frost. There was Nichols and Keats. A man of many interests.

He brought the drinks back. Mine in an old fashion glass, his in the tumbler. He handed me mine and motioned me to sit. I sat on the leather sofa. The newspaper and various magazines were strewn across the coffee table and over the floor between us. Forbes, Architectural Digest, Newsweek, Discover, Golf Digest. It was quiet. I glanced down at the front page of the newspaper. I'd done this a hundred times before. "I'm sorry about your wife," I said. I'd said that hundreds of times, about wife, husband, mother, father, son, daughter; fill in the blank. It never got any easier.

"I know you've talked to the police, but I thought you might answer a few questions I have."

Mann swallowed nearly half his drink, then very deliberately set the glass on the end table and sat back. His eyes, red and tired looking, were steady on me. "Not 'ntil you ansher my questions," he said. His 'S's shushed as he spoke. "Barbara was killed in your office. I want to know what the fuck my wife wush doing in your office."

I realized he was more than a little drunk and more than a little angry. On the other hand, I don't blame him. I would be too, if I was him. I tasted my drink. It was strong. "She was worried. She thought she was being watched," I said. "She had a feeling you were in some kind of trouble." It wouldn't hurt to make it sound a little dramatic.

Mann was silent, his gaze steady on me.

"She wanted me to look into it," I said. I took another gulp of my drink and wondered if Mann was too drunk to be offended if I got up and added some water. "Are you?"

"Why would she think I was in trouble?"

"You haven't answered my question, but I'll give you that. First, our conversation had just begun. She mentioned some securities that had been cashed in. She also mentioned unusual behavior by you, namely unexplained absence. I'm sorry, but that's as far as we got."

Mann looked past me out through the big plate glass window toward the garden. There were steel rods with bird feeders hanging from them and birds fluttering around the feeders, but I knew he wasn't looking at the birds. Finally he said, "I'm not in any trouble and my wife's dead. So what's your interest?"

"Tamara Phillips asked me to look into her sister's murder."

He gave me a sharp look. "The black woman?" He asked, his face growing red. "What the hell is her interest?"

"Sisterly, I would guess." I wondered why I was trying so hard not to aggravate him.

"Half-sister. If it's true."

"Right."

"Well?"

"They had just gotten to know each other. Other than that, I wouldn't know. I think she would just like to find out who killed Barbara and why." His look told me he didn't really care what I, or Tamara thought.

"It's none of her god damn fucking business."

This wasn't going very well. I put my half-finished drink on the coffee table and moved to the edge of the cushion. "I'm sure the Sheriff's investigator inquired into you and your wife's relationship?"

He looked at me. I couldn't tell if it was hate, anger, or grief in his face. "That'sh none of your fucking biznish," he said.

I tried staring him down. Finally I said, "Let's try this. Someone hired a shooter to kill your wife. Is there anyone that you know that would want your wife dead?" My question seemed to shake him. His red eyes looked a little moist.

He stared blankly down at the floor, and after a long pause, slowly shook his head. "No," he said in nearly a whisper. "No."

"You two met in Las Vegas, I understand. When was that?"

He didn't answer. I could barely see his chest moving. I wasn't going to get anything more out of him. Not that I got anything anyway. I took a card out of my coat pocket and laid it on the coffee table.

"You think of anything you haven't told the police, call me. I'll show myself out." I stopped in the hallway and looked back. Mann hadn't moved. My impression was, he had nothing to do with his wife's murder. I left.

-9-

The Funeral
Monday am September 5th
Damp, 68 degrees

We were at Saint Francis de Sales cemetery. There was not a speck of blue or a hint of a sunbeam in the sky. I, in my black trench coat, stood to the right and slightly behind Tamara, listening to Father Bennett's prayer and trying to be aware of the small group of mourners standing around the casket. John Mann stood beside Father Bennett. Deep grief ages a person, if only temporarily. Mann looked ten years older than he did only two days ago. I knew now, with certainty, that he had nothing to do with his wife's murder.

A man I guessed to be John Mann's brother, Robert stood at the foot of the coffin beside a thin, dark haired woman in a long dark coat. A young man maybe twenty-one, twenty-two who looked to be a young version of John Mann. There were others, a heavy set balding man in a gray suit, a woman, maybe in her fifties, dressed in dark slacks and a mid-length coat with a fur collar, a young man with a small goatee wearing a leather bomber jacket. Still others. Associates. Employees. Extended Family. Hard to tell which. Danny Khanh, standing some distance away caught my eye, nodded toward Tamara and smiled.

It had been a policy that I had instated in homicide cases years ago; A Sheriff's detective would attend the funeral of the murder victim. Part of the theory that you never know what you know until you know it, so observe everything. There's a pattern to all human behavior. The solution to the crime, or any question for that matter, is to understand the pattern.

Father Bennett ended the service with prayer and a blessing and with guilt, I made the sign of the cross. It had been a long time since I had attended mass and I wasn't sure I had a right to the blessing.

The mourners dispersed quickly without approaching John Mann, who stood stone cold, staring out at the hills beyond the field of gray granite headstones. The dark haired woman and the man I assumed was the brother, approached Father, said something I couldn't hear then turned away, leaving Tamara, me, and Mann alone at the grave. Behind me cars started. I looked around and saw Danny was gone. I knew he had taken photos and would spend the day trying to identify all the mourners. I touched Tamara's elbow and she turned to me. Her eyes were red and wet. "Let's go," she said softly.

Most of the cars had wound their way through the cemetery and filed out through the iron gate leaving only two vehicles left. A black Lincoln and behind it, my BMW. When we walked past the Lincoln, I saw that someone in a dark suit was behind the wheel. I pressed the button on my key chain unlocking my car doors, and heard my name called. Behind me, John Mann was coming through the headstones.

"Pittaro," he snarled. "I need to talk to you."

Tamara stood with one hand on the open door, the other on my arm. "John," she said, as he stopped in front of us. "I wish there was something I could say."

His face was as gray as cast iron and just as hard, his eyes, dark and cold as if something raged behind them. His breathing was deep and seemed to come out in a low growl in the way an animal would send a warning.

He looked at Tamara and his eyes seemed to soften, but only for an instant before he focused back on me. "Pittaro," he said, there was white spittle at the corners of his mouth. "They tell me you're good at what you do."

"Who's they?"

"Never mind. I checked on you. You have a reputation for being tenacious. I want you to find out who hired her killer."

"Sheriff's working on it, John."

He shook his head violently. "No. That ass hole couldn't find a peter pan in a whore house. I want you on it."

John Mann looked at Tamara. "I understand he's working for you. Good. As of now he's also working for me. I'll cover any costs above what you're paying him."

"Do I have a say?" I asked.

Mann stared at me and shook his head slowly from side to side. "No," he said. "How much for a retainer?"

I told him.

"The check," he said, "will be in the mail in the morning." He turned around and walked to where the Lincoln sat. He opened the passenger side door, stopped and looked back. His tone had softened only slightly as he said, "Find out who killed her, Pittaro."

-10-

Tuesday, 10 am,
September 6th
58 Degrees with high of 70
Wind from the NW

I was up early, swallowed a half of a cup of reheated coffee, put on my blue nylon windbreaker and was out the door with Nisha as the sun was cresting in a clear, cloudless sky. Down Wilson, right on Clifton, to Pinewood and through Moore Park. The air was cool. The leaves on the poplar and birch had started to turn yellow and too soon would litter the lawns and sidewalks. The seasons seem to come around faster lately. We stopped to check the bank along Rice Creek where it goes under Gardner for any new or interesting animal scents. Then back west on Hampton to Cevert and right on Wilson. Two miles. Not a heavy workout, but better than nothing. I really should think about a health club.

After fresh water and food for Nisha, I brushed my teeth, showered and shaved. I slipped on a clean pair of jeans, and a blue cotton shirt, then pulled on my boots, clipped my gun to my belt and got my brown suede jacket from the closet. "I'll be back around noon, girl," I said to Nisha. She looked at me as though she understood, and I wasn't too sure she didn't. In the car, I checked my watch, time for one stop.

I stopped at the Stop and Go on the corner of Perkins and 11th Ave, got a black coffee and two fried doughnuts to eat on the way, and headed downtown.

Berring Harbor is on a wide bend of the Temperance River. It began life as a water stop on the St. James and Western railroad. In 1851, the railroad built a spur track off the main line that served railroad owned stock pens. The town was incorporated in 1858. There is nothing left of the original town now; Or the rail yard, or the packing plant, or the grain elevators. Most of the citizens wouldn't know where the pens had been, even though the city celebrates its heritage with Stock-Yard Days over the first weekend in September with a pageant at the high school and a parade.

There is an insurance company, Midwest Life, occupying that parcel now; A whole campus of glass and gray stone buildings, of green lawn, and islands of shrubbery, and mature trees. There's a software company, and mail-order warehouse. The mail-order warehouse has recently built a new building off the interstate on the west edge of the city behind the Berring Harbor Mall, across County Road 15 from the Berring Harbor Business Center.

Jerry Whitfield has a little office next to B's Breakfast Grill on Old Main Street in the 'left behind part' of the city. Large gold stick-on letters on the plate glass window next to the door said, Attorney at Law. Over the past few years, there has been a movement by some of the local business' to spruce up the neighborhood, hence the gold lettering.

I parked across the street in front of the Tae Kwon Do Center, got out, brushed the doughnut crumbs from my shirt and crossed the street.

I'd seen Whitfield around the courthouse. He's a tall, slim man with pale skin, freckles, and a lot of red, curly hair. Sort of reminded me of Raggedy Ann. He got up from behind his desk when I came in. "Vic Pittaro," he said. "It took me a few minutes to put a name on a face when you called. Sheriff's Department, right?"

He was wearing a light blue Anchor button-down shirt with a red tie, charcoal slacks and black tassel loafers. He gave me the practiced smile that I assumed he uses on all prospective clients. When he reached his hand out I noticed the sleeves were a little short. We shook. His grip was a bit too reassuring, a lawyer's grip.

"Retired," I said. "I do private work, now."

"I read that in the paper. I'll keep that in mind. I might have some occasional work for you." His look turned deeply sincere. "You mentioned Tamara Phillips over the phone. Terrible thing about her sister. I'm sure Tamara's devastated."

"Yes," I said.

There was a dead spot in the conversation, as if he was trying to read something into my short response. I let it lay.

"Well," he said. "I haven't had breakfast yet. What say we go next door to B's and get a bite? We can talk over some bacon and eggs."

"Sure," I said.

B's is a small, narrow place that had all the smells of breakfast. A counter ran from the plate-glass window to the back, along the right wall with maybe eight stools covered in red vinyl along the front. Several of the vinyl seats were cracked, one had a pie-shaped piece of red plastic missing. The cash register was on the near end of the counter with the cooking area behind. There were two doors on the back wall. One said 'Restroom', the other door was open and looked to be storage and where the dishes were done. The woman in a white frock and equal amounts of gray and black in her hair, was putting serious effort in scraping the grill. I assumed she was "B".

There were four tables with chairs along the other wall. The walls were bare. No prints, no pictures, no decorations to spoil the ambience. The restaurant was quiet. There were two men at the far stools nursing mugs of coffee. One had on denim coveralls and a plaid shirt. The other one wore work shoes, jeans and a white t-shirt with the sleeves cut off, to display well-developed biceps and pectoral muscle.

"I'm surprised you have no girl Friday to answer a bank of phones and such," I said as we sat at the first table.

Whitfield chuckled. "After Roger Phillips' murder I left the prosecutor's office and went west. I tried the big law office route."

The large bosomed woman that had been scraping the grill came with water, two cups and a pot of coffee, and set them on the table. She had a pleasant earthy face, no makeup. The letter 'B' was embroidered on her smock, over her left breast. She greeted Whitfield and looked at me. "What's the 'B' stand for?" I asked.

She smiled. "Depends on my mood."

"We'll try to be good," I said.

She took our orders. Whitfield ordered French toast and sausage. I ordered whole-wheat toast. "I didn't like the politics of the big time law office," Whitfield said, "or the fact I didn't have a choice of clients."

I poured the coffee and added a dollop of water in mine to cool it. Whitfield added cream and three packets of sugar to his and began to stir. "So, I moved back here. I have a girl, Sandy, comes in once or twice a week to do billing and tidy up my mess if she can get someone to watch her kids. I take the clients I want and pass on the others."

I sipped at my coffee. "Sounds perfect to me."

Whitfield put his spoon down and leaned his elbows on the table. "I know how thrilled Tamara was to discover she had a sister." He shook his head. "It's tragic, is what it is. A shame." He drank some coffee. "Anything I can do to help Tamara. What can I do for you?"

I tested my coffee and put the cup down. "What can you tell me about Barbara Mann?"

"Barbara Mann? Not an awful lot. Tamara found a birth certificate in Jefferson County Records when she was searching for something on George Hobbs, Tamara Phillips' father. She asked me, or rather hired me to look into it. The child's name listed was Barbara Jean Kaine. Turned out Hobbs had a daughter with another woman, and," Whitfield flipped his hands. "Voilà. Barbara Mann."

"Amazing. I'm sure you vetted her?"

"Yes. The internet. Once I had her Social, it didn't take long to come up with Barbara Kaine Mann. When I told Tamara, she asked me to look the woman up. I arranged to talk with her. I think Tamara wanted to be sure before she committed herself, you know what I mean? Discovering she had a sibling?"

I nodded. "Fair job investigating, for an attorney."

"Easy enough, now days. But I can tell you, I felt like I did a good thing bringing Tamara and her sister together."

Whitfield looked past me.

I picked my cup up and blew across the top. "What was the other woman's name?"

"Barbara's mother? Don't recall off hand. It's in the file, I'm sure. I'll get it for you. Listen--- I understand you taking a personal interest. She was killed in your office, and from what I've read in the paper, you're damn lucky to be alive."

I shook my head. "If I'd been his target, I probably wouldn't be." I sipped my coffee, and put the cup down. "John Mann hired me to look into Barbara's murder."

"I see. How the police doing with it?"

'B' came with our breakfast and a reed basket filled with an assortment of those little plastic cups of jelly. Whitfield proceeded to flood his French toast and sausage with syrup. I found grape jelly and peeled it open and went to work on my toast. "So far all they've found out, is the shooter's name; Julius Santos, a gunnie out of Detroit," I said.

"Yeah, I heard that. So the question is, who hired him?" Whitfield cut off a corner of his grilled toast, slathered it in the syrup on his plate and forked it into his mouth.

A woman came in and stood at the cash till. She had a lot of auburn hair. Her slacks were dark, black or a very deep blue, and covered a well-shaped bottom. 'B' turned from the grill to the register.

"I'm surprised," I said. "I didn't think the Sheriff's department had released any details about the shooter."

Whitfield swallowed, sipped his coffee. "Ha," he said. He wiped his mouth with a paper napkin. "Courthouse grapevine, Vic. Very efficient."

I nodded. He wolfed another bite of french toast. Maybe he was afraid I was going to steal some. "What can you tell me about Barbara?" I asked

He chewed, swallowed, and gulped a swallow of coffee. "I'll get you a copy of my file, though there's not much to it."

I ate some toast. "So how did you come to get hired by Ms. Phillips?"

"I knew Tamara when I worked for her husband, Roger in the County Attorney's office." He displayed his lawyer smile. It was then I realized, though he was talking to me, he wasn't looking at me. He was looking past me at the woman in the tight pants. I drank some coffee.

We sat that way for several minutes. When the woman left, Whitfield went back to his french toast, then focused his attention on the sausage links. When he finished, he looked up at me. "After Roger was murdered, I thought now's my chance to strike out on my own. big mistake," he said. "I moved back to Berring Harbor just after last Christmas. I think it must have been maybe the second week of January. I was in the courthouse and ran into Tamara."

'B' came over and refilled his cup. She looked at me. I shook my head and put my hand over my cup. She laid the check on the table and walked away. I picked the check up.

I watched him stir three packages of sugar into his coffee. The two bodybuilders paid their check and left.

"We talked for a while in the hall," Whitfield said. "Mostly about Roger and that she was doing some genealogy on her family. I told her I'd just moved back and had opened an office and was hoping for a client or two. Now that I think of it, she probably knew I needed the business. She probably took pity on me when she asked me to try and locate the person who she thought might be her half-sister. I mean, I'm mainly an attorney."

Outside, on the street, the traffic ranged from heavy trucks, semi-trucks, pickups, the occasional automobile. A city bus lumbered past, heading toward the heart of town. This was the part of Berring Harbor that used to be the heart of the young city, now gone to neglect.

"What was your impression of Barbara Mann?"

"Oh, I never met her in person. Just gave the information to Tamara."

"So, you never actually met her?"

He shook his head. "Nope. Talked to her once over the phone."

I paid the check, left a tip for 'B' and we left. "Couple more things, Jerry," I said outside the café.

"Sure."

"John Mann, the victim's husband. Do you know him?"

"Mann Construction. Know of him. That's all."

"Jamie Adams. Name familiar?"

He shook his head. "Nope."

"Bobby Rico?"

He shook his head, again. "Sorry," he said. "What's with this Rico and the other one? What was that name?"

"Adams. Just names that came up," I said.

"Nope," he said. "Wish I could help, but anyway, thanks for breakfast."

"Sure." I said. We shook hands and I left.

-11-

Tuesday September 6th
4:20 pm, 77 degrees
Humidity 89%
Possible Thunder Storm

It was 4:40 pm when I got back to my office. I parked in my spot in the back and walked around to the front. The air was heavy and still, giving a sodden feel to traffic moving along Division. Across the street, over the trees in Liggett Park, the sky was darkening.

Inside, the atrium was quiet. Kitty's desk was clean and locked. She'd left at 4:00. The door was open to the insurance agency and there was a light on. I waved to the new girl in Time to Travel. A pretty, young black girl named Rachel. Unlike Kitty, Amanda hadn't come back after the shoot-out. Not that I could blame her. The door to Bob Ward's office was closed and the office was dark.

I unlocked my office door and went in. The air was hot and there was still the acrid smell of bleach the cleaners had used. I left the door open. I hung my jacket on the coat tree, then toed the rubber doorstop in place, went behind my desk, and propped the window open. It didn't help. I turned the fan on and felt the stir of the thick, acidic air, then turned it toward the door. At least it would blow some of the caustic smell out.

I went back and stood at my office window, watching dark grayish-green clouds roll and fold in from the west. The traffic on the street had a ponderous sound. Across the street, a group of joggers threaded their way through strollers and walkers along the park walkway. I wondered what Tamara was doing. A woman hurried past taking furtive glances at the sky, determined to make her destination before the storm hit.

As I watched, a light rain began but the sky was promising greater things. Suddenly the winds began, lifting street debris into the air. I'd had breakfast with Jerry Whitfield and lunch at the sub shop and had enough coffee to set my hair vibrating. Now, here I stand bloated and confused watching afternoon traffic move slowly along Division Street in both directions. All to what end?

The air was filling now with everything the storm could fling into the air. Paper bags, plastic cups, newspaper, leaves and branches ripped from the trees of Liggett Park. Head lights were on. Wipers slapped. People were running, commuters trying to beat the storm. Get home, batten down the hatches. I stood there watching. What seemed improbable was the traffic moving both ways. Across the street the trees roiled as though their leaves might be stripped free. I thought about Tamara and wondered where she was. I wasn't obsessing. It only happened maybe fifty times a day. I glanced around letting my gaze settle on the spot where Barbara Mann had been sitting when she was killed.

When I looked, up Danny Khanh came through the doorway. "What I can't figure out," I said. "Is why it is that the people who work in the city live outside the city and the people who work outside the city live in the city?"

A gust of rain and wind slanted in through the window and spattered rain on the sill.

Danny shrugged out of his blue nylon windbreaker and hung it on the back of one of the two chairs. He wore dark slacks and a blue short sleeved shirt with the collar open, and a 9mm in a shoulder rig. "Grass always greener?"

I lowered the window, leaving it open several inches. "Always is," I said.

Danny went to the coffee maker, pulled the carafe and smelled the contents. "Aged more than a day?"

"This morning."

"Care if I make some fresh?"

"Sure. Why not, I could use some."

I sat at my desk and opened the file that Whitfield had copied for me. It wasn't much. Barbara Ann Kaine. Born in 1976. Attended Benjamin Harrison High School in Jefferson City and graduated in 1994. She was a receptionist for something called Crosley Manufacturing; Graduated from Bishop Barber School. Worked as a stylist at several places for nearly two years, then went off to L.A. to become an actress. Had social security activity at numerous places in the Los Angeles area including at Timeline films. Also, Las Vegas at a place named Ba'rebas On The Strip. A certificate of marriage to John Mann issued in Clark County, Nevada. No mention of any arrests.

Danny had come back from the service area with the coffee carafe of water and proceeded to make coffee. When he had the Mr. Coffee gurgling he hooked his toe behind the leg of a chair, and swung it toward the desk and sat.

"'S'pose you're going to tell me that with Tesch's help you got it solved," I said. "And the perp in lock-up."

"You're looking at an ace detective, but unfortunately, no. No clue has shown itself."

Something was niggling in the back of my mind. A clap of thunder rattled the window. "I'm missing something," I said.

I know sometimes in the rush of things, things slip by. Not supposed to happen to a trained detective. Should be able to recall everything. I looked at Danny. "Something she said before she was killed. She said there were people in Bayfield who might wish her harm. And something called the Manley Athletic Club."

Danny smiled. "Cute name. Think it might be a clue?"

"Might be if we knew what it meant?"

"Maybe," Danny said. "someone should go down to Bayfield and ask around."

"Maybe. Be better if I was official, though."

Danny's shoulders sagged and he shook his head. "This conversation sounds like dialogue from a B movie."

"Life is a B movie, Detective."

Danny stared at me. "Jesus. You're a mess."

I didn't say anything. I got up and went to the window in time to catch another a streak of lightening and roll of thunder.

"I got the photos of the funeral developed," Danny said. "If you want to see them."

I shook my head. Tamara at my side. No. Me standing at her side. "Okay, enough," I said, mostly to myself.

"There has to be something in her life that would be a motive," I said. "Let's look at it this way. Someone was tailing her and possibly her husband. Why?"

Danny stretched his legs out and crossed his ankles. "See where she went?"

"Okay. See where she went. We don't know why. Why kill her in my office if there was no connection with me."

"Say she had discovered something that disturbed her," Danny said. "Something that she wasn't supposed to know, and someone was afraid she would tell you."

"But, how would the shooter know she was coming to see me?"

"He didn't. He's just tailing her. So he followed her here."

The coffee maker was gurgling and steaming. Danny got up, got the mugs and several packets of sugar from the top of the file cabinet, poured the coffee, set one in front of me and sat back down.

I closed Whitfield's Mann file and moved it aside. "Don't forget, Santos was a shooter, not a thinker."

"Ah ha," Danny said. "that means Santos calls the person that hired him to keep tabs on her. He tells this person she's in the office of Victor Pittaro, master detective. That's when this unknown person orders her killed."

"You'll make a good detective, someday."

-12-

Tuesday September 6th
6:30 pm

We were in my kitchen, sitting at the counter. Tamara sat on the kitchen side with a cup of tea. I had a cup of this morning's coffee.

She was wearing black Capri's and a rose-colored button down blouse with the top two buttons opened. A gold chain showed at her throat. Nisha was lying in front of the dishwasher watching Tamara. Outside, it was gray and raining. Not a loud heavy rain like earlier; a fine, quiet mist. A soaker.

It had been a week since I'd made a complete ass of myself and sitting here made me a bit weak, but I was determined to recover some of my dignity. "I sincerely apologize for the other night, Tamara."

She tilted her head slightly and smiled, dimpling her cheeks. Her dark eyes were bright with humor. She reached across and gave my hand two quick pats, and pulled back.

"Any developments, Vic?"

"Steve Tesch has Danny Khanh as the lead detective on it. And Danny's keeping me up to date."

Tamara watched me say nothing, expecting. "So far," I said. "In a case where a spouse is murdered the surviving spouse is the one looked at first. That seems to be where Tesch is focusing his energy. My instincts, however--- I don't believe John Mann has anything to do with his wife's death."

She watched me. I couldn't tell if she shared my sentiment or not.

I looked down at my coffee. There seemed to be an oily film floating on the top. "Tamara," I said, looking up. "Maybe it's the cop in me, but how can you be sure that Barbara was who you say she was?"

Her face was without expression.

"I'm sorry, but I have to ask."

I liked looking at her face, into her eyes. "I'm not doubting you," I said. "Or Barbara, it's just that--- Jerry Whitfield gave me a copy of his investigation. There's really nothing definitive in it other than the birth certificate listing a "George Hobbs" as the father."

Her gaze slowly shifted away from me to the window above the sink. "I know what you're thinking, Vic" she said. "Part of me questioned it too, and part of me knew the moment we met. It depended which part I would listen to at any moment. Make any sense to you?"

I didn't say anything.

"I would lie awake at night playing scenarios through my mind, I'm ashamed to say." She turned her cup of tea in her hands as she talked. "But in my heart, I knew it was true. Still---

"Still?"

"We talked about it a lot, Barbara and I. Can you imagine it? A black woman and a white woman sitting in my kitchen trying to deal with the probability that we are sisters. Preposterous. We needed to be sure. We decided to go the genetics clinic at the University in Jefferson City and get tested. We did and the test proved we had the same father."

Nisha shifted positions, still keeping her eyes on Tamara.

"You still have that policeman look on your face," Tamara said.

"It's just---" And then I stopped.

Her large, dark eyes glistened. "She was my sister, Vic." She got up and walked to the sink and looked out window. "You think it's more than coincidence that she lived in the area?"

"That question has crossed my mind."

"I don't believe in coincidences, Vic."

"I have a problem with them, too."

"That's not what I mean," she said. "It's something else. It could not be a coincidence that I began the search for my father when I did, after years of having no interest; Of finding that I have a sister, discovering that we could have passed each other on the street."

I could tell she was thinking.

"Vic. Everyone who passes through your life does so for a reason. Everyone you meet, even for a moment, changes you in some way." She turned back to me. "Do you believe that?"

"I don't know," I said.

She came and stood at the end of the counter and leaned toward me. "Barbara came to me with a problem and you came to mind. I sent her to you." She rested her hand on mine. "And here we are, now. Coincidence?"

-13-

Wednesday September 7th
9 am

The room was small, about 8'x12'. The walls were painted white. There was a sink, a desk, a padded table, and the bench I was sitting on. Doctor Stanton Lloyd sat on a wheeled stool at the small desk with a computer monitor. "That's typical with tinnitus, Mr. Pittaro," he said, looking up from the folder he was holding.

Doctor Lloyd is an emaciated little man, somewhere between fifty years old and my age, or older, with fine white hair that barely covered his scalp. The long, white smock he wore hung on him like a starched sheet. He closed the folder, took off his heavy black-rimmed glasses and spoke in his soft melodic voice. "The buzzing is caused by damage to the otic nerve, which is caused by excessive, sustained audio."

"Such as?"

"Well, constant or sustained frequency. Not necessarily of a high decibel level. Could be factory noise. Even continuous use of the telephone could be the cause. What do you do?"

"I'm sorry?" I said, leaning forward.

"What is your work?"

"Retired from the Sheriff's office." So, I'm going deaf. That's sweet. A deaf PI.

Doctor Lloyd tapped his glasses on the closed folder then put them back on. He took a pencil from the breast pocket of his smock and made a note on the front of the folder.

I asked the only thing I could think of. "Soooo, what can I do?"

"Well, you're not going deaf. However, the noise may increase over time. Also, you may notice it more when you're fatigued. A hearing aid might help. It won't get rid of the humming, but it might overpower the noise to where you won't have to strain so hard to hear."

"That's it?"

He nodded. "I'm afraid so," he said.

I'd consider sticking one of those damn things in my ear if it would filter out all the bullshit I hear. "I see," I said. This is the part where he awaits my reaction. "And if I don't get a hearing aid?"

"It's not going to change the prognosis." He pushed his stool back. "There have been some studies that indicate caffeine may affect the nerves in the inner ear, causing fluctuations in the static volume. If you're a heavy coffee drinker you might test that theory."

He waited again. Finally he said, "I'll send the results over to Doctor Preston." He jammed his pencil back into the breast pocket of his smock, got up and went to the door. "Let me know what you and he decide," he said, and went out.

-14-

Wednesday, Two pm
September 7th
60 degrees, Partly Cloudy

Robert Mann lived near Sweet Water Trace about twelve miles southwest of Bayfield. I felt good. I'd run two miles, showered, shaved, had a healthy breakfast of cereal, fruit, and coffee. The rest of the day will be de-calf. Nisha had had her breakfast, her pain medication and her duty walk, and was now resting on her rug in front of the sofa.

The rains had quit during the night and today the sun was high and warm. The air was still. Just right for a drive in the country and I was dressed for it. I wore an ash gray Arrow shirt with a button down collar. My slacks were charcoal, my boots were ankle high and black, which matched my holster, and I had on my glen plaid jacket. Perfect for early fall.

I drove south out of Berring Harbor over the Temperance River Bridge with the top down on my car. There wouldn't be too many more days like this one left this fall. On the right was the harbor and the marina. The boat slips were full and it would be another month before they were all hauled and stored for the winter. At the foot of the bridge, on the right, is the Harbor Restaurant and behind it, a boat yard with its rows of weathered wood cradles. On the left is Jackson's Marine, an amalgamation of structures, some concrete block, some frame, some steel, all painted a flat blue. Used to be they sold boats. Now Jackson's Marine sells four-wheeled ATV's, jet-skis, paddle boats, dirt bikes, boats and, as the huge billboard in front says, a "Complete Line of Marine Accessories".

The next two miles are what marketer's dreams are made of: sandwich shops, car washes, discount stores, burger joints. strip malls, drive up-banks, car dealers, muffler shops, take out pizza, service stations. At the light, I caught State Highway 29 and the scenery continued. Mexican restaurants, family restaurants, steak restaurants, Kohl's, more auto dealerships, Super Target, Italian restaurants, movie theaters that took up whole blocks. Home centers that took up whole blocks. When I went over the Interstate, corn and bean fields appeared and I had to wonder at what must be giddiness on the faces, and the shine of money in the eyes of the farmers who owned those fields of corn and beans. In thirty minutes I was through Bayfield.

Chessman Estates is a gated community just over the county line, two and a half miles south of Sweet Water Trace off of County Road 10. I had the Internet map Kitty had printed out for me in my hand as I turned in between the stone pillars. A sign at the edge of the road read, 'Chessman Estates. No Trespassing. Admittance for residents and invited guests only.' "Good thing I called first," I said to myself.

A stand of red sumac grew on the right where the terrain rose. On the left, was a man-made lake with young trees along the edge, all the same height. I could see several very large homes on the far shore. I followed the lake around to the left. An athletic looking woman in gray cotton shorts and matching sweatshirt with cutoff sleeves jogged along the asphalt path between the street and the lake. Her blond hair was pulled back and banded.

Scenario. Kid's in high school. Husband at the office too late too often. Jogging will alleviate the frustration for only so long. At a stop sign she glanced my way, smiled and crossed in front of me as

I slowed. The excessive bounce of her breasts beneath the sweatshirt was hard to ignore. I didn't.

I found Empire Place where Kitty's map said I would and turned right. Robert Mann's home was a sprawling Victorian house set in the center of a green velvet lawn. A red brick drive curved up to a turnaround and a three-car garage. A white fieldstone walk curved from the drive to the front stoop. Inside the curve was a stone fountain surrounded by a large stand of green hydrangea with large white flowers drying around the edges. There was a panel van parked with 'Quality Home Cleaners' parked in front. I parked beside it, grabbed my blazer from the other seat, got out and slipped it on. Mainly to cover the gun on my belt.

A woman opened the door on the second ring. She was a thin woman nearly as tall as I am, with a narrow, hollow-cheeked face, a sharp prominent nose, and a tight, thin-lipped mouth. Her complexion was that of someone who spent an excessive amount of time in the sun or a tanning bed. Her hair, the color of a brown paper bag was cut in a style that gave her a man-ish look. She wore black slacks and a white silk blouse with the tails out and tied in front revealing her navel on a gaunt midriff. She was not an attractive woman.

"Yes?' she asked in a hoarse, matter of fact voice.

"Vic Pittaro, Ma'am. I phoned earlier to see Mr. Mann."

"I wasn't aware Robert was expecting anyone. And you are from---?"

She stopped and waited for me to fill in the blank. "I'm a private investigator, Ma'am," I said. I handed her my PI license. "I'm investigating Barbara Mann's murder."

She studied it soberly for a moment, then handed it back. "I'm Janet Mann, Mr. Pittaro. Come in please." She stepped aside. "Robert is on the phone."

I stepped into the foyer. The floor was polished flagstone and on the right an oak staircase rose to the second floor. There were framed prints on the walls and an oak coat stand stood in the corner. "This way, Mr. Pittaro. I'm sure Robert won't be long."

She stepped around me and reached back to close the door. She seemed to be around thirty, but there were faint lines around her eyes and at the corners of her mouth. I could see the half-visible outline of the blue veins in the back of her hand.

I followed her down the hall, through a formal living room with a stone fireplace on the far wall and out through double French doors onto a large flagstone patio surrounding an oval swimming pool. The smell of chlorine was in the air. There was a glass-top table with four wrought iron chairs under a green umbrella, a scattering of outdoor furniture and at the edge of the patio, in a huge wood planter, the largest poinsettia I had ever seen.

"Will this be okay? And, could I get you a drink?"

"This will be fine and no thanks."

"Coffee, maybe?"

"Coffee would be nice. Black please, thank you." I'll start the test this afternoon.

I walked to the edge of the pool and looked down into the chlorinated water.

Ripples, the workings of the re-circulating pumps, fractured the surface making the bottom deceptive.

Robert Mann came through the French doors. "So, Pittaro, what can I do for you? The Sheriff's office, right?"

Robert Mann looked to be much younger than his brother and had recognizable facial features, but there the comparison ended. He was tall and thin to the point of being gangly. He had a wild head of light brown hair, a pale angular face with a day's growth of whiskers, and wore round, rimless glasses. He looked like an emaciated version of a young Albert Einstein.

"Have we met before?" I asked.

Mann's cell phone chimed. "I've seen your picture in the news occasionally over the years," he said, reaching for the cell phone on his belt. He was dressed in dark slacks, a pale blue oxford shirt with short sleeves and fawn colored suede loafers with no socks. The kind we used to call hush puppies.

He raised his hand stopping our conversation, turned his back to me and walked to the raised deck on the far side of the swimming pool. Must be some important business deal to intrude on a family's grief, I guessed. The price of being important.

I went back to studying the pool. There was a diving board on one end and concrete steps on the other. A Styrofoam lounger floated near the deep end and several floatation devices were scattered around the apron. Beyond the pool, lay a half acre of green lawn that ended at the edge of the wood line. Very private. To the right of the patio, a waist high white brick wall rose enclosing an area with a stainless steel grill and what looked to be a wet bar. With my back to Robert, the cicadas in my ears drowned out anything I might have overheard of his conversation.

I turned when I glimpsed Janet Mann. She carried on a silver tray a white china coffee service and a crystal snifter of what I assumed to be brandy. "For Christ's sake, Bob, can't you even ask the detective to sit?"

"Please sit, Detective." She smiled at me and set the tray on the glass-top table, and I made myself as comfortable as I could on one of the wrought iron chairs. She poured coffee from a chrome server into two cups, handed him one, and offered cream and sugar.

I waved a hand over my cup noticing little heat. "Thank you, black is fine," I said. Good thing I had a whole career of cold coffee behind me.

She sat across from me. I watched her open a small gold cigarette case. The kind that holds maybe six cigarettes. "Do you smoke?" There was something inauthentic about her. Theatrical, but in the way of a not too accomplished actor.

"No," I said.

She took one out and lit it with a pencil lighter. She took a big drag and let the smoke out through the corner of her mouth, then lifted the snifter, drank and put the glass down. "Terrible thing about John's wife," she said. There was a puffiness under her eyes and the cobweb of lines at the corner of her mouth and eyes were more numerous and deeper than I first thought. It was then I decided that this was not her first brandy of the day.

"I know that the Sheriff's detectives have already talked with you and your husband, Mrs. Mann. What I'm interested in is Barbara Mann."

She smiled at me. It was a theatrical smile showing a lot of teeth. "Janet, Detective Pittaro. Please, call me Janet."

"Fine. I thought maybe by talking with you and Mr. Mann I might learn more about her; What she was like, her personality, who her friends were."

"What would that have to do with finding who killed her?"

"Well first, we know who killed her. The shooter is dead. His name was Julius Santos. What the

Cardinal Red

authorities are working on now is finding out if someone hired him. That's their responsibility."

Her eyes went big. "Really?!" She put her hand to her mouth. "Someone hired this man to kill Barbara?"

I shrugged, uncommittedly. "The Sheriff's detectives are looking into it, yes." She glanced across the pool at her husband.

"John Mann hired me to assist the authorities independently and maybe uncover a motive." Technically, I was also working for Tamara, but then I would be in the position of trying to explain the Mann family tree. I sipped my tepid coffee, waiting.

"Oh," she said. Holding her cigarette in her fingers, she lifted her drink to her lips and took a swallow. "Well," she said. "I don't know what to say. Bob and I didn't know Barbara very well. And of course, we were both mystified when John married her. We were worried she was some sort of opportunist."

"Do you still feel that way?"

She looked at me for a moment, saying finally, "I'm sorry, I don't feel comfortable answering that. I do know John thought the sun rose and set on Barbara."

I nodded.

"I still don't know why knowing who her friends were would help in any way." she said.

"I don't know if it will, but that's what I do. I ask questions in the hope that eventually something will mean something."

Robert Mann came across the patio clipping his cell phone to his belt. "We've already talked with Lieutenant Tesch," he said. "I don't know what else we could tell you."

Janet Mann stubbed her cigarette out in the ashtray, got up and moved to the chair to my left. "Sit, Bob." She pointed to the chair across from her. "Mr. Pittaro is a private detective. Your brother hired him. He said the authorities think that someone hired that man to kill Barbara."

Robert sat across from me in the chair his wife had vacated. "Oh?" he said.

"I'm no longer with the Sheriff's office, Mr. Mann. Your brother hired me to look into his wife's murder. But, yes, that's the assumption they're working on."

"Call me Bob. Everyone does."

His cell phone rang again. Mann got up, got his phone and walked away as he answered it all in one motion.

"That's the way it's been since we announced his candidacy," Janet said. "We've been assured of the party endorsement." She drank some more of her drink.

I nodded and smiled. "Wonderful," I said.

"Robert is so concerned, so civic minded." She took another cigarette from the gold case, closed the case, then lit the cigarette. She took in a lung full, then blew it out as if she was blowing out birthday candles. "We know he'll make such a great state senator," she said

"I'm sure he will. But that's not why I'm here."

She was turned slightly, facing me. The smell of alcohol was strong on her. "Oh, of course. I'm sorry."

Robert came back to the table and sat down. I turned to Janet Mann. "You said you were both mystified when Barbara and John got married?"

"Well, a Las Vegas dancer for God's sakes?" Her gaze flicked to Robert and back to me. "We would have hoped he would have done better. John is extremely practical and we thought from the beginning she was just looking for a sugar daddy. Doesn't surprise us that her past came back. I'm sure that was it."

I took my notebook from my pocket. Paged slowly through it with a practiced, thoughtful look. "Do you know a man named Bobby Rico?"

Robert dropped his head in thought. As he raised it, his eyes flicked to his wife, then to me. "No, I don't believe I do," he said.

"No. Don't know the name," Janet said.

I turned the page, then put the notepad back. "Jamie Adams?"

Robert shook his head.

Janet reached, patted her husband's hand. "Jamie Adams, sure. We've met him often, Robert."

She turned her attention to me. "I believe I last talked with him this past spring at the County Cultural Center, the fundraiser. Remember, Robert?"

Robert opened his hands and shrugged.

"Can't remember everybody," I said, turning back to him. "Tell me what you can about Tamara Phillips."

"We've never met her," Janet said. "But from what I've heard, she's Barbara's supposed sister?".

I nodded at her and smiled, then Robert, then back to Janet. "There's some doubt?" My neck was getting sore.

"She's black. What does that tell you."

-15-

Thursday September 8th
Raining, 69 degrees

It was late afternoon. The sky was gray and heavy with falling rain, making it seem much later than it was. We could hear it on the roof, a steady purr, like something stuck in a fan. We had the lights on and were sitting at the glass-top table in Tamara's kitchen with the rainwater streaming down the patio windows, smudging the view of what, I couldn't tell. She sat across from me. This evening she was in faded jeans with a blue smock over a white t-shirt. The jeans, t-shirt, and smock were paint stained. We were having iced tea with a wedge of lemon on the lip of the tall glass.

"Barbara knew something," I said. I traced the moisture on the side of my glass with my fingertip. "Or, maybe someone just thought she knew something."

Tamara was watching me with intensity.

"But, I can't go with that because that gets me nowhere. I have to go on the assumption she knew something that somebody didn't want known."

"And when you find that out we'll know why someone wanted her dead."

"And maybe who," I said. "Did she ever mention a fitness club called the Manley Athletic Club?"

Tamara shook her head. "No." She thought a moment. "Mann, Manley. I think I would have remembered it."

I nodded.

"So what's our next move?" she said.

I dropped the lemon slice in the tea and sipped. If caffeine makes the static worse I don't need coffee. "Have you met John's brother, Robert and his wife?"

"Robert, yes. Janet? No." Tamara said. "I do know Barbara felt that Janet didn't like her. That she didn't like it when John married her. But you've met John. I don't think he much cares what anyone thinks. Why?"

"I drove down to Sweet Water Trace yesterday. I just wondered if you'd met them."

She seemed confused. "Because of how they felt about Barbara?"

"It's more like talking to anyone who's connected to the victim."

"Barbara," Tamara said, pointedly.

"Yes. I'm sorry. Barbara. I'll try not to talk like a cop."

She looked at me intently, then her head moved in a thoughtful nod. "But," she said, "you are a cop, aren't you?"

I nodded, and looked at her. She put her elbows on the table and tipped her face into her hands. I could hear her breathing. I wondered if she was crying. And if she was, what could I say? The rain continued its purr on the roof and ran down the windows.

We sat that way for a while. Me thinking deep thoughts, Tamara I'm sure, thinking thoughts deeper still.

When she finally looked up, her eyes were red. A smile grew slowly on her face. "I was in my studio when you called," she said. "It's where Barbara and I had our best conversations."

She got up and went and looked through the rain-fouled windows. It had gotten darker, but I knew what she was seeing. I'd been there, done it. Staring through a rain-washed window always makes the past seem clearer, as if the distortion magnifies our memories.

I let the sound of the rain envelop us. When she finally turned away from the window she said, "Come, I want to show you my studio."

I followed her through the kitchen past the living-room, and down the hall to her studio.

Her studio was probably the most inhabited space I'd ever been in. The back wall was glass, overlooking whatever was beyond. There were two skylights. The kind that capture the light and funnel it into the room, though they weren't doing much of a job at it today. She turned the switch and a fluorescent light came on.

The wall on the left was solid and lined with shelving; the kind of board and bracket shelving one would find in a garage. The shelves were full of various sizes of cans and boxes. There was a shelf of books, stacks of magazines. There were two heavy work tables, one small, one large. The large one held miscellaneous tools. There was an easel with a work in progress, a small paint stained table with boxes of brushes, tubes and jars. Next to me on my left, was a very abused, paint-stained wooden desk with a computer and an oak captain's chair of the same vintage and condition. Scattered around the room were completed paintings. I was speechless.

"Well?" Tamara said. Her face was alight.

"Awesome," I said. But I was thinking, she wanted me to see this. "But more than that, it's a you that I never would have imagined." I waved my hand taking in the room. "How did you come to this?"

She was leaning back against one of the heavy tables facing me. "After Roger's death," she said. "There were a lot of what next feelings. I was working in the State Attorney's office as you know, and I didn't want to anymore. It gradually it came to me, it wasn't what I wanted to do next with my life, it was what I didn't want to do. This was one of the things that opened to me."

I shook my head in admiration. "Amazing."

She nodded and grinned, then the grin softened. "Barbara and I spent hours here." She stopped talking and looked past me. It was quiet. The rain had stopped or at least slowed. "Eight months," she said wistfully. "We learned a lot about each other in that time. Probably because neither of us had thought we had siblings."

"She was an artist?" This surprised me, and I guess it showed.

"No," Tamara said. "Barbara would sit at the desk while I worked, and we'd talk. Sometimes she would work at the computer."

I looked down at the desk and computer, turned the chair out and sat. "Talk to me about Barbara," I said.

"We've already done that." She said.

"Yes. Some. What were you working on when I called?"

"This," she said. Her smock nearly reached her knees and was so paint streaked I wondered if she cleaned her brushes on it. She stepped to an easel with what looked like drawings on heavy paper. "Lately I've been working in watercolors," she said. "I'm sketching out a landscape."

"So Barbara would sit here and you two would talk while you painted."

"Yes."

"So, do whatever you were doing when I called and we'll talk about Barbara."

Tamara looked at me for a long minute then laughed. "You expect me to work in this light?"

I smiled, and looked around, humbled. "You're right. What was I thinking?"

Her smile was wide and refreshing. She came, stood beside me. "I wanted to show you where and how we became sisters. I wanted to show you how everyone who comes into your life, even for the briefest moment, affects your life. The smile you give to a stranger, the touch you give to a friend, changes both lives."

I was stilled. I was sure I could hear the blood flowing through my veins. I couldn't pull my eyes from her face. All I could think of was the kiss. Finally, fearing I would blubber, I cleared my throat. "Tell me---" I cleared my throat again. "Tell me everything you can think of about Barbara."

Cardinal Red

When I looked at my watch it was 7:15. Tamara had found a chair and had refreshed our tea. We'd talked for over two hours. I don't know who I learned more about, Barbara Mann or Tamara. It was Barbara's murder I was trying to solve, and in that case one didn't know what was important until it was solved, so I'd always worked with the idea that the more you learned the better. As for Tamara, it was personal. The more I learned about her the more nervous, and infatuated I became.

I went home. The night air was warm and damp. I let Nisha out and stood on the back step while she nosed around looking for the right spot. I looked up at the dark, black sky.

-6-

Saturday, September 10th
Third Day of Overcast Skies

It was noon Saturday and I was in my office. I had the Daily Herald spread open on my desk and, with my reading glasses perched on the end of my nose, was reading the comics. Pretty pathetic I know, but what's one to do when one doesn't have a life; Nisha lay beside the desk, her front paws cradled her snout. Her eyes were closed and snoring sounds rose from her.

I couldn't see Kitty from my desk but I could hear her giggle and a voice I knew was Bob Ward. Ward has the office next to mine. He's the owner and sole employee of Ward's Mobile Home Sales. A small man, maybe 5'5" and pushing 200lbs, balding and delusional, he envisions himself an operator. Spencer Hynen will have him for lunch if he finds out good old Bob is hitting on his daughter. I heard the switchboard ring and heard her answer. Ward stopped in my doorway and said, "How they hanging this morning, old man?"

He was wearing a pink flowered short sleeved shirt and light brown cotton slacks. He was smiling his happy smile.

"Good morning, Bob." I said, a went back to my paper.

I had gone through the obituaries and the sports page, baseball was the only sport I paid any attention to, and was checking my horoscope when I heard Nisha move. When I looked up, Kitty was standing in my doorway, several thick blond curls covering half her face. She had her knit bag, which served as her purse slung over her shoulder. "You leaving, Kitty?"

"Yes," she said. She seemed hesitant, then stepped through the doorway and knelt beside Nisha. "You're such a beautiful girl, Nisha."

She let Nisha lick her hand, then stood.

"Something wrong, Kitty?"

"No. No," she said. She glanced quickly right, then back to me, then to Nisha. "No, nothing's wrong,

Mr. Pittaro. Just wanted to say goodbye to Nisha before I leave."

She left. I went back to feeling sorry for myself.

Danny Khanh came through my office door carrying a paper cup with a plastic spoon sticking out of it. He wore dark slacks, a white turtle-neck and a mahogany colored corduroy jacket that bulged under his left arm. He hooked a client chair with his foot, spun it parallel to my desk and sat. Or rather, he slouched with his feet straight out in front of him, and with the spoon began scraping the last dredges of what must have been soft ice-cream from the nearly empty container.

"Come in. Grab a chair. Get comfortable," I said. I'd removed my glasses and held them by the bow. "Can I get you coffee now that you've finished your lunch, or whatever? How about a drink, a cigar?"

"Spectacles?" he said, pointing to my glasses.

Nisha had struggled up and was now poking her nose at the container in Danny's hand.

I dropped the glasses on the desk and scowled. "My eyes are tired and sometimes I use them for reading."

Danny grinned. "Sure," he said. "And yes, a drink would be good."

I glared at him a moment, then got the bottle of Myers from the drawer, the two glasses from the top of the filing cabinet, then went back to my desk and poured us each one. "It's nice the management of this place allows dogs," Danny said.

"I told them she's a seeing-eye dog."

Danny smiled, and took his drink. "A seeing-eye for a private eye that needs glasses," he said. "Fits."

I ignored him, put the glasses back on and went back to the paper. "Here it says in 1940 life expectancy at birth in the U.S. was 61.4 years for men, 65.7 for women. Now the comparable figures are 75.4 and 80." I got my calculator out.

"For me, that's 21,900 sunsets," I said. "Or sunrises, depending on how you look at it. I prefer sunsets. 'Course, you're half my age, but how many sunsets have you seen? How many loves have you had? Or lovers? More importantly, how many do you remember?"

Danny had his elbows on the arms of the chair holding his drink with both hands in front of him. He had turned his head and was watching me. "Feeling a bit old, are we?"

"Ancient. But my point is, Barbara Mann didn't get to see all of her allotted sunsets."

"Vic, I've checked. You've been involved in over a hundred homicides cases in your career, including two officer-involved shootings where you were the officer involved. Is there something special about this one? Other than the woman was killed here in your office?"

"You got into my personnel file?"

Cardinal Red

Danny had sipped his rum and was looking into the glass. "Be better with some ice," he mumbled.

"Beggars probably shouldn't complain."

"You're right."

"So?"

"So, no. Not your personnel file. What I could find on the internet and in the Daily Herald's morgue. While you were my superior I felt checking your bonafides was inappropriate. But now, with you being my mentor and all, so to speak, I wanted to see what I was getting myself into."

"Mentor? Jesus Christ."

Danny straightened in his chair, finished his drink, and poured another. I still had half of mine.

"So, what is it?" he asked.

I shook my head. "I don't know. It seems more personal. Happened here in my office. Tamara's sister. Retirement. Unsure of what's ahead. Maybe a little of all of it."

I still had a swallow left in my glass, but why let it run dry. I added another two fingers and put the cap back on, then I rocked back in the chair and sipped. "I like it room temperature," I said.

The air was quiet except for the traffic noise out on the street.

Danny grinned. "What do you make of the husband? You saw him."

"He'd been drinking pretty heavily." I thought about it for a moment. "I've seen a lot of bad acting.

His grief seemed genuine. 'Course, I've been fooled before. What do you know about Robert Mann?" I asked.

Danny sipped his drink. "The brother?"

"Yeah."

"You mean besides the fact that he's a Cookton County Commissioner, and he's running for a seat in the State Senate?"

"Yeah."

"Not much else. Unless you consider the rumors that he's got his eye on the Governor's chair."

"In the course of this investigation, have you talked with him?"

Danny had relinquished the paper cup to Nisha who had in turn lost interest and had returned to her relaxed position, leaving it on the floor out of my sight. I assumed this, as I had seen neither one drop it into the wastebasket.

"Nope. Why?" he asked.

"I drove over to Bayfield Wednesday morning and had a chat with him and his wife. Looks like a couple of 1960's counterculture retreads, while living and acting like capitalists. I was just wondering if you'd talked with them, and your impression."

"Damn," Danny said. "Tesch never asks me my opinion."

"How about financials?"

"He's got Schnider on that and phone records. 'Course, Mann Brother's is a private company. You know how that goes."

I nodded. "Only the immediate particular can be so investigated without a warrant. But, John Mann will cooperate."

"You're assuming that."

"He will." I got up with my drink in my hand and went to the window. There was a steady stream of traffic up and down Division. There were people walking the sidewalk. Down the street at the light where Seventh Avenue crosses Division, and in front of what was once the South Town Bakery, where Sal had made the best, greasiest Old-Fashioned doughnuts in the city and is now an empty building, people stood waiting for the walk light. In the park, up toward the knoll, where the Liggett Park band shell stood, kids hung around in clusters plotting their next felony. The band shell hadn't been used as intended in a long time and was becoming a place to hang out during the day and a place to score at night. "A time for everything and everything in its time, or something like that."

"What?"

I turned to face him. "The audiologist said I have tinnitus, and need hearing aids."

"What?" Danny said.

His face was blank, then he winked. I shook my head. "Just what I need now," I said, turning back to the window. "A smart ass tailing me around."

We were quiet for a while, and I went back to staring out the window. I could hear Nisha's steady breathing, interrupted by the occasional heavy sigh. How many loves have I had? One. Mo. How many lovers? Enough. How many sunsets? One especially poignant one two years ago in the hospice atrium.

"There's something wrong with those two." I turned, and leaned back against the sill. Danny had his hands folded over his stomach, his head down. "Can't put my finger on it." I said.

He didn't look up. "Who?"

"For Christ's sake. Who were we talking about? Robert Mann and his wife."

"Easy their, mentor."

I lowered my head, shaking it side to side.

-17-

Saturday Afternoon
September 10th

After Danny left, I rinsed out the drink glasses and put them back. Nisha watched me, her tail thumping randomly on the floor as though her anticipation about getting up and leaving wavered with her desire to remain still. I went to her, bent over, snapped the leash on, and coaxed her to her feet.

I locked my office door and we went out, locking the lobby doors behind us. We went down the steps slowly and down the sidewalk to my car parked in my designated spot. With some effort, Nisha got in and up onto the passenger seat. I closed the door and went around to my side, got in. I started the engine and we left.

There's a sub shop on the corner of Seventh and Collins. I stopped, went in and got two Italian Subs with double meat. One, skip everything, just the meat, the other with everything and a large black coffee. The hell with it. Ninety percent of what one hears is just noise, anyway. I carried the bag out to the car and set it on the hood and opened it. I opened the sandwich with just the meat and gave it to Nisha in the front seat.

I opened the coffee and set it on the hood next to the bag and leaned against the front fender of my car and ate. It must have been in the lower 70's but no sign of the sun. Lately, the weather had been as gray as my mood. I needed some sunshine. I thought of Tamara. She always seemed a ray of sunshine. I thought of sunrises and of sunsets. I thought of Barbara Mann and I thought of all the sunrises she would never see. I finished my sandwich and was drinking my coffee, and I got to wondering why a hotshot hoodlum from Los Angeles would be here, in fly-over-land, at the Cookton County Cultural Center. I thought about that while I finished my coffee, then I got my cell phone out and punched in the phone number of Guy Jackman in faraway Los Angeles. Dick Tracy never had it so good.

Cardinal Red

At the traffic light, a polished blue semi-tractor with a lot of chrome and a large piece of earthmoving machinery on a lowboy trailer rumbled. The light changed. I turned away as a female voice answered with, "The Wine Cellar may I help you?"

I covered my other ear with my hand and said too loudly, "Is Guy in?"

The voice said, "Who's calling?"

I squinted and pressed my hand hard against my ear. "Sorry about the noise," I said, trying to shut out the roar of the chrome pipes as the driver of the truck went through the gears. "Victor Pittaro, from Berring Harbor."

I think she said, "I'll ring the office."

In the time it took Guy Jackman to come on the line the rumble from the truck had faded. "Hey, old man," he said in that distinctive alto voice I remembered so well. "How you doin'? I bet you're calling to accept that position I offered you?"

"No, I'm not. And if I remember right, you're older than I am."

He laughed and said, "Yeah, but I'm better looking." Then laughed again.

"I know. It's been a long time."

I've known Guy almost all of my life. We started elementary school together. After high school graduation, Guy joined the Marines and was stationed in Japan. It was the early 70's. I learned years later, long after he'd returned home and married, that as a

Marine, he'd been a security guard at the American Embassy in Saigon on April 29, 1975, when the Embassy came under attack by the North Vietnamese Army. During the evacuation of the Embassy he had fired on and killed several North Vietnamese that had scaled the wall.

With the first gulf war, came the flashbacks. He became despondent and racked with fits of anger. His marriage disintegrated and broke up. In '93 he moved to Los Angeles and opened a wine shop on Santa Monica Blvd. Though we keep in touch by phone once or twice a year, I've seen him only once since; when Mo and I were in California in '96 for the USC/Northwestern game.

After several minutes of chit-chat I said, "I know this is a long shot, but you know anything about a guy named Bobby Rico?"

"Some," he said. "I know he's connected."

"A wise guy?"

"So I've heard."

I wonder if I uncovered a clue. I said, "You know anyone that could put me in touch with him?"

"I know he likes good wine."

"Damn! Maybe I shouldn't know these things about my old school buddy?"

"Whether you're talking the Southern California film business or the mob these people have the money to develop a high shelf taste. Why is Monroe County's top cop interested in Bobby Rico?"

"I'm retired, Guy. I'll fill you in when I get out there."

"Retired? Damn! I must be doing something wrong."

"I doubt it. How about a Jamie Adams?"

"Never heard of him."

-18-

Monday
September 12th
Cloudy Sky, 67 degrees

I had met Tamara for lunch at Gabriella's, on the bluff overlooking the Temperance River. We were at a table in front of the big plate-glass windows in the glassed-in veranda. The temperature was sixty-seven with an overcast sky. The maples and birches along the river were starting their color change. The weather forecast was for light showers.

Gabriella's is bright and airy, which is surprising with all of the oak trimming. There are probably twenty tables covered with white tablecloths. On each table is a cut glass bowl with a floating candle that would be lit for the dinner trade. Below our window, the ground dropped sharply through the trees to the river's edge where a pair of mallards moved effortlessly in the slow current.

Tamara was having shrimp scampi with linguini and was sipping ginger ale. I had a glass of the house red wine; which was going wonderfully with my sausage and peppers. Probably the best sausage and peppers I've eaten outside of my own kitchen.

"What about Nisha?" Tamara asked.

"My neighbor will watch her. See that she's fine."

"I would love to. Los Angeles. God, it's been years." She was wearing a black silk blouse with an open, burnished-silver collar and a string of pearls at her throat. She looked regal. I broke off a piece of baguette, distracting myself. "Great. I'll have Kitty make the plane reservations for Wednesday, and see if she can get us rooms at the Roosevelt."

She speared a shrimp with her fork, cut it in half and ate it. "Ummm," she said. Then her look turned serious. "Who is this man again, we're going to talk with?"

I had sopped up some sauce with the crusty bread, ate it and taken a swallow of wine, which emptied the glass. "Bobby Rico," I said. "We're going to try to talk with him."

"I remember Barbara mentioning the name," she said. "He was her agent when she was in Los Angeles. The man she saw at that event in Bayfield."

"Yes. Probably more than an agent."

"You mean pimp."

That stopped me for a second. I was learning that I couldn't dance around with this woman. "He might be a pimp," I said. "But, that's not what I meant. He's purported to be mob connected."

Our waiter came by, I pointed at my wine glass. He picked it up and looked at Tamara's glass of ginger ale. She had barely touched it.

After the waiter left I said, "I thought we might confirm his relationship with her, and in the process discover what his connection to Bayfield might be. We know he knows Jamie Adams. And we know he attended a fundraiser at the Cookton County Cultural Center with Adams."

"And that is strange."

"Yes. Bayfield is a long way from Los Angeles," I said. "It stretches the imagination to think his interest is the art of Cookton County."

The waiter brought my wine and left. We ate in thought for several minutes. She liked to eat, I was learning. Savoring everything. My thoughts were of the possibilities of the two of us in LA for a week. I wasn't sure what hers were, but I speculated wishfully.

"Short notice, I know," I said. "And, I'm sorry about that."

Tamara drank some ginger ale, then patted her mouth with her napkin. "Would we have time for some sight-seeing?"

"If we got our business taken care of in the first few days, we'd have the weekend, and besides, it's on John Mann's dime."

She nodded her head and smiled, and I felt myself melting.

***

I was aware of her perfume as we walked across the parking lot to her car. I opened her door and tried not to focus too directly no her legs as she got in. "Vic," she said. "I'm excited about LA."

I leaned on the open door. "I'll make the arrangements and call you."

She smiled. I closed the door and she drove away. I turned away, sucked in a deep breath, then let it out slowly, self-conscious about staring after her. I walked to my car, leaned against the door and called Kitty and asked her to book two seats on a through flight into LAX for Wednesday morning. Late morning would be preferable. My guest would be Tamara Phillips. Then, I called Guy Jackman.

-19-

Wednesday pm
September 14th
At 34,000 feet
No Turbulence
Clear Skies

I watched Tamara rummage through her purse and come up with a package of Dentyne. She was wearing an ivory silk blouse with a fine gold stitching on the collar, worn with the two top buttons opened, and a charcoal wool skirt. Her black flats had drifted beneath the seat in front of her, and her legs were crossed at the ankles. Her stockinged legs looked very good. Her dark caramel complexion, in the odd cabin light, looked as delicate as a fine pastry. I felt as I always did when I looked at her.

She caught me looking, smiled and offered a stick of gum. I declined and turned to the window musing over the prospect of spending the next few days with her.

The cabin attendants had made the last walkthrough with their plastic waste bags and the captain had turned the seatbelt light on. I had my face to the glass looking down on the San Gabriel Mountains. We banked right and then left and minutes later I was watching the honeycomb of Los Angeles sliding below the trailing edge of the wing as the plane slowly sank toward the runway. Systematic squares, evenly divided as though some being had laid out colored graph paper carefully cut to lie flat between the brown mountains and the blue of the sea. Gradually, contours began to emerge and I could see where the colors stretched into breaks in the mountains; The flowing, twisting diagonal lines that were the jammed interstates. I heard the whine of a motor and watched the aileron slide out and down as the pilot dumped air. The ground came quickly now and I could feel Tamara's hand tighten on my wrist. The squares turned into recognizable houses, tree lined streets appeared, automobiles, gray warehouses, blocks of semi-trailers, then a thump, wobble and the roar as the pilot reversed big engines bringing the plane to a sudden slow. When the plane had slowed to a crawl, a cabin attendant's voice came over the speaker welcoming everyone to Los Angeles. She was thrilled that we had chosen this airline to fly, and that it would please her and the rest of the crew to no end if when we needed to go hurling through space at five-hundred miles an hour in an aluminum tube again we would again choose this airline. And by the way, it's 2:45 in Los Angeles with sunshine and 70 degrees.

Forty-five minutes later, with my sport coat slung over my shoulder, I was following Tamara through the sliding doors onto the sidewalk at LAX, pulling Tamara's large suitcase and my black suitcase. Tamara had a flowered canvas carry-on slung over one shoulder and a black purse over the other. It was another ten minutes before we were sitting uncomfortably in the crowded shuttle for the ride to the car rental agency. Thirty-five minutes later we were driving down Century Blvd. The agency had upgraded me for only another eleven dollars a day, to a nearly new Silver Charcoal Buick. What the hell, I'm on expense account, right?

I turned left onto La Cienega avoiding the 405. It's a good thing to do in the late afternoon in LA. I'd been here before. Why do they call these freeways the 405, the 401, the 5? In the Midwest we'd say Interstate 94, Interstate 90, Interstate 80, or Interstate

35. Maybe they figure they live a faster lifestyle, they don't have the time to say those longer words.

We were quiet. I heard a siren. The thing about these huge cities like LA, or Chicago, or NYC, there's always a crisis somewhere. One can always hear a siren. In the west, which means out over the ocean, random dark clouds were breaking the afternoon sun. I turned the air conditioner to low. Tamara was watching out the window. She seemed to not be seeing anything in particular. I know how that is. A circus does it for me. Not just going to a circus. Just seeing a circus poster will do it. Mo loved the circus, a carnival, or a fair. It was the action, the bustle of people. She would stop anyone she thought might be interesting and begin a conversation. The amazing thing was they would soon be talking about personal things, or their families. Things I'm sure they never dreamed they'd be telling a stranger. At a traffic light I said, "When you and Roger were here you must have had a wonderful time exploring LA."

We passed the oil fields. The pumps were rocking up and down, doing their thing. "Not really," she said. "We were here for a football game. We lost so there were no parties to attend. We stayed in a hotel in Pasadena. Roger wanted to see the ocean so we drove to Santa Monica and spent the afternoon on the beach then on the way back to the hotel we spent some time in Hollywood walking down Hollywood Boulevard."

I felt her watching me. "How did you know what I was thinking?" she asked.

"I recognized the stillness. I get there sometimes, myself."

"You'll have to tell me about her sometime."

"Yes."

We were quiet. We crossed Wilshire, and Beverly. We crossed Melrose. Beneto's Bistro was still there. In fact, not much had changed, at least in this part of the city. We passed an empty three-story building with plywood over the doors and windows and an abandoned auto repair shop surrounded by a rusted and weed-gown chain link fence. An attempt had been made to renovate some of the buildings. There were boutiques, sandwich shops, used furniture stores and a deli. An unshaven man in a filthy black peacoat trudged along the sidewalk pulling two shopping carts he had lashed together and loaded with, I imagine, everything he owned.

I turned right onto Santa Monica Boulevard. The traffic was what I expected. Heavy. I was catching every light and invariably a horn would honk behind me the moment the light turned. Rain was speckling the windshield. I turned the wipers on interval. At La Brea I turned left, crossed Sunset and got stuck behind a white and yellow city bus stopped across from the Hollywood Gym. I made a right on Hawthorn. At Orange I made a short left and swung into the drive of the Roosevelt Hotel.

We checked in, left our luggage with a bellhop and took the elevator to the sixth floor. "Way too much stone and marble and brass for my taste," I said as the elevator door opened.

"I like it," Tamara said.

"Really?"

We stepped out to a carpeted hallway, lit by shell-like sconces along the wall that directed the light toward the ceiling. "It's from a different time," she said. "A more elegant, more aristocratic time."

"Feels damn cold to me."

"Yes, in a way it does," she said. She smiled. "Let's hope the rooms will feel warmer."

"Let's hope," I said.

They say Marilyn Monroe's spirit resides here. I'm sure others have walked this hallway as well. Grant. Bacall. Hutton. I followed Tamara a half step behind down the subtly lit hall in awkward silence, my mind concocting preposterous Gable-esque images. Ridiculous. I chided myself as I followed the brass number plates on the doors. I don't even own a smoking jacket.

At room 636 Tamara slid her key in the slot and opened the door. Quick, think of something intelligent to say. "You ready for some dinner?" Was all I could come up with.

"I'm famished. Give me about forty-five minutes after our luggage comes."

"What sounds good?"

Cardinal Red 157

"You choose. But not too elaborate. It's been a long day."

My watch said 5:10. "I'm right next door in 638. Just ring me when you're ready." I turned to my door, then turned back. "Tamara, I'll get the bell hop."

When her door clicked shut I was still standing in front of mine staring at where she had been. If there is a door between the rooms I'll be awake all night thinking about her. I heard the deadbolt snap in place. Well maybe a drink or two will help.

The room was hotel modern. Thick carpet, king sized bed, sitting area, writing desk with computer connection, and a large ornate armoire standing beside the entertainment center. And, no door to the next room. All the amenities one could want, including a well-stocked wet bar. I shrugged out of my sport coat and tossed it on the bed, then found the thermostat and turned the air-conditioner on. I opened the liquor cabinet and scanned my selection of the little bottles. Blue Label, Grand Marnier, Jack, a blend or two, and a pick of imported beer, but no Rum. Well shit! Beer makes me pee, Jack gives me a headache and the price of the Blue Label would give me a guilt trip. Maybe later I'll go find a liquor store. Right now, one whiskey wouldn't hurt.

I went out to the ice machine at the end of the hall. On the way back, I stopped at her door. I could see if she would like a drink. I stood there, my thoughts too heavy in my throat to be spoken. So I went back to my room, took off my pants and fixed my drink.

***

I was standing at the window sipping Crown Royal over ice, looking down onto Hollywood Boulevard, trying to blot from my mind the sound of her bathtub being filled in the next room when the bellhop came with my luggage. I had him set it on the luggage stand, tipped him a ten spot and shut the door.

I unzipped the suitcase and debated whether to use the dresser drawers or live out of the suitcase. Mo would have used the dresser. She would have laid everything out on the bed, shaken out the wrinkles, then refolded each item as she arranged the drawer. One drawer for underwear. Hers on one side mine on the other. That would have been the extent of the co-mingling of clothes. My shirts would have been hung on hangers and I would be allowed one drawer for slacks, jeans and whatever. The rest of the dresser would be hers.

I took my shirt off, gave the collar and underarms a quick frown of disapproval and tossed it onto the bed, then carried my drink with me into the bathroom. I set the drink and my watch on the back of the commode. I showered and shaved and brushed my teeth. Cleanliness is next to Godliness, you know. I bagged my dirty clothes, put on clean boxers and socks, then stretched out on top of the bedspread. My mind wouldn't settle. Mo's been gone nearly four years. So why do I have this guilt feeling in my gut like I'm doing something wrong? I'm not.

It was 7:15 fifteen when the phone woke me. "Vic, I'm so sorry. I fell asleep. I'm so sorry. I guess I was more tired than I thought."

"That's alright, Tamara. Fact is, I was asleep when you called. Would you like to go get a bite?"

"Ten minutes? I promise."

As I dressed, I found myself whistling.

We drove down La Brea, crossed Sunset, Fountain, and Santa Monica Blvd. We passed Pink's and made a right on Melrose heading west. There must have been thirty people standing on the sidewalk in front of Pink's. Why people would stand in a line for twenty minutes for a hot dog is a mystery to me.

Melrose Avenue in West Hollywood looks as if you mixed the 60's, the 70's, and the 90's all together and tossed them out like a roll of dice. It's both aged and ageless, and radiates energy. Busy with young people. You won't find the fountain of youth hidden behind a storefront but there's a palatable air of vitality. San Francisco has Hyde Park and Fisherman's Wharf, Minneapolis has Uptown, and Jefferson City has Lake Blvd. Places that seem to breathe away your years just by you being there. I can only imagine what it must have been in the days of the flower children.

Tamara chose the restaurant. Albano's. 'The best pizza west of Brooklyn' the sign read. I've never been in Brooklyn but I don't doubt their claim. It's a small place with maybe six tables. We sat at a small table in the nook near the front window. The autographed pictures and posters that cover the walls have obviously been there a while as many people in the photos have long since gone to the big sound stage in the sky.

The waitress was a pretty, thin, blond girl about eighteen or nineteen. One of the thousands trying to make it in Hollywood. I ordered black coffee, Tamara ordered ice tea. "Are we going to see Mr. Jackman in the morning?" She asked.

"I told him I'd call."

"And you think he knows this mobster."

"Bobby Rico."

Our drinks came. We ordered a brochette pizza with tomatoes, garlic, olive oil, and fresh basil.

"Is there any reason for me to be nervous?" Tamara had opened a pink package of Equal and poured it into her glass and was stirring viciously.

"These guys are business men, mostly," I said. "Might not appreciate answering questions, but no. No reason for you to be nervous."

Cardinal Red

She unwrapped her straw and sampled her drink, then turned toward the windows.

Los Angeles can be hot this time of year, and was now. The sun had dropped into the ocean but there's enough asphalt in Los Angeles to radiate heat until it rises again. That doesn't stop the action, though. The sidewalk was busy with youth. The young women in knee length black boots. Miniskirts. Orange hair with green streaks, green hair with orange streaks. Colorful knit shawls. Laced leather bodices. Every combination of outerwear imaginable. The males in torn jeans, or some in black leather pants. Boots, muscle shirts, with hair just as colorful as the females. And some, both female and male, with jewelry hanging from ears, lips, nose, eyebrows and probably from places I can only imagine. I'm nearly sixty years old, and yet I feel comfortable here.

Our pizza came on a large porcelain pan. As we ate we watched the passing street life outside our window. Occasionally, I could feel her turn and smiled at me. "You like this, don't you?"

"This?"

Her smile was soft and knowing. She opened her hand with a slight wave. "This place. This area. You like it here, don't you."

"Yes." I nodded. "I do. There's an energy here that I can feel. I like it."

She nodded, slowly turning her smile into an understanding grin.

***

We went back to the Roosevelt. I turned the car over to the valet and we went in. We got in the elevator. I punched number six. We stood close. I felt a little light headed, but I think it was probably my pulse, not her perfume.

At her door she slid her key through the slot and turned to me. That horrendous night at her house came slamming back. I went still. She touched my arm. "I'll be ready in the morning, Vic. I promise."

-20-

Wednesday Evening
September 14th
It Never Rains in
Sunny California

I was nursing a glass of rum over ice, drinking sparingly, looking down on Hollywood Boulevard. It was dark, but the street was lit with color. I could see Mann's Chinese Theater. And further down the block, the Kodak Center. There were people on the sidewalks, some of the males in t-shirts and shorts. Many of the females, in sleeveless blouses and miniskirts. Others, in sweatshirts or quilted jackets.

Traffic was heavy and slow. I sipped a small swallow of rum. A bus stopped, two men and a woman got off. Two kids, one dressed in black leather, the other in faded jeans, t-shirt and spiked hair dyed pink got on.

I looked at the bed against the wall. Tamara was on the other side. Was it possible to have a friendship with a woman like Tamara and not have these desires for more? Maybe not. And how do I deal with it when she doesn't have the same feelings?

I swallowed the rest of the coffee, tossed the empty cup in the wastebasket, turned the lamp off, and went to bed.

***

The wake-up call came at seven. I shaved in the shower and brushed my teeth. I pulled on my gray slacks and from the dresser I got a pale blue Oxford shirt. I buttoned it leaving the two top buttons open. I got my blue blazer off the hanger and slipped into it, picked the room key and the car keys off the top of the armoire and was out the door by seven forty-five.

We had breakfast in the hotel dining room. Tamara looked stunning in a white blazer, an olive green blouse and white slacks. The white accented her milk caramel complexion perfectly. Her shoes were two-inch heels with narrow black straps across her foot and around her ankle. She wore a gold necklace and a diamond tennis bracelet. It struck me that maybe I should at least button up my shirt.

I had coffee, whole-wheat toast, and a boiled egg that came in a silver eggcup. Tamara had tea and a bagel. As she stirred a teaspoon of honey into her tea she said. "Tell me about Guy Jackman."

I watched her as I explained Guy's Vietnam experience, his troubled marriage and how he came to end up in Los Angeles. When I finished she said, "And you think he knows this mobster."

I had a mouth full of toast. I swirled it down with a swallow of coffee. "When I asked if he knew Bobby Rico, he said maybe."

A furrow appeared over her nose. "Funny way to answer. Do you think--"

I took another swallow of coffee. "Do I think he's in business with the mob? Knowing Guy I doubt it, but people change. At any rate, if he knows Rico we might get an introduction and if he doesn't he may know someone who does."

The woman sitting at the next table was talking in hushed tones to a big thick-necked man seated across from her. Her hair was permed, fingernails red, and her cheeks rouged. Probably the man's wife. He wore crisp blue jeans and a shirt that must be Southern California's version of a Hawaiian shirt stretched tightly over his ample stomach. He wiped the back of his neck with the white napkin then tossed it onto the table knocking a fork to the floor. "She's knocked up, for God's sake! What did you expect me to say to her!?"

The woman had a handkerchief in her hand. She pushed the empty dishes aside and leaned toward him. "She's your daughter, Fred."

"Bullshit! She's not coming home with a bastard nigger kid."

The woman looked over at me and tried an embarrassed smile. It didn't quite work. I could see her wet eyes. She reached out to her husband. "Please, Fred," she pleaded. "Please."

Fred turned in his chair and stared at me. His face was red. I could see beads of sweat on his face. He looked at Tamara for a long moment, then back at me. I smiled and waved a finger at him. "Come on, let's get out of this fucking dump," he said.

After they left, Tamara looked at me and started to say something, stopped then smiled at me. I shrugged. "If I said I was sorry about that it wouldn't change anything, and if I kicked his ass it would make me feel better but it still wouldn't change anything."

Tamara reached out and put her hand on top of mine. "I know," she said. "I guess you're right. People don't really change."

"Well, some people mellow some."

She nodded, concern tightened her face. "Not that ass," she said. And I knew her empathy was for the wife, the daughter and the baby.

-21-

Sunset Boulevard
Thursday am,
September 15th
84 degrees, Hazy

'The Wine Cellar' is on Sunset, between Sweetzer and Fairfax. I parked around the corner on Laurel Ave, locked the car and we walked back down toward Sunset. It's hard to classify Sunset Blvd. It's contemporary, nouveau riche, modern, and Fat Burger modern, all mixed together with a few classics thrown in. And it's not just the architecture. The evenings draw thousands, flooding the clubs and sidewalks, and filling the street with many a Lexus, BMW's, and motorcycles.

We went right at the light on Sunset and walked down to a dark red brick building with a deep green canopy over the entrance. To the right of the entrance was a long plate glass window with displays of wine bottles behind the glass. To the left was a smaller window. Both windows had black, square, wrought-iron bars over them. Across the front of the canopy the gold lettering read, 'The Wine Cellar'.

"Heeeyy paisan!" Guy Jackman shouted as we came through the door. The neighborhood we grew up in was mostly Italian. Though his lineage is more kidney pie, he has always fashioned himself an Italian. He came from behind the counter with his arms out.

Guy is a lean man and about two inches shorter than I am. He has a round face with a blue shadow of whiskers and a thin black mustache. His dark brown hair was darker than I remembered, without any visible gray, and long enough to be styled. His tan had a deep healthy look and when we embraced, I'm hesitant to use that word, he smelled of expensive cologne. He stepped back and looked at Tamara then looked back at me and said, "It's been a long time, my friend." Then he turned his attention back to Tamara. "You are a beautiful woman, Ms."

He lifted the Ms. into a question. Tamara smiled.

"Guy, this is Tamara Phillips," I said.

Tamara reached her hand out and Guy took it and held it. For a moment I thought he was going to kiss it.

"Please, this way," he motioned to the open door behind the counter then guided us into his office. The carpet was light blue, the office furniture was all matching light oak. There was a black leather couch against one wall and two straight chairs with black leather arms in front of the window. The window was the small, barred one that faced the front giving a sidewalk view of Sunset Blvd. The walls were hung with photographs. Mostly movie stars or celebrities. Most of them autographed.

"Vic, Tamara, please sit," Guy said, motioning toward the couch. He swung a leg over the corner of his desk. "When did you get in? Where are you staying?" He had on a maroon short sleeved shirt with a button down collar and a yellow silk tie. His slacks were charcoal with a sharp crease down the front and the black loafers he wore had leather tassels.

"The Roosevelt. We got in yesterday afternoon. Say, you find the fountain of youth or something? I thought that was supposed to be in Florida someplace."

Guy smiled. "It's all in the mind, Vic. All in the mind." His eyes were on Tamara as he spoke.

The door opened and a small, tan woman in a white shirt and tight black slacks came in carrying a tray with a bottle and three wine glasses on it. She set the tray on a small square table beside the door. "Thank you Sherry," Guy said. Sherry turned, smiled at him and went out the door.

Guy went to the table and with a corkscrew very professionally pulled the cork from the bottle and poured the wine. "I was saddened to hear of Maureen's passing, Vic. She was a beautiful woman and I can tell you that I envied you and your marriage. My relationships don't seem to hold up."

I couldn't help glancing at Tamara beside me. "I seem to be lucky in that area, I guess."

He served the wine, propped his haunch back on the corner of his desk and lifted his glass. "Good to see you, my friend."

I held my glass up and looked through the deep crimson liquid then took a sip. It was very good and it must have showed.

Guy watched with approval. "Small vineyard. Fellow by the name of Divanti makes about four dozen cases a year. Always saves me ten cases."

"It's a long way from the dago red we used to drink as kids, Guy."

"I think about those days quite often."

"Yeah," I said.

Tamara smiled. "I'm anxious to hear about them."

I turned to Tamara. She was holding her glass to her lips with both hands. I winked. "Some other time," I said.

"So you're a private cop, now? When did this happen?"

"Few months ago. Too many years have passed to learn something different, now."

"Wrong, Paisan. Now's the time. Find something to keep you young." He smiled at Tamara, lifted his glass to her.

I shrugged and shook my head.

"You mentioned on the phone," he turned back to me. "That you were investigating a murder? And that somehow Bobby Rico's involved? Berring Harbor is not really in Rico's sphere of influence."

"His name came up is all. The strange thing is, I have two clients. A law firm involved in probating a contested estate and the murder of Barbara Mann who was murdered three weeks ago. Bobby Rico's name comes up in both cases. By the way, Barbara Mann was Tamara's half- sister. "

Guy turned his attention to Tamara and I watched the old charm I remembered come bubbling up. "Tamara, I'm so sorry," Guy said.

"Thank you," Tamara replied

Guy sipped his wine. "So what would seem to be two separate unconnected cases is somehow connected. And, you don't believe in coincidence."

"I was a cop for over thirty years, don't forget."

Guy smiled and nodded. "So where does Rico come in?"

"Barbara Mann mentioned Rico's name just before she was shot."

"Mentioned his name to you?" He looked puzzled.

"Yes. She was killed in my office."

"Jesus."

"The shooter was a pug out of Detroit by the name of Julius Santos."

Guy shook his head again. "Was, you say? I gather he's no more?"

"I killed Santos."

Again Guy shook his head. This time with a brief smile, which I took to be what he had expected me to say.

It was quiet for a moment. Through the window, the traffic along Sunset moved at a stop and go pace. Guy was looking from me to Tamara and back.

"Barbara had told me that she felt her husband was in some kind of trouble. That's when I sent her to see Vic," Tamara said.

"Jesus." He said again. "I'm so sorry, Tamara."

"Guy," I turned from the window. I had finished my drink. I set the glass on the tray. "What can you tell me about Bobby Rico?"

"I don't know how I can help you. Like I said when you called, we see him often. Maybe three, four times a month. Fashions himself as somewhat of an operator, I think. He has a place on Santa Monica near Highland called Sunshine Entertainment. Furnishes exotic dancers, strippers."

"And prostitutes," I said.

Guy shrugged. "Probably."

"How connected is he?"

"I couldn't say, Vic. But I know somebody in organized crime. Captain Weismann. At Parker Center. You know where that's at?"

"I remember."

He thought for a minute, then grinned as if he'd thought of something humorous. Maybe you won't have to go downtown," he said. He went around to his desk and reached for the phone. He looked at me and smiled at Tamara. After a moment he spoke Spanish into the phone. The only Spanish word I know is taco but I gathered by the way his voice rose and fell he wasn't ordering lunch.

Out on Sunset, a red and white LA County ambulance went by with horn and siren blaring followed by an engine company. As quiet returned, Guy hung up the phone. "Detective Hernandes at the Sherriff substation on Santa Monica in West Hollywood is the one to talk to."

"I know where it's at," I said.

"Tomorrow morning. Anytime between 9 and noon."

I looked at Tamara. We had planned to spend the morning at the Getty Museum. She smiled, nodded, and shrugged.

-22-

Thursday Two pm,
September 15th
88 degrees, Hazy

Go off Santa Monica two blocks in both directions and the area is mostly multi-story, multi-unit housing with a few single-family homes sprinkled in. But, along Santa Monica the mixture is dingy restaurants, boarded-up storefronts, sound stages in windowless concrete buildings, and fenced in lots crammed with the trucks and trailers with names like Production Support and Studio Services in black lettering on the doors. I parked on Wilcox, made sure the car was locked, then we walked back down to Santa Monica.

Sunshine Entertainment occupied the right half of a two-story, sand colored brick building on Santa Monica Boulevard between Cahuenga and Cole. I seldom notice a building as anything other than a functional structure. I noticed this one however, with its dark cocoa colored brick cornice, arches, window ledges, corners, and the turquoise shutters and door frames. An odd mix, but it worked. I liked it. Maybe I wasn't going to like what went on inside.

There were three doors in the entrance way. The one on the left seemed to open to a motorcycle showroom. The windows were dark, showing only a gleaming black road hog with a lot of chrome displayed against a flat black background. The center door I assumed led to the upper floor. Tamara pushed open the door to Sunshine Entertainment and I followed her into the small waiting room. The furniture was mismatched; a blond wood-framed sofa with beige cushions, with lamps and armchairs of various styles. Across from the door was a desk with a thin screened computer monitor and a phone council. The receptionist sat behind the desk. She was a pretty, flat-chested girl in a white sundress with pink flowers. She was thin, and freckled with long, wild peroxide-blond hair that seemed to have been blow-dried by a tornado. There was red ribbon precariously anchored in the fine, platinum flax. Her head was tilted, cradling a phone against her right ear, and at the same time she worked a crossword puzzle.

She looked up at me, then at Tamara. "Hold a minute, Mark," she said in a voice as clear and tiny as an ice crystal.

"My name's Vic Pittaro. This is Tamara Phillips. We'd like to talk with Mr. Rico, please."

"Is he expecting you, Sir?" I had never heard a voice like hers from anyone over the age of four.

"I'm a detective," I said. I hesitated, waiting. Never offer more than necessary.

She looked at Tamara and back at me. "Okay. Just a moment," she squeaked.

She put the pencil down and punched the phone council. "Mr. Rico, there's a policeman and a woman here to see you." There was a long pause then, "Mr. Rico will be with you in a few minutes," she said in her child's voice. She pointed at the chairs. "Sit if you like," she said.

We sat. Me with my gun jabbing me in the right kidney, Tamara, beside me with her legs crossed, her white skirt riding up revealing leg and thigh the color of smooth caramel. I don't know which disturbed me more.

After a few minutes of near torture, a soft ring sounded on the receptionist desk. She answered, said 'yes sir', then pointing said, "Right through that door, Sir."

***

The walls of Bobby Rico's office were lined with framed pictures of starlets, strippers, and dancers. The furniture was leather. On the couch, with his legs stretched out, sat a man in a blue sport shirt, gray slacks and leather sandals with no socks. His nose looked to have been broken at one time, a scar ran the length of his jaw. He was chewing a toothpick and looked relaxed but I sensed the look was deceptive.

Bobby Rico sat in a swivel chair behind a large mahogany desk. He was a slim man with thick black hair, in a silk sport shirt, pale blue, with the top buttons open. He had a gold herring bone chain at his throat, what looked to be a Rolex watch on his left wrist, and a woven copper bracelet on the other. He sat with his forearms flat on the bare desk, his nails nicely manicured. Behind him, through the plate glass window, was a view of a parking lot and far in the distance, high against the green hills, the famous Hollywood sign.

"I'm Vic Pittaro," I said. "This is Tamara Phillips."

Rico glanced at Tamara then back at me. I didn't know what to think. Most of the time it was the other way around.

"I don't recognize you, and I know most of the local boys," Rico said.

I took my ID from my wallet and handed it across the desk. "I'm a private detective."

Rico looked down at my ID, then over at Broken Nose and laughed. "A gumshoe from flyover land, Jake. Looks like I need to have a talk with that ditz out front about letting yokels in." He shook his head. "I don't know what's worse, a smart one or a dumb one."

I turned my head and looked back at Jake. He was grinning.

Rico held my ID up to me. "What can I do for you Mr.---ah?" He looked at my ID again. "Right. Mr. Pittaro."

It didn't look like we were going to be offered a seat. That was all right. I wasn't interested in being new best friends either. "I'm interested in what you can tell me about Jamie Adams."

"Never heard of him."

"Look, I'm not here to bust anyone's balls. Adams is involved in a civil action. I was hired by the defendant's attorney in the case to look into Adams' business here in L.A. You were in Berring Harbor last April as a guest of Jamie Adams. How did you come to know Mr. Adams, Mr. Rico?"

Bobby Rico rocked back in his swivel chair and clasped his fingers together over his chest. He looked over at the couch. "You ever hear of Berring Harbor, Jake?"

"Nope."

"The name Robert Mann mean anything to you?" I asked.

"Nope."

This was not going well and I was getting a little nervous with Nose behind me. I looked at Tamara. On the corner of the desk was a Rolodex. I pushed it aside and turned and rested a hip on the desk. At this angle I could see Jake the Nose without turning my head.

I took the copy of the Jefferson City Chronicle article from my jacket pocket and laid it on the desk. "I think that's your picture and your name is there on the guest list."

Rico pulled the article toward him and looked at it. "Yeah, that's me all right. So?"

"Recognize Jamie Adams in the picture?"

"What if I do?"

"What does that have to do with Sunshine Entertainment?" Jake the Nose said.

I looked at Jake. "Well, we yokels kind of wondered what the connection might be between Robert Mann, Jamie Adams, and Mr. Rico, here."

"You're a funny guy. Real funny, ain't he Bobby?"

Rico leaned forward in his chair. "I'm tired of this. We're all done here. Jake, show these people out."

Jake stood.

I rose from the corner of the desk, opened my jacket and put my hand on my gun. "You're right," I said. "This is getting tiresome."

Rico lifted his hand and the Nose stopped close enough to where I could smell his cologne.

I felt Tamara step close to me as Jake and I looked at each other. I hadn't imagined him being as tall as he was, or as fit. It wasn't hard to picture him as a heavy in an action movie. I broke eye contact first and turned to Rico. "We, Ms. Phillips and I, thought we could just have a pleasant chat with you. And we, Ms. Phillips and I, thought a friendly chat would accomplish more with less hassle than it would if the questions came from Captain Weismann. Guess I should have realized Berring Harbor is a long way from LA in more ways than just distance."

"Fuck you. You're nothing here," Rico said. He glanced at Tamara. "Pardon the language Ma'am, but why the hell should I be answering any of your questions?"

Tamara pulled a photo from her purse and handed it across the desk. "Do you know this woman, Mr. Rico?"

He glanced at the photo and handed it back. "Ah, no. Should I?" He shifted his look to me.

"The woman in the photo is Barbara Mann, my sister," Tamara said. "She's dead. Murdered. Her last name may have been Kaine when you were her agent."

"I was her agent?"

"She was a dancer," I said.

"Dancer," Rico said to Jake.

"Dancer," Jake replied around the toothpick firm in his teeth. He had moved back and was leaning against the wall next to the door pretending to look relaxed.

Rico rocked back in his chair, put his hands together, and touched his chin with his fingertips. "Ms. Phillips ---"

Rico moved his mouth to let me know he was thinking. He punched a button on his phone and said, "Trixie, look through the files in the bottom right drawer of your desk for a file with the name of Kaine on it and bring it to me."

I heard Trixie's voice on the speaker. I heard a bus go pass on Santa Monica. We watched each other. I watched Rico. Jake watched me. Tamara watched Jake and me. Nobody was going to get away with anything. Finally Rico said, "Ms. Phillips, I place a lot of girls. I don't recognize the photo, or the name. Probably not the name she used anyway. If there is a record, which I doubt, you may have it."

He looked at me. "Mr. Gumshoe, Jamie Adams is a pip-squeak. He likes to think of himself as a big shot player because he's put some money in a couple low budget B movies. He's not smart enough to realize he's being taken for a ride. The real players out here love to see these hayseeds show up with their bank accounts. I was in Jefferson City on business. Adams had invited me to this function, as he called it, and as long as I was in the area I thought it might be fun. I was wrong."

"Yes, Trixie," Rico said.

"I couldn't find anything, Sir."

Rico punched the intercom off without responding. "There you have it. Now get out."

I looked at Tamara and we moved toward the door and passed Jake the Nose. As we went through the door Tamara turned to Rico and said with just the right amount of sarcasm, "Nice talking with you, Mr. Rico. You've been a big help."

I followed her out onto the sidewalk and down to the corner. I stopped, looked at her, and shook my head. "What?" she said. Her cocoa complexion seemed to darken. The tendons in her neck stood out like two cables.

"Rico," I said.

She stared back at the sandy brick building. "He's an ass," she spat.

I nodded. "I couldn't have said it better myself."

-23-

LA County Sheriff's Sub-station
Friday, September 16th
Three pm. 73 degrees, Hazy

It was already in the mid-70's with a faint haze over the Hollywood hills. I stood in front of a low, brown-brick square building that is the L.A. County Sheriffs Sub-station in West Hollywood at a little after ten the next morning watching the morning traffic move along Santa Monica Boulevard. An orange and white transit bus went by traveling toward Hollywood, trailing the scent only natural gas leaves. Across the street, a shabbily dressed woman, young, maybe in her twenties, pawed through a waste container searching for anything of any value while her male companion rested his backpack against the side of the building.

I'd had a bagel and coffee alone in the restaurant in the Roosevelt dining room and I think the coffee had turned my stomach sour. Tamara had slept in. Anyway, that's what she said she was going to do.

I went up the three steps and through the door into the Sub-station anteroom, a small, stuffy, windowless room painted lime green with a narrow counter and a plate glass partition that separated the entry from the rest of the building. There was a pass-through and a speak-through in the glass like you see in some banks and I could feel a breath of cool air come from the openings. On the left was a windowless door and on the far wall a recruitment poster, attempting to show the diversity of the Los Angeles County Sheriff's Department.

Beyond the glass I could see four desks. On the back wall was an office with blinds on the windows. That would be the commander's office. The narrow corridor on the right, behind the desks, led back to whatever was in the back. Probably where the doughnuts were kept. Two of the four desks were empty. A uniformed deputy sat behind the one closest to the glass. His nametag read, 'Graham'. He was tilted back in his swivel chair with his feet on his desk looking up at me, his big hands folded behind his

Cardinal Red 187

head. He looked to be in his 50's and it showed in his face. His facial features were large and his skin had a gray cast. He showed no willingness to affirm my presence, but his eyes were open. It would be a violation to sleep on the job. Back in the corner at the fourth desk, the chair was slid back and computer was on. There was a navy blazer hung over the back of the chair.

I took my card from my coat pocket and slid it through the pass-through and spoke into the speak-through. "Detective Hernandes is expecting me."

It was a strain for Graham, but he managed to get his feet off his desk and sit up in his chair without tumbling to the floor, but I could tell from the look he gave me that I had disturbed him. He reached for my card without a word, studied it a moment, turned and shouted, "Hernandes!"

He turned back and studied the card some more. A moment later a tall, high-waisted woman came from the hallway carrying a coffee cup. She wore a white short-sleeved blouse and slacks that fit well and were either a very dark blue or black. I couldn't tell.

"What is it, Graham?"

"There's a shoofly here to see you. Says you're expecting him."

Shoofly! The last person I knew to use that word was Raymond Chandler.

I couldn't make out what the woman said through the glass but Graham nodded toward the door at about the same moment I heard the door buzz. So I took my cue and pulled the door open.

"Detective Hernandes, I'm Victor Pittaro." Her handshake was brief. I put her in her mid-forties though she could have been older. She was within an inch of my height, with auburn hair, styled short. She had a pleasant face, dark eyes, a wide mouth, and there were freckles around her nose. She wore no jewelry. Her blouse, I decided, had a sheen and was probably silk, which set off her southern California complexion. She looked fit enough to come out ahead in a tussle, and the 9mm Beretta on her right hip gave her extra points. Oh, and the slacks were black.

I showed my license. While she examined it I said, "Guy Jackman called you?"

She hadn't yet asked me to sit so we were standing beside her desk.

"Yes. That asshole," she said.

I didn't know what to say to that, so I ignored it. "I'm working a murder investigation and I was hoping you could give me a little of your time."

She was still studying my license. "And you know Guy Jackman, how?"

She said his name like you would say the word viper. I ignored that too. "We grew up together," I said.

"Here?" she asked, pointing a manicured fingernail to my license, to the state insignia embossed across the top.

"Yes," I said.

"Well, I'll be damned." She handed my license back then seemed to study me a moment then said, "Well, I guess none of us are without our crosses to bear."

I put my license back in my jacket pocket. I was beginning to think my old buddy had set me up. "Detective, there are two names that keep coming up in the investigation. One of them, Bobby Rico, comes up in NCIC. I have that. What I would like is to find someone who can fill me in with the details. The other name is Barbara Kaine. The victim. Evidently, she worked out here in the entertainment industry for a while before moving back home and marrying. I asked Rico about her, but he claimed he'd never heard of her. I'm sure he was lying because she had told me his name just before she was killed."

Hernandes looked at me strangely, like she was trying to follow what I had said and couldn't.

"Barbara Kaine had come to my office to ask me to look into a problem. Before she could say much a shooter by the name of Julius Santos walked up to the door and shot her."

Hernandes gave me a quizzical look. "In your office?"

"Yes."

"And --- this Santos?"

I nodded.

She studied me for a moment. "I see," she said.

"You talked with Mr. Rico, then?"

"We've talked."

"Enlightening, I presume. When I talked with Mr. Jackman yesterday I was led to understand that you were a police officer." She was looking straight at me. I recognized the look.

"Monroe County Sheriff's Department Retired, Detective."

"I see. Mr. Jackman has a deceitful way of representing things."

She took some time studying me, to the point where I was beginning to feel uncomfortable. I couldn't wait to get my hands on my old friend Guy. Finally she said, "Let's see if we have anything on the woman. What was her name?"

"Barbara Kaine."

She sat and went to her rolodex and spun it with a pencil, stopped, turned it again, stopped, and said, "Let's see if I can get what you want with a phone call."

I looked around, took a chair from the next desk and sat, without being asked. She identified herself, name and shield number, to whoever was on the other end of the call and asked for the ticket on Bobby Rico then tapped her pencil on the desk while she waited. From somewhere in the back, I heard a man's laugh, then a man in light khakis and a colorful cotton shirt worn loose over his waist came down the hallway. He gave me an uninterested glance, and went to an empty desk. Finally she said, "Great, Rollo. Just a sec." She cupped her hand over the mouthpiece and looked at me. "Where are you staying?"

"The Roosevelt."

She went back to the phone. "Rollo, have a copy couriered to Homicide Detective, Victor Pittaro at the Roosevelt. Thanks."

She had surprised me and I guess it showed on my face. "Slick," I said. "Thanks."

Her smile evaporated some of the hardness in her face. "Alberto Rollo works Vice. I'm sure he knows Mr. Rico well." She turned to her computer and began keying. "The woman, spell her name K-a-n-e?"

"K-a-i-n-e," I said. I was beginning to like Detective Hernandes and I was getting anxious to have a little chat with my old pal, Guy Jackman.

"Do we know when she was supposed to have been in the LA area?"

"Between '94 and '99."

"A middle name or initial?"

"Marie," I said, leaning in.

She angled the screen toward me and highlighted a name. "Here's a Barbara Marie Kaine, arrested in July of '97 for soliciting and again in March of '98. Served no time. In June of '98 she was arrested at the Blue Bird Lounge in Westwood for disorderly conduct."

I recalled the image of the Barbara Kaine walking into my office and I remembered the contradiction I'd felt.

Detective Hernandes looked at me. "Probably code violations but it doesn't say. No time served." She chuckled to herself. "Guess what name she gave the arresting officer?"

"No," I said.

"Yes." she said. "Kandy. With a K."

"Imagine that," I said. I stood up, spun the chair back to the next desk. "Thanks for your time, Detective."

"Well, I hope I was somewhat helpful."

"It all helps," I said.

"That's the way it usually works." She stood. She handed me her business card. "Little by little, it comes together."

I glanced at it and stuck it in my pocket. "Usually," I said.

"Yes. And Mr. Pittaro," There was humor in her smile. "tell Mr. Jackman that I said to go take a flying fuck at a rolling doughnut."

"I'm sure that's been suggested to him before."

"Yes," she said. "I'm sure it has."

I gestured a tip of a hat and left.

-24-

Roosevelt Hotel Pool
Friday 4:30 pm
September 16th

I made my way back down Santa Monica Boulevard to Hollywood wondering if I had learned anything new. By the time I turned into the Roosevelt I'd decided I had only confirmed what I already knew. I parked under the canopy, turned the rental over to the valet and went up to my room. There was a message waiting to call the concierge. I did. Ms. Phillips would be in the pool garden.

And she was. She was sitting in a plastic chaise near the pool in a black one-piece suit with a silver satin band around the waist reading Sunsets, by Lyn Miller LaCoursiere. There was a small drink table beside her with a tall glass with a straw. Behind her was a flood of green fern, Bird of Paradise, and behind that, some kind of palm. I stood back unnoticed in the humid air and watched her. There was a presence about her that was more than her cocoa complexion or her physical presence. It was as if she was in motion while perfectly still. The word elegant came to me. I walked over, hoping that I wouldn't blurt something stupid. "Hi," I said.

I looked around for a place to sit. She smiled, marked her place then scooched her legs to the side making room on the chaise. "Here," she said.

I swallowed hard trying not to stare, then gave up. "Elegant," I said, making a point of admiring her legs.

Her smile remained as she rolled her eyes. "So, what have we learned about Barbara today?"

She reached for the drink. I looked around, then went to the other side of the pool and came back with a metal chair, set it facing her, sat, and told her. Which didn't take long.

"So other than what we surmised, the only thing we really learned was her stage name."

"Yeah. That, plus there is or was something between Detective Hernandes and Guy."

"Speaking of Guy," Tamara said. "What was that about you taking him up on some proposition?"

"After Mo died he offered to set me up in Santa Monica with a wine shop. He called it 'The Wine Cellar Annex'."

She smiled. "And you turned him down?"

"Couldn't imagine myself living here."

"Oh, I can. I can imagine you living here," Tamara answered.

I started to respond then couldn't think of anything. I was having trouble keeping my attention focused on our conversation. "Hungry?" That's it, I thought. Go from one hunger to another.

"Famished."

-25-

Sunday Morning
September 18th
Clear Sky, 78 degrees
Breeze off the Ocean at 5-8 mph

We had dropped off the rental Buick and had taken the shuttle to the LAX terminal and were now sitting in one of those highly marketed Italian fast food places waiting for our flight to be called. Tamara was picking at her thirteen dollar salad trying to find a lettuce leaf with a modicum of life left. "Did we learn anything?"

"I don't know. Doesn't seem like it, does it?" I studied the lasagna on my fork, then stuck it in my mouth and washed it down with some very bad coffee. "Do you think we'd have been better off with the airline food?"

"Probably," she said.

Tamara was wearing black twill slacks, a black top and a short sleeved Sateen jacket with wide lapels. A string of pearls adorned her neck. She reached across the table and laid her hand over mine. "I might be crazy, Vic. But--- well, even though we didn't learn anything about Barbara's murder I feel like I am doing something. When Roger was murdered, Jimmy Keenin was identified as the killer and arrested the next day. It felt like I had nothing to do but to grieve. Oh, I dealt with the funeral, and the trial and all, but I had no purpose."

A gray-haired man with a gray mustache came in followed by a younger man. Both were trailing small, black pull along luggage. Both were dressed alike in long tailored trench coats with the belts hanging loosely, and silver wings pinned to the collars. I watched them walk to the counter. I watched the black woman with the red and white paper ball-cap take their orders, and all I could think of was how nice Tamara's hand felt on mine.

"I feel guilty about the last three days, Tamara. We could have flown home yesterday, or even Friday."

Tamara smiled at me. "I know. Staying was partly my idea, too." We sat quietly for a time picking at our food.

Watching her speak had several advantages. Between listening over the noise of the terminal and the buzzing in my ears, I had to read her lips to follow her words. And to read her lips, I had to be looking into her face. I liked that. We had spent the past three days together exploring LA, and it was probably the most pleasant time I've had in years. "We travel well together," I said.

She smiled that non-committal smile again and pushed the plastic plate of salad away. "I loved the promenade in Santa Monica. But I think the Getty Museum was the highlight."

"What about Universal Studios?"

"Fun. But, giving what we're about to do, I could have done without the plane crash in the War of the Worlds exhibit."

"You're right," I acknowledged. "And, I could have done without this." I wiped my mouth with the paper napkin, balled it and dropped it on top of what was left of the fake lasagna. I pushed the plastic plate aside and rested my arms on the table. "But, I really enjoyed this time with you."

Her eyes smiled. "And you're fun to be with," she said.

My face felt a little warm.

When we got back to the gate and seated, I reached into my jacket pocket for the packet that Detective Rollo sent over on Bobby Rico and handed it to Tamara. "Nothing in it that would connect him with Barbara's murder," I said, "or any clue as to why he would be connected. Except---"

"Except?"

"He seems the only one in this mess, so far at least, that would have the connections to hire a man like Santos."

She turned the manila envelope in her hands. "So," she said. "We keep him on the list."

I nodded. "High on the list," I said.

"And his only connection's to Berring Harbor are Jamie Adams, or the Cookton County Cultural Center."

"Or both," I said.

Tamara opened the packet containing Rico's sheet. The first page was a summary. She read it aloud. "January, 1986 assault. May, 1987 possession with intent. Served ninety days in county jail. May, 1991 arrested on suspicion of murder. 1991 released, insufficient evidence."

She looked up. "Nothing since."

"That's street stuff," I said. "He's several rungs above that now. The rest are the dispositions of the charges, arresting officer's names, investigator's names, assistant district attorneys, arresting officer's statements, witness statements. Detective Rollo stapled his card to the back page with a note to call him if I want to know what he knows but can't prove. I'll call him first thing in the morning."

-26-

Sunday Night,
September 18th

It was nearly midnight as we jostled down through buffeting winds and heavy rain. The cabin was dark, except for a few tiny reading lights. Odds were, however, that not many passengers were sleeping. Beyond the cabin window the night is as black as a cave, except when the lightning flashes. Rivulets of rain streaked horizontally across the outside glass. The pilot dipped the right wing sharply and suddenly, as if someone snapped on a switch, the lights of Jefferson City appeared in the blackness glowing like balls of yellow fuzz then almost instantly the wheels slammed the runway. Tamara's fingers dug into my forearm, the plane danced for a moment then settled onto the glistening black asphalt.

We got our luggage and a taxi. My car was at Tamara's, twenty minutes away. By the time we hit the interstate, Tamara had her eyes closed and her head resting against my shoulder. I sat quietly, listening to the work of the wipers, afraid to move, afraid to disturb her. The lights of Jefferson City gave in to the wet blackness of fields of what I knew to be wheat and corn. What the hell had we learned in LA? That Jamie Adams had spread a fair amount of money around Hollywood but he had a reputation as a bungler. That Bobby Rico did have a connection to Berring Harbor through Jamie Adams, or the Cookton County Cultural Center, or Robert Mann. We learned nothing about Barbara Kaine-Mann, and that didn't set right. Didn't even seem enough to justify the plane fare.

The cabbie took the 3rd St. exit and we went into Berring Harbor the back way, along the river. The rain had quit, leaving water standing in the intersections. The beacon on the top of the radio tower flashed a red halo. I cracked the window and inhaled the damp, heavy air. Water slammed the bottom of the taxi as we passed under the railroad bridge at Grand Avenue and 3rd. The CCI truck terminal was washed in yellow yard lights giving the whole complex a surreal look. Tractors lined the fence, their green paint glistening wet. Two tractor/trailer sets were lined up in front of the office.

Tamara sat up when we turned onto Tower Street and I realized she hadn't been asleep. I got out when we turned into the driveway and stopped. Tamara pulled our luggage from the trunk. I paid the fare, put my bag in the trunk of the Sebring while Tamara dug for her keys. She was behind me, her carry-on over her shoulder, the light from the streetlight across the street, behind her. "Come in for a moment, Vic."

A Dante like image of the last time flashed through my mind. I winced to alleviate the pain. Never again. I closed the trunk lid and turned. "Are you sure? You must be tired."

She took my hand, turning, smiling. The streetlight reflected in her black eyes and made her Jamaican face glow. "I'm sure," she said. "Just for a few minutes."

I swallowed feeling immature, and feeling embarrassed about the feeling. "Lead the way. I'll get your luggage."

I stood, my back to the fireplace and sipped my rum and coke in the dim light of the recessed lighting over the mantel. Dumb to be standing here, I thought. There was no fire. Just seemed like the place to wait. Like in some '40's movie on the classic movie channel. I could see the light slipping beneath her bedroom door down the short hallway. Any moment now she will come through that door and into the room in a satin robe.

She came out barefoot and had shed the jacket but still wore the black slacks and blouse. I felt the tension spill from my chest. "You look refreshed," I said.

"Thanks, Vic. Sorry if I took too long?"

I sipped at my drink, mainly to keep me from stumbling. This was not going well. "Tamara I really should be going. That red-eye flight took a lot out me and I'm sure you're tired too."

"Yes, I am. I just wanted to tell you that even though we didn't uncover anything useful in Barbara's murder, the time with you was very pleasant."

"Well, you never know what will turn out to be important. What I've learned over the years is to just keep asking questions. Most of the time things eventually start to come together. But I'm glad you came, too. In fact, it's been the most pleasant six days I've spent in a long time."

Tamara smiled and looked up at me. I saw the mantel lights reflected in her dark eyes. I felt the butterflies rise in the pit of my stomach. My throat tightened. I swallowed. "I have to say, I wasn't sure you would go."

She took my drink from my other hand, set it on the mantel and stepped so close I could feel the heat of her body. "If you would like to kiss me again, I would like that," she said softly.

My throat felt thick again and I couldn't open my mouth fearing my heart would pop out. I could smell her perfume, her hair. A scent I don't think I will ever forget. She came up on her toes and we kissed. A long, soft, lingering kiss. When she backed away she said, "Call me tomorrow, if you like."

I heard the door close behind me, heard the latch turn and saw the hall light go off. I stood there long enough to regain my balance then went down the three steps and walked to my car. I felt like whistling.

-27-

Monday Noon,
September 19th
72 degrees,
Light Cloud Cover

The Monday lunch rush was in full swing and I needed coffee badly. I hadn't slept much and it wasn't the jet lag. I hadn't been able to get Tamara's scent or the taste of her lips off my mind long enough to fall asleep.

Danny Khanh and I were sitting at a high table at a chain bar/restaurant in the Rock Creek Mall. I was wearing a beige polo shirt, my wool-blend sport coat to hide my gun, and washed out denims. Danny wore blue jeans and a plaid shirt that hung loosely over his waist. The bottom part of his holster showed below the hem of his shirt.

I had checked my watch twice before the waitress showed up with two menus and two glasses of water. She was in uniform. White short-sleeved blouse, tight black slacks, and a black apron. She set the menus on the table, smiled a meaningless smile and left. "Think she'll come back?" I asked Danny.

Danny shrugged. My eyes burned but my guess was it was more from a lack of sleep than the cigarette smoke that hung over the bar. But the price was worth it.

When our waitress came back it was apparent she was rushed and didn't want to waste any time. I ordered pastrami on rye, fries and coffee black. "The coffee now, please." Danny ordered a fully dressed burger and a bottle of Budweiser with a glass. I looked at him, frowned, and half-turned away. The diners seemed to be evenly divided between men and women, and also equality divided between shoppers and retail workers.

"And by the way," he said, "you look like shit."

My coffee arrived, as did Danny's beer. I nodded and began spooning ice from my water glass into my coffee. When I thought it was about right I leaned forward and took a huge gulp. It was hot and strong. About three of these, I thought, and I'll be all right.

The room was dressed for fun. Mirrors with gold lettering. A lot of brass. Colorful neon beer signs. Focused lighting highlighting the mahogany bar and the glasses and bottles behind it. Bartenders in black vests over white long-sleeved shirts with the sleeves rolled up.

The three suits at the table behind us left. In a matter of minutes, the table was cleared and wiped and another set of lunch diners was ushered in.

The waitress came with my pastrami sandwich and Danny's burger. She refilled my coffee, looked from me to Danny and back to me, then laid the check next to my water glass. Guess she thought I looked the more affluent of the two.

I had taken a bite of my sandwich and was looking at it, surprised at how good it tasted. The bread was fresh with a crusty crust and the pastrami was stacked thick with just the right amount of brown mustard. I tried the fries. They were cold.

How did your LA trip turn out?"

"Didn't learn anything that fits into this. Had a tete-a-tete with a hood named Bobby Rico, which was interesting. Seems he never heard of anybody. But according to Barbara Mann, she knew him in LA as a talent agent."

A sliver of lettuce clung to the corner of Danny's mouth. "And I suppose talent agent is a euphemism for---?"

"You're too cynical, Danny."

Danny took a swallow of beer and wiped his mouth with his napkin. "So, how's this Rico connected to this case?"

"Don't know that he is. I just thought since Barbara Mann saw him at a fundraiser for the Cookton County Cultural Center, and recognized him from LA, and he was there as a guest of Jamie Adams, and I'm involved in both cases, I should find out something about him."

I shrugged. We watched an Asian woman in a white satin blouse and a gray wool skirt with a slit up the side walk by. When she got to the bar, she turned and looked back.

"Too fricking bad," Danny said.

"What's too fricking bad?"

"That I wasn't this hot when I was single."

"What makes you think she's not looking at me?"

The ice in the water glass had melted and I was busy spooning water into my cup the waitress had just refilled. I sipped the coffee, added two more spoons of the water and a packet of sugar, and stirred.

Danny smiled and turned his back toward the woman. "And the official investigation?" I said.

"Not much. Schnider pulled cell phone records on both. Husband and wife. Nothing unusual. John Mann had the company financials released and the Sherriff sent them to the States' financial guys."

"Really!" That surprised me. "Tommy Schnider's good with that sort of thing. Hu-mmm."

Cardinal Red

Danny slanted a look at me. "Something I should know?"

I shook my head. "Just thinking," I said. "Political connections. Elections coming up. And Erskine is a politician."

"A-ha." Danny said. "Robert Mann's senate campaign. See, I'm learning. Tesch said I'd learn if I stuck with you."

"Tesch said that?"

Danny smiled. "Well not those exact words. More like, 'if he does learns anything, don't forget who you work for.'"

I finished my sandwich and pushed the plate away. The waitress hustled by. I pointed at my empty cup. She stopped, looked at the cup, at me, at Danny, at his empty bottle, picked up the check, and left. "Robert Mann." I said.

"What?"

"Something's off there with those two."

"Robert Mann and his wife."

I nodded. We were quiet for a bit. The waitress came back with Danny's beer and my coffee, and dropped the check on the edge of the table. My cup was two-thirds full. Danny's glass of beer had an eighth inch of foam. He lifted the glass, looked at it a moment, shrugged, and said, "You think they're involved?"

I dumped some water from my glass into the coffee, and sipped some. "I didn't say that," I said.

We were quiet again. My coffee cooled. I stirred a packet of sugar in and drank some more.

Danny poured the last of his beer and was turning his glass with his fingers. He stopped, "So, where do we go from here?"

I shrugged. After a long pause I said, "I don't know. The brother and his wife seem to be the only connection to all the parties. Maybe I'll just make a pain-in-the-ass of myself and see what comes of it."

Danny smiled and shook his head. "Should be easy," he said.

***

The next morning I had taken care of Nisha and was on my way to prove Danny Khanh right. It was the only plan I'd come up with. I stopped at a Pastries Plus on the way out of town and bought an egg and sausage sandwich, two old-fashioned doughnuts and a large coffee too go. The traditional cop's breakfast.

The traffic on State Highway 29 moved at steady speed and I settled in. I wonder what Tamara's doing? She did ask me to call. I glanced at my watch. 10:10. I dug my cell from my pocket, then tossed it on the seat beside me. Don't do it, I chided myself. I slid Magic by Bruce Springsteen in the CD player. Magic is what I felt when I thought of Tamara. It didn't work. The words ran together with images of Tamara so vivid they over-shadowed the music. Her large dark eyes. Her scent. Her kiss. I punched the CD button off and I thought about the weather. The weather report in the paper indicated the recent pattern of rain every other day had ended. We'll see. It was a beautiful day for mid-September. Many people claim fall as their favorite time of year, though I think they're very short sighted. And I have to admit fall is somewhat agreeable. The temperature is pleasant, the days roll on, clear and bright. It's nature's plan to mesmerize us, to lull us into a stupor before slamming us into the dark of winter. But I'm wise to her.

I could call and ask Tamara to a late lunch. Yes! Probably be back in town by one. Generally doesn't take me long to make an ass of myself, as recent events prove. I tried whistling for several miles, then finally found 'NPR' on the radio.

By the time the sandwich and one of the doughnuts were gone I was coming into Bayfield. I stopped at a Quick Stop, used the bathroom, bought another coffee and was back on the road.

I drove up the red brick drive of Robert Mann's home, parked and got out. I was wearing gray slacks, a powder blue shirt, and my black ankle boots that zipped up the side. I grabbed my blazer from the other seat, got out and slipped it on and went up the fieldstone walk to the front stoop.

I punched the doorbell and could hear a faint chime come from inside. I waited. The stone fountain was still running. The flowers were gone from the hydrangea, leaving brown nubs where the blooms had been and the leaves had a dry look to them. I rang the doorbell again and in a moment Janet Mann opened the door.

"Yes?" she said.

Her pause was barely noticeable as her cigarette voice mellowed. "Oh, Detective," she said.

She looked as she had before, except the slacks were gray and her top was a blue flower print faded to nearly white. "Please, come in. Robert's not here. He's usually at the shop until about four."

"I won't come in. I just wanted to ask you, Bobby Rico told me that he had met you." Which was untrue.

"And you'd said you didn't know him. I just wondered if you could clear that up for me?"

"Oh. Well---" She looked up. "I---I just don't recall the name."

I've learned over the years, most people, when trying to squirm from under a gotcha, will portray innocence by making solid eye contact.

Her look was direct and determined. "Where was it I was supposed to have met him?"

"He didn't say. Just that he'd met you and Robert last April."

"Well, I---"

She looked down briefly in thought. "Bob and I meet so many people. April you say?"

I nodded.

"Could have been at the County Cultural Center in Jefferson City," she said. "I just don't recall."

I nodded again. "Okay. Thanks for trying." I turned and stepped away.

"That's all you wanted?"

"Yes. Thank you."

"You drove here from Berring Harbor to ask me one question when you could have just called?"

"I had nothing better to do," I said, and walked to my car.

In my rear view mirror, I watched Janet Mann framed in her doorway looking after me, until I was beyond the driveway curve.

-28-

Jefferson City,
Wednesday Noon
September 21st

The Castaways Gentleman's Club is in the Oak Hill district of Jefferson City, on the corner of Halsted and Rose. It's a two-story sand colored brick building with plywood covering the second story windows, sandwiched between a three-story brick faced concrete block building on one side and a vacant lot on the other. There was an alleyway between Castaways and the vacant lot. Halfway down the side of the building, a man stood with his back to the street urinating on the brick. Thirty-Two years ago, when I was a rookie patrolman on the Jefferson City force, the building was a movie theater. Later it was a furniture store. Today the marquee proclaimed 'Nude Dancers Every Night.' The marquee has served each new enterprise well.

I parked on the street alongside the vacant lot overgrown with weeds and secured by a high wire fence. The square metal sign on the chained and padlocked wire gate read property of Jefferson City Parks Dept. Hard to imagine what was being protected.

I locked my car and walked back to the Castaways. The glassed in poster boards on either side of the entrance, that in my time held movie posters or later, 'No money down' furniture ads, now held prints of nude women with black squares arranged in delicate places. The plate-glass windows were painted black three-fourths of the way up.

I hesitated inside the door and quickly scanned the room. No place looks more dingy or seedy than a strip joint in the middle of the day. There was a long bar along the left side of the room. A raised stage on the right with a walkway that extended out into the room. The televisions that hung from the ceiling in every corner were all dark but one. Two men in work clothes sat at a table drinking beer, watching a replay of a basketball game on the one that was on. I knew it was a replay because that's what it said in the bottom corner of the screen. The rest of the tables were vacant. A slow afternoon.

A man in a gray linen sport coat and dark slacks stood at the far end of the bar talking with the bartender, a black man who looked like he could have been in the Chicago Bears defensive line when he was younger.

I went toward the server station in the center of the bar. The bartender started my way. "What'll it be?" he said putting a napkin with a beer logo on the bar in front of me.

"Jamie in?"

"Jamie?"

"Jamie Adams."

"You ah cop?"

"What makes you think that?"

"You look like ah cop, an your carrin' on the right hip."

"Good eyes," I said. "Name's Pittaro." I took a business card from my shirt pocket and laid it on the bar. He picked up the card, read it, then walked down and handed it to the man at the end of the bar.

I recognized Jack Adams as he walked over. "Jack," I said. "I'd like to talk with Jamie if he's around."

Jack Adams was Jamie's older brother. He looked like his father when his father was young. Jack laid my business card on the bar, looked at the bartender and nodded, then said to me, "What's this about?"

I watched the bartender pick up a phone. "Just doing some background for a client," I said. I turned back to Jack. "Client said she knew Jamie. Thought I'd ask."

Jamie came thru the office door. Gray pinstripe suit with charcoal slacks that seemed to be custom made. Pale blue shirt unbuttoned at the throat. Black loafers with tassels. Jamie was smaller than his brother with a narrow face, a sharp nose. His dark hair looked like it was styled and he wore a thin Hollywood moustache. When he turned to say something to the bartender I noticed he wore a small silver ring in his right ear and one of those short pigtails that hung over his collar.

He stopped beside his brother. "What the fuck you want, asshole. It's all settled with the bitch, haven't you heard?"

"I heard. That's one of the reasons I stopped by. To congratulate you. From what I heard your stepmother was far more generous than you deserve."

He stared at me for a hard intimidating moment. "Fuck you," he said. "You're not welcome here. Take a walk." He made a dismissive gesture with his hand, turned his back to me, leaned his elbows on the bar and tried to pretend I had left.

Jack had taken a step back. The bartender was trying to look busy washing glasses.

"Jamie. Jamie." I said. I looked around. The two men watching the television had stopped watching and watched us. "The other reason I stopped by," I said. "has nothing to do with Janet or the estate. I have a client that said she knows you. Barbara Mann."

Jamie turned his head and looked at me. "Connie," he said over his shoulder. "Give me a tonic with some ice."

"Had a client," he said to me. "I read the papers."

"Right."

"If you think I had something to do with her murder you're fucking crazy."

"I'm not suggesting anything. She said she knew you is all. I just wanted to confirm what she said."

Jamie gave me that stare again. "I don't remember." Connie came over, laid a napkin on the bar in front of Jamie and set down his drink.

"She said she had met you at the Cookton County Cultural Center last April."

He smiled faintly. "I don't remember." He picked up his drink and sipped. "But it could be. I'm very civic minded and very interested in culture."

"Sure," I said. "Know a Robert Mann?"

"Nope."

"Janet Mann?"

"What the hell is this?"

"I take that as a no?"

"You're getting smarter."

"Bobby Rico?"

"Never heard of no Bobby Rico."

That was a lie. His eyes gave it away. And I had the feeling that I was going to get nothing more from him. Which is just what I gotten since I'd walked in.

"Okay, Jamie. Thanks for your time." I picked my card from the bar, stuck it in Jamie's jacket pocket and walked past the two men at the table toward the door.

Jamie said, "Pittaro."

I turned back. Jamie was smiling. "Good luck," he said.

I went out the door and walked to my car and drove back to Berring Harbor. I'll have to think about this, see if I did learn anything.

-29-

September 23rd
Friday Night
68 degrees

I forced my eyes open and reached for the phone and knocked a half glass of water off the bedside table onto the carpet. "Shit!" I dry mouthed.

"Yeah?"

"Vic. I'm on my way to the scene of a shooting on Collins Avenue. The Lieutenant wants you there."

From the tube on the dresser, Leno was telling me to stay tuned for Jimmy Fallon. Nisha lifted her head from the rug beside my bed.

I was coming to, slowly. "Danny? What-- what the hell time is it?"

"11:30. The Lieutenant wants you there ASAP."

"What's it have to do with me? Who's the victim?"

"No identification on the body. The only thing they've found so far is your business card."

"Mine!" That woke me up.

Nisha roused and was inspecting the wet spot in the carpet. "I'm at home, Danny. I'll meet you out front."

I threw the blanket off, sat up and rubbed the sleep from my eyes. I'm at home? What a dumb thing to say. Where the hell else would I be?

"Ten minutes," Danny said. I heard the click.

"A shooting. Who the hell could that be?" I said aloud. Nisha yipped and shook her head. "You want to go out, right girl?"

I got my boots and black leather jacket from the closet, sat on the sofa and pulled on my jeans and boots.

In less than ten minutes we had toured the back yard and were back inside. I hung my gun on my belt, and when I walked out the front door Danny Khanh was waiting in a black sedan.

***

I've spent some professional time in the area over the years. Collins Avenue runs north and south along the eastern edge of Berring Harbor. The west side of Collins is city, the east side belongs to Monroe County and as such belongs to the Sheriff's Department. It's a place most people avoid unless they're after some of the specialty merchandise that's traded there. The County Board mostly turns a blind eye to the area believing that the drug dealers and prostitutes if put out of business along the avenue, would just turn up somewhere else. And the city is content to keep the area on the fringe. It's a policy of containment both governments deem favorable. It also offers a place for some of the more righteous in the area to fulfill their dark needs in reasonable anonymity.

When we turned onto Collins I could see a cluster of official vehicles, lights swirling through the dark, turning the street into a carnival midway. Knots of people, mostly young and black, congregated noisily in the street. We drove slowly through them, past city squad cars, an EMT wagon and county cruisers, then made a u-turn in the middle of the street and slid up behind a black sedan angled in against the curb in front of a grimy, three-story brownstone. The top windows along the front were boarded up with sheets of plywood. Several of the first floor windows were broken out. A uniformed city patrolman stood guard at the door. Danny flashed his shield and went in.

I followed Danny past the patrolman into the foyer, dark but for the lights pulsing through a broken window from the vehicles in the street and the dim glow from a light at the top of the stairway. The smells were of piss and cooking grease and cabbage. They grew stronger as I followed Danny up the stairs to the second floor. Light spilled from an open doorway where a sheriff's deputy, who I didn't know, stood talking to someone inside the apartment. As we approached, the stink of Steve Tesch's cigar struck me. I almost preferred the resident odors.

Danny flashed his shield at the tall, young deputy. The deputy nodded. As Danny went through the doorway the deputy extended his hand stopping me. "He's with me," Danny said to him. The expression of the officer's stern face didn't change as he looked at me. Then he dropped his hand.

As I stepped inside the apartment, the stench hit me. I was thankful for the cigar smoke. A black body bag lay on a gurney that obviously contained a body. An EMT I knew from the county hospital stood beside it. I had been in apartments like this before and always in unpleasant circumstances. There was a living room with a soapstone sink, a refrigerator, and a gas stove on one wall. There was a chrome dinette and four chrome chairs with pale blue vinyl seats. There was a day-bed sofa combination done in black. Opposite the daybed was a colored television on a discount store television stand. On the right a door opened into a bedroom with a broken down dresser with cigarette burns on the top, cheap fold-up tables used as bedside tables. The vinyl flooring was worn through in places and curled away from the wall in others. A yellow light from a single bulb came from the ceiling fixture.

Danny was standing beside the open window. Steve Tesch was squatting near a pool of drying blood in the middle of the room with a cigar stuck in the center of his mouth. He saw me, blew a cloud of smoke and struggled to his feet. "Clarence," he mumbled. "Unzip the bag and let Vic have a look."

Clarence tugged the zipper down and I looked down at the very dead face of Jamie Adams. I turned and looked at Tesch.

"You know this bum?" he said around his cigar.

"Name's Jamie Adams."

Tesch held my business card in his fingers. "Had this in his jacket pocket. The perp missed it when he, or she, went through the pockets."

I scanned the room again, then looked back down at Jamie Adams. I'd seen my share of these, but was hard to picture Jamie here in this place. Then again, some men get their kicks slumming. "Any idea what went down?"

"Sure. The hooker had someone waiting when they came through the door. No mystery there." Tesch pulled his cigar from his mouth and blew smoke down toward the floor. "Clarence."

The EMT unzipped the bag nearly all the way and spread the bag open. Blood had soaked his white shirt, tie, and jacket. "I make it one square in the chest," Tesch said. "The ME will tell us exactly."

"Yeah."

"Any reason he would have your card in his pocket?"

"Awhile back Attorney Felton Ridge hired me to look into Jamie Adams' gambling habits. Ridge is Janice Adams' attorney. Jamie was contesting Clyde Adams' will, leaving the entire estate to his wife Janice. It was settled last week."

"You're saying this joker was Clyde Adams' son?"

I nodded.

"Well, I'll be damned. A long way from the house on the hill to this shit-hole." He jammed the cigar in the corner of his mouth and turned toward the door, and mumbled, "Clarence, get it out of here."

-30-

Saturday Morning
September 24th
68 degrees,
Blue Sky

My morning began like it had for the past four or more weeks; Patient, as Nisha struggled to her feet, then made it awkwardly down the three steps to the walk and the lawn. Burdened, as I waited for her to do what was necessary. Pained, as I watched her hunch and struggle to move her bowels. I could only imagine the agony she was in. How much longer could I put off the inevitable?

We breakfasted together. Then, while she found her spot on the rug in front of the couch, I cleaned the kitchen. When I had everything washed and put away, including what I had left in the sink the night before, I sat on the couch beside her and pulled my boots on. I ran my hand over the shiny black fur of her head and down her back. "You're in charge until I get back, Nisha. I've got a murder to solve. Although, so far I haven't had much luck." I thought I could detect a look of understanding in her dark face.

She watched me clip my holster behind my right hip and put on my, well worn, brown leather, 3/4 length fall jacket. "I'll be back, girl," I said. She put her head down on her front paws and I left.

It was 9:10 when I joined the commuters heading to work. There would be insurance to sell, patients to treat, mortgages to approve, everything that keeps the economic engine of Berring Harbor running. Barbara Mann wouldn't be part of it, though. Neither would Jamie Adams. They were dead. Murdered. It seemed incredible to me that there could be a connection between Barbara Mann's murder and Jamie Adams', and yet that was the only thing that connected me to both cases. What circumstance could have brought those two together? Was it the connection with Jamie's legal battle with his father's young wife over the estate? Didn't seem likely.

Cardinal Red

With the hum of the traffic in my ears, I let my mind slip back to earlier times and the last time I'd seen Clyde Adams alive.

I was a rookie on the Jefferson City Police Department. Clyde was in the Fire Department. Fire Station One shared the same building with the Police, as well as some other city offices.

Who can say why some relationships start and end. We became friends in spite of the fact that Clyde was nearly fifteen years older than I was. We were close enough during those years that he was at Mo's and my wedding. Shortly after I left the Police Department to join the Monroe County Sheriff's Office, Clyde left the Fire Department to join his father-in-law's company, and in time became President and CEO of The Houser Group, the largest development company in the state. I bet I hadn't seen him more than a few times over the years until one morning last January.

I was behind a city bus. We caught the light on the corner of Seventh and Division behind. The lights changed and when the bus moved, I turned right onto Division.

It's a bit ironic now, but one morning as I opened the office, Clyde showed up a frail, diminished man. I recognized the look instantly. God, how I recognized the look. It had taken Mo seven months to die and I'd watched every minute of it.

Clyde sat in my client chair, on that cold, stone-gray morning, in a pink tasseled stocking cap and a quilted poly fiber parka that looked three times too big for him. "I heard you had retired, Vic." His voice was strong when he spoke. "Then I heard you started this shop. That surprised me."

It had snowed during the night, I remember. I'd had to shovel the layer of the heavy white stuff from the steps and pulled a muscle in my lower back in the process. I remember it because it had ticked me off. I work out, I run, I lift weights. I take care of myself. And I can't hear certain sounds. I wondered what it must be like to be old and frail. "It's more just something to keep me busy, Clyde. At least that's the way it seems to be working out."

"Maureen, now there was a good woman, Vic." He was looking around the office as if he were following a shadow. "You were one lucky asshole," he said.

"That she was, but you didn't come all the way into the city just to shoot the shit." There was something not right here. "What's going on, Clyde?"

"I've got a new wife now. Cynthia died, you know."

"Yes. Must have been several years ago now, if I remember." This was not the wealthy, on the ball, business tycoon that I knew him to be.

"Five years," he said. "Five years." He stopped moving and looked at me. That's when I noticed how bright his eyes were. "I married Janice Rue two years ago, Vic. Younger woman. Met her at a party. Men like us, we need a younger woman, Vic."

"Well, I---"

He gripped the arms of the chair as if he were going to stand, but didn't, instead he bent so far forward I thought he might tumble from his chair and hit his head. "I killed Cynthia, you know," he said.

If I showed surprise, and I thought I did, it didn't seem to register on him. I remember glancing toward the office door. "Clyde," I said. "You shouldn't say crazy things. Somebody could overhear---"

"She didn't want to fuck anymore. Well, not me exactly." He stopped abruptly, then he giggled. "No. No. No. By not me, I mean I didn't kill her myself. I hired it done. A man can do that, you know."

He looked down at the desk and was quiet for a moment, then sat back quickly, got to his feet and went to the window. The only sound was the traffic out on Division Street. I remember thinking, 'here was one of the biggest movers in the county losing reality'. Not the man I knew.

Suddenly he turned, pulled his stocking cap off. "Vic, when I'm dead, and that may be soon, I need someone to look after Janice's interest. Jamie is no good. He's into some bad things with people I don't trust. I have a good lawyer, Felton Ridge, but I've had several conversations with Jamie. He'll do anything he can to break the will."

It struck me that Clyde's eyes were clear and focused, his speech strong. He sat looking at me with the look I remember. "I can trust you, Vic," he said.

***

It's a seven minute drive to my office, and by the time I parked, mumbled good morning to Kitty, and unlocked my office door, it was 9:25. I tossed my jacket over the back of a client chair and sat heavily in my chair.

It had been over a year ago that I'd had that conversation with Clyde Adams.

I remember looking down at the check for five grand he had laid on my desk. I remember looking at the wasted skeleton of Clyde Adams and when he'd said 'killed old Betty, or rather I had her killed'. I wondered what the hell I had just agreed to do.

-31-

Monday Noon,
September 26th
72 degrees,
Indian Summer

I was sitting on a white-painted wrought iron bench in Collins Park watching the boats in the harbor. The few that hadn't been pulled and covered with blue shrink-wrap and put in the boatyard for winter storage. It's a more interesting place when all the slips are full of cruisers and the people. But, it's quieter now. Joe Bass' Crestliner hasn't been pulled yet. The last time I was on that boat it was with Mo, the week before she was diagnosed. It seems everything and every place has a memory. I felt the emptiness creeping in and I wondered what she would think of my infatuation with Tamara. Luckily, several sea gulls had spotted me and decided to shill me. I welcomed the distraction.

I had gotten a hot dog and black coffee from the Harbor Sandwich Shop, and had folded the paper wrapper back and taken a bite when Danny Khanh walked up with a sandwich in sealed cellophane, coffee with cream in a paper cup, three packets of sugar, and a bag of chips in his hands. The sandwich wrapper said Italian Sub in red and green print.

He set his coffee and the chips on the bench beside me and stood there, staring down at me, his brows pinched like he smelled something ripe. "What?" I said.

He was staring at my hot dog as decidedly as the gulls were. "What?" I said again, wiping mustard from the corner of my mouth. I indicated the sandwich he was holding. "You think that's better? Who knows what's stuffed in that roll. They press it and shape it to look like what it said on the package and jam it into a cut open roll with a piece of fake cheese. At least a hot dog is honest."

Danny smiled and sat. "I got a copy of the preliminary ME report on Jamie Adams for you in the car," he said, as he tore the packets of sugar open and dumped them in the coffee.

Cardinal Red

"I can see why you had to leave it in the car, you'd had to carry it in your teeth." More seagulls had spotted us. The ones that had landed strutted around looking at us expectantly.

"Watch this," Danny said. He broke off a small piece of bread from his sandwich and tossed it beyond the squalling gulls inciting what could only be termed a gull riot, and which attracted more of the damn birds.

"Now see what you've done," I said.

Danny sampled his coffee, then took a bite of his sandwich. He chewed and swallowed, then took another swallow of coffee. "I can pretty much tell you what's in the report," he said. "Shot twice, once in the chest 3 centimeters to the left of the sternum between the 4th and 5th rib with a 32 caliber. He was probably dead before he hit the floor."

He lifted the top off his sandwich, looked at it, put the top back. "Strange thing is," he said. "The second was shot in the neck, after he was down. After he was dead."

I looked at him. "No blood under the neck wound?"

Danny nodded. "Not much," he said.

"The two slugs came from the same gun?"

Danny nodded. "Yup. The bullet hit him in the neck and passed through. We dug the slug out of the floor. Would have missed him all together if it had been another inch to the right."

I thought about that. Why shoot him a second time if the first one did the job? Amateur? The first one went into the heart.

"So why the second shot?"

"Make sure?"

I shrugged. "Humm."

We each enjoyed our sandwiches, though I'm sure mine was better.

"How's the plan working? And by the way, you've got mustard on your chin."

I wiped my chin with the paper napkin. "Plan?" I said.

"The pain-in-the-ass plan."

I shrugged. "I drove down to Bayfield Tuesday morning and asked Janet Mann again about Bobby Rico. She still couldn't remember meeting him. Wednesday, I went into Jefferson City and had a semi-intelligent conversation with Jamie Adams, then went back to Bayfield and talked to Robert Mann. On Thursday, I caught Janet Mann just as she was leaving for an appointment and asked about Jamie Adams again and the Manley Athletic Club. Irritated the hell out of her. Interestingly, Jamie Adams was killed two days later. Even more interesting is that I'd mentioned his name to Bobby Rico in Los Angeles just the week before."

My coffee was gone. And now that the food was gone, all but two of the gulls had left. The two that were left, stood a dozen steps away, watching.

Probably the rear guard. Make sure we weren't trying to pull something.

"You don't believe in coincidence?" Danny had stuffed the cellophane from his sandwich into the paper cup and crushed it into a ball. The two gulls watched intently.

"Coincidence or divine intervention," I said. "I try not to make a judgment about either. I just find things curious."

A female jogger came along the asphalt path toward us wearing red shorts over a dark blue leotard. She wore an orange t-shirt over the leotard top that said 'Why Not' in black lettering across the front, and an orange and black headband that held her blondish hair back. As she jogged past she glanced our way. She wasn't huffing and her 't' was stained dark under her arms. I smiled back but I'm sure she didn't notice as she was already by. We both turned and watched her until our interest gave out.

"She smiled at me." Danny said, grinning.

"Sure she did," I said. "You think they all do."

His grin turned into a short laugh. "So," Danny said. "Adams opens the door, takes a step back and the shooter shoots him."

I shrugged. "Jamie Adams wouldn't have opened the door for just anyone."

"So he knew his killer."

I nodded. "Or, killers. Was there any indication that he'd been there for a period of time?"

Danny looked at me. "Killers?"

"Think about it. Why would someone shoot a body that was already dead?"

"Tell me," Danny said.

"How about, to better implicate the second person."

Danny smiled. "The second person, maybe being a novice at murder, and maybe unfamiliar with guns and such, and therefore being greatly nervous, might miss or almost miss the body he was shooting at."

"Would account for the second shot," I said. "You have a better theory?"

Danny shook his head. "Nope," he said.

"What else do we know?"

"The room is rented by a pimp named Lonny Joyce. Kelly talked to him. Claims he hasn't had any of his girls in it for weeks. Seems business is slow. Claims he never heard of Jamie Adams and can't imagine how this Adams guy got in."

I nodded. "Sure."

We sat for a while. Two more joggers came by. One with a small, white, ugly dog whose legs were a blur as it tried to keep up. The way it was panting, I suspected its heart would give out anytime.

"You think the brother and his wife are involved?"

"You know what I know."

I looked at him and shook my head. "Maybe we both should give this up and become parking lot attendants."

"Probably," Danny said.

I stood. "I think I'm going to have another talk with John Mann."

-32-

Tuesday am
September 27th,
64 degrees,
Sky, Crystal Blue

The morning was cool. I had on a blue cotton turtle-neck sweater, my new stone-washed blue-jeans that I had recently bought at Robertson's, and my gray wool sport coat. A picture of style, I was.

The air smelled of fall. A kind of dry dustiness of the drying of leaves, and browning of the grass along the street. Tamara says this is her favorite time of year. I can only think of the cold and ice to come.

I parked under the sign that the building manager had stuck on the side of the building the day after I had signed the lease. A sprinkler hose was running on the strip of lawn between the sidewalk and the street. I locked the car and stared at the sign. It read 'Pittaro Investigations;' I still wasn't sure I was doing the right thing. The Jennings vs. Blanden Paper investigation had only involved one morning of camera work and one morning in court testifying. The only other clients I've had so far are Tamara and Janice Adams, and they involve dead bodies. At this rate my new career would involve more corpses than the past one. I walked across the lawn next to the building to avoid the sprinkler and went in.

"Good morning, Mr. Pittaro," Kitty bubbled when I came through the door.

"Good morning, Kitty." I tried not to let her effervescence get me down. "Any messages?"

"Yes, sir. A Mr. Felton Ridge called," she handed me a pink note. I took it and read it. In her delicate hand it said, call back ASAP, and gave a number that looked like it might be a cell phone. He had called at 8:50. I wondered how Jamie Adams' murder affected him. From what I knew he only represented Janice against Jamie, not brother Jack. It might be interesting to talk with Felton.

"Mr. Ridge starts his day early, I see."

Kitty handed me my mail. "Yes, sir. The phone was ringing when I came in."

"Thank you, Kitty."

The phone in front of Kitty buzzed and a light flashed. She smiled as she reached for the phone. "Mr. Ward's office."

I unlocked my office door, scooched the rubber stop around, jammed the door open, and hung my coat on the tree.

If I make coffee at home in the morning, most of it goes to waste. Here at least I usually drink it, or most of it. I dumped the dregs of yesterday's brew down the sink in the washroom across the lobby and in a few minutes was waiting anxiously for fresh. If you're really anxious and need the caffeine to get the brain switched on, you pull the carafe at a third full and pour a cup. It's just what I did. I blew once into the cup then sipped just enough to taste. It was rich, and hot, and like a shot of adrenaline. I carried it to my desk. Just what I needed if I was going to talk to Felton Ridge.

Felton answered on the second ring. "I need to see you," he said, without saying hello.

Felton Ridge is one of the most prominent attorneys in the county, with an office in the Fidelity Building a block from the courthouse. With my only paying client being Janice Adams about to come to a screeching end, I didn't want him to think I was scratching. "Good to hear from you too, Felton. How about late this afternoon or tomorrow morning. First thing in the morning would be best."

"No. Now. I need to see you now. I'll be there in twenty minutes."

"Felton I---" he hung up. When I put the phone down Kitty Hynen was standing in the doorway.

"Mr. Pittaro, could I talk with you?"

"Sure, Kitty." I motioned toward a chair. "Come in."

She sat in the brown chair across from my desk and folded her hands in her lap. "What is it, Kitty?"

She hesitated for a moment, then took a deep breath. "It's Mr. Ward. I don't want to get him in trouble or anything but---" Her eyes were on me and I had the feeling she was trying to read me. "You see," she said, finally. "I know he drops his wife off at the elementary school at 8:30. She's a teacher, you know."

"Yes, I know." She dropped her gaze to her lap, and I saw she was rubbing and twisting at her fingers. "Go on, Kitty," I said.

"Well, he keeps asking me to meet him for breakfast at Berkman's. I always tell him no, that I can't but he keeps asking me. I thought that if I could tell him that I had to start coming in early, like 8 am, that I had to do some computer work for you, before you came in like billing, or correspondence, or something. I could also have your coffee made for you."

Cardinal Red

I'm sure my expression showed surprise. "I'm sorry, Mr. Pittaro," she said. "I should have never brought this up."

"No. No, Kitty. You did the right thing." This I hadn't expected. I cupped my chin in my hand for an instant. Hum. Bob Ward. Well, well. "Kitty, I'll take care of it. Give me a day or so. In the meantime, if he asks say no."

She smiled weakly and looked down at her hands. "Then can I tell--- She looked up at me. "Can I come in early, then? I won't charge my time for it."

"No," I said. "That's not right. You come in at 8:00 and put your time in for the extra hour. I'll take care of it with the management company."

I could see the relief on her face. "Thank you," she said, and smiled.

Felton Ridge walked into the office at 10:15. I looked at my watch. "Felton, how the hell did you make it from your office downtown, to here in twenty minutes?"

He was not a big man, probably 5'8" five eight, I'd guess 145-150 lbs. Though he looked maybe forty, I knew him to be older. His hair was light brown and trimmed neatly. And, I imagined that it always did. Everything seemed proportionate with his small body style. His oval face, his blue eyes, his small slim nose. "I try to be precise," he said.

He surveyed my office quickly. "May I sit?"

I waved an open hand toward my client chairs. He was carrying a black leather attaché. His suit was a dark blue pin stripe, his shirt white and his tie blue silk. The whole ensemble probably cost more than my monthly mortgage payment.

He set the attaché on the desk and pulled a chair to within an arms-reach to my desk, sat and adjusted his trousers so the crease wouldn't sag.

"You seemed desperate on the phone, Felton. I hope the homestead's not on fire."

"Not desperate, Pittaro. Overwhelmed."

"And I can be of help, how?"

"I'll start at the beginning so we don't get confused."

"The 'we' I assume was just to be inclusive."

Felton ignored me and went on. "I've been Clyde Adam's personal attorney for over twelve years."

I nodded, approvingly.

"According to Clyde's will, and I assure you I am not thrilled with this, I am now Chief Executive Officer pro tem of The Houser Group, until the executive board appoints a new CEO, which won't be until the board meets in the spring. I don't need this or want this."

I rocked back in my chair and folded my hands together. This was going to take a while.

"In that capacity, and because of the litigation between Janice and the sons, which as you know was

Cardinal Red 251

settled before Jamie's murder, I had an auditor go through the company finances."

"And," I said. "You've discovered some chicanery."

Felton shook his head. "No. No. Clyde was too involved. Even toward the end. What the auditor discovered was that The Houser Group was quiet heavily invested in Pine River Estates."

"Mann Construction," I said. This thing was turning into a hair- ball.

"Yes," Felton said. "Which would not necessarily be a bad thing, but---"

"Aha, the but…"

"Yes," he said.

I sat forward in my chair and laid my arms on the desk. "Let me stop you there for a moment," I said. "What does this have to do with me?"

Felton seemed to lose a bit of his professional, lawyerly, demeanor. "I was Clyde's attorney, but also his friend." Sentiment showed in his voice. "I don't want to see Janice or his reputation hurt. And, Clyde respected you."

"Okay," I said. "So, what's the but?"

"I'm hearing that Mann Construction is broke, which if true, means the Pine River development is dead, which means The Houser Group is out a $118,000,000."

That surprised me. "Wow," I said. "Very interesting."

-33-

Tuesday Afternoon
September 27th
80 degrees, Partly Cloudy

"Come in, Pittaro." John Mann, wearing chinos, a beige safari shirt and moccasins with no socks, turned and walked into the study. I stepped through the door into the foyer, closed the door behind me and followed. I knew the way. I'd been there before.

"Drink?" Mann said. He had gone behind the bar and was pouring an amber liquid into a short glass of ice.

"Sure," I said. I went to the windows that looked out on the garden, the lawn, and the thick wooded area beyond. The lawn had brown spots and needed cutting. The flower garden was weedy and looked neglected. The whole scene smelled of seclusion.

"Scotch?"

"Fine. Heavy on the water."

I pulled a leather-covered barstool around and sat.

Mann set a glass on the bar, added ice, Scotch, and a splash of water, and set it on the bar in front of me.

He took a swallow of his drink, set it down and frowned at me. "Over a fucking month," he said. "And nobody can find out who killed my wife."

I took a sip of my drink, then held it up and admired the gold crystalline color. Top shelf. Very nice.

"Mann Construction is broke. Tell me about it."

"What the fuck are you talking about?"

"That's the word I hear. You're broke and Pine River is dead."

His face was getting red. "Are you out of your fucking mind? Where'd you hear that shit?"

"Anything to it?"

His face was fully red, now. "No. What the fuck's the matter with you?"

"Manley Athletic Club. Heard of it?"

"No."

"You know a man named Bobby Rico?"

"Jesus Christ. What is this shit?"

"Know anything about the Cookton County Cultural Center?"

"No. That bitch of a wife of my brother's got Barbara involved in it. I've no interest in that shit."

"You've never been there?"

"No."

"Did your wife and Janet Mann get along okay?"

"Sure. Barbara got along with everybody. What the hell is this?"

"Mann, you don't have to prove to me you're an asshole. Seems everyone who knows you thinks so. At least everyone I've talked to. So let's stop wasting time."

He stared at me for a long minute as if he was sizing me up. I slipped off the stool and stood, my back against the bar. He was about my weight and maybe an inch taller and it was possible he'd been in as many tussles as I had, his attitude would account for that, but I had him in temperament. "You're not up to it, Mann," I said. "You're too hot headed. Just sit down and we can have a calm discussion."

He opened his mouth to say something, then closed it and sank onto the sofa. He sat quietly, his elbows on his knees, his head in his hands, his breathing heavy. I let him be for a bit, took my drink behind the bar and added water, and came back.

"The Sheriff's Department has interviewed me three times," he said in a resigned voice. "Tesch seems to think I had something to do with Barbara's death."

He looked up at me. His eyes were wet. "I loved her," he said. His voice was feeble, like he didn't have the strength in him to get the words out.

He shook his head slowly from side to side. "They've gone through everything. My personal finances. Phone records. Income tax returns. They just brought the computers back yesterday. I swear to God Pittaro. She was the love of my life."

We were quiet for a moment. I waited, watching his chest rise and fall with his breaths.

"Any truth to the rumor about financial problems?"

"We had a stretch last spring, then we got the State Highway contract. Things got better. Robert is the CFO. Ask him." Mann's voice was heavy. "Have you come up with anything?"

"So far, I don't know anything more than Tesch. Do you have a theory on why she was killed?"

Mann shook his head slowly without looking up.

"What I want to do," I said. "Is learn everything I can about Barbara. I need to talk with her friends, her hairdresser, the housekeeper. Anyone who she may have known. Even if the Sheriff's investigators have already talked with them."

He was still shaking his head from side to side. I couldn't tell if he was agreeing with me or not. Or, even if he heard me. "I need to learn everything I can," I said. "And, I will get personal."

He looked at me sideways.

I shrugged. "You're paying me," I said. We were quiet again.

Finally he said, "Whatever you need to do, do it."

"For a start, I need to get a sense of her here. I need to spend some time here, where you and she lived. I will try not to disturb anything, but it's what I need to do. Even the bedroom."

He stared at me for several long seconds, then picked up his drink from the end table, drained the glass, got up and went to the bar. He added ice with the silver tongs then topped the glass off with Scotch. "Do what you need to do," he said, and walked from the room. I did.

The house had an open floor plan. I crossed the hall to the living room. The room was painted eggshell or ivory, I could never tell the difference. There was a huge bow window facing the front lawn with lace curtains to the floor. The furniture was white, plush, and formal. There was a low, glass coffee table. The carpet was white with a small light blue pattern. There were photos of Barbara and John in gilded frames. There was a black marble fireplace that looked like it had never been lit. There were paintings on the wall that I would guess were originals.

I walked through the rest of the house. I went up the stairs. There were two bedrooms. The first bedroom had a full bath and looked out onto the front lawn. If it had ever been used, it had been used sparingly. There were vacuum cleaner tracks in the carpet. The second bedroom was the master bedroom decorated in off whites and blues. There was a gas fireplace set in brown brickwork of various shades. The room faced the rear yard. There was a large bed. I think it is called a California King. On one side of the bed, was an end table with a lamp with a soft blue ceramic base. Beside the lamp was a digital clock. Next to the clock was a picture of a woman on a beach in a bikini. I picked it up and looked at it. The woman was laughing. Her hair was blowing. Water showed along the edge of the photo and there were dunes behind her. The woman was Barbara Mann. I set the photo back.

On the other side of the bed was an identical lamp on an identical table and a framed photo of both Barbara and John, and a television remote. I went around and sat on the bed and picked up the photo and let the room seep into me.

There were two straight backed chairs with brown leather upholstery and a blue leather recliner. There was an oak armoire with antique brass hardware. I opened the doors to reveal a flat screen television on the upper shelf. Below the television were two shelves of books. Novels, mostly.

Against one wall was an oak bureau and an identical bureau on the opposite wall. One obviously hers the other obviously his. I went through his first, everything neat and folded, then hers and found nothing revealing. Next to her bureau was a five drawer oak jewelry box on turned legs. The kind that have side doors that when I checked held gold and silver necklaces. I opened each drawer. I went to the windows. Large windows with heavy drapes with gold thread that looked out onto the green expanse in the back yard.

Barbara Mann was a smart, intelligent woman. I'd learned that in the few minutes we'd had together. Since, I've learned she'd seen more of the smarmy side of the world than most. That would seem to have toughened her. She had told Tamara she feared for her husband, not herself. She told me that it may have had something to do with the business. Whatever it was, it got her killed.

There was a walk-in closet. One side his, the other side hers. Everything hung straight and orderly, and organized by item. There were shelves of shoes in shoeboxes, though probably not as many as Mo had.

In the master bath, I went methodically through everything. The medicine cabinet, the vanity under the double sink, the linen closet. When I was done I knew what kind of shaving cream John used and the brand of feminine deodorant Barbara Mann used. But nothing that said 'if I'm murdered, this is who did it and why.'

Downstairs I went through the living room, the study, and the office. There was no reason to try to get into the two computers, even if I could. Danny would get me any pertinent information. When I was done I went out through the glass doors to the patio. John Mann sat in a deck chair next to a woven metal table staring at the distant tree line. An empty glass sat on the table.

I pulled a chair out and sat. "You didn't answer me when I asked if the name Rico meant anything to you."

Mann didn't say anything. I persisted. "What was the ten thousand dollars for?"

He turned toward me. "I never heard the name until you mentioned it. The money was to bail out that fucking brother of mine."

"Robert. Bail him out of what?"

"Gambling debt."

"You paid off his gambling debt. To whom?"

"I don't know. I met Robert and some guy at a motel in Jefferson City. I gave Robert the money and I left."

"This was when?"

Mann seemed to be thinking. This was a good sign.

"The end of May," he said. "Just before Memorial Day."

"And you don't know who the guy with Robert was?"

"According to Robert, he was a lawyer representing some Vegas casino."

Mann turned back to his distant stare.

Humm, I thought. That might be a clue. But a clue to what? I got up from my chair and left.

-34-

Late Afternoon
Saturday October 1st
69 degrees
Still Indian Summer

My kitchen window faces west. The late afternoon sun was low enough to spill its shine straight through the window in a dust-mote filled yellow column that splayed across the room, turning the dark brown-sugar color of Tamara's skin nearly golden. She was sitting on the corner stool at the counter wearing blue jeans faded to perfection and a maroon, buttoned down short sleeved shirt with a crest of a bird on the breast pocket. She wore a silver herringbone necklace with a silver pendant.

I was leaning against the sink. I had on blue jogging pants with a silver stripe down the outside seam and a loose, sweat stained gray sweatshirt with the sleeves cut off and neck cut out. I needed a shower. Nisha and I had been out wandering through the open meadow behind the townhouse complex and along with my odor, my sweatpants were covered with weed chaff and burrs. "I'm sorry about the way I look Tamara," I said. "Nisha and I just finished our walk."

"I should have called first, but, well---"

"No. No, it's okay," I said. I filled Nisha's water bowl with tap-water and set it on the kitchen floor, then got a glass for myself and turned and looked out the window. The red autumn sun hung low on the horizon, the rusts, and oranges, and yellows of the fall woodlands beyond were in shadow. The days are becoming shorter and life is moving faster, I thought, and yes, if you'd have called I would have looked and smelled better. The Goddess seems to be working against me. As usual.

I swallowed enough of the water to ease my dry-mouth and dumped the rest in the sink. It had been almost two months since Barbara Mann's murder in my office. Almost two weeks since LA and that goodnight kiss in front of her fireplace. We'd only talked briefly on the phone since.

I looked at Tamara. "I wish I could tell you that since we came back from Los Angeles I've learned something new. But, I can't. Danny Khanh got me a copy of the murder book on Barbara, but there was nothing in it we didn't know. The shooter, Santos, had a sheet in both Ohio and Michigan and had done time in Jackson for armed robbery."

"Murder book?"

"The case file. Everything pertaining to the investigation up to now."

Her mouth tightened. "And, I suppose the Sheriff's Department has got other things to work on," she said.

I shrugged. "I'm sure Tesch and his investigators are doing what they can," I said. But I had a feeling Tesch wasn't and I wondered why.

"I can make a pot of coffee, Tamara. Or I have instant coffee, or tea?"

"Instant coffee will be fine if you have cream or milk." She had kicked off her shoes and her bare toes were curled around the bottom rung of the stool. Her toenails were painted the color of a red plum. As were her finger nails. As was her lipstick. I wondered if it was the detective in me that was noticing these things or this damned attraction to her.

"It'll have to be milk," I said.

I lit the fire under the teapot of water on the stove and got two mugs from the cupboard over the sink and set them on the counter. Bachelor pads don't have cups and saucers, they have mugs.

Nisha had drunk her fill and had found a comfortable spot in front of the dishwasher and was watching Tamara, with what looked to me as distaste.

"Looks to me like Nisha is a bit resentful having another female in her territory," Tamara said.

"Looks like that to me, too," I said. "Nisha, this is Tamara." Nisha's stare didn't waiver.

"She's an Akita, right? And her muzzle has some gray in it. I would guess you've had her in your life for a long time."

"You know your dogs. Twelve years, almost." I got the instant coffee from the cupboard I used for a pantry and put a spoonful in each cup.

Tamara turned her attention away from Nisha, spread her arms across the counter and looked at me. "If I were to guess, it would be that you've always had pets. For Roger and I, it seemed we were always too busy."

"I was gone a lot at night at the time we got her," I said. "Mo had been diagnosed and I guess I thought a dog would be good company for her. Turned out well, though I think her loyalty was directed more toward me than Mo." I suddenly felt very sad. It surprised me.

"Nisha's not doing very well. The arthritis in her hind quarters is getting to the point where she struggles to stand up. She's in pain."

The teapot began to whistle. I got the milk and sugar, fixed our coffee, pulled the other stool around the end of the counter and sat.

Tamara had leaned back against the wall and stuck one foot out as if she was examining her toes. I liked watching her.

"Tell me about Maureen," she said.

We were silent for a few moments listening to Nisha's breathing. I looked at her. "Well--- sure," I said. I went to the fridge and got several cubes of ice from the freezer. Through the kitchen window I could see the sun hanging over the distant woods. "Want your coffee cooled down?"

Tamara had turned back to the counter and was fixing her coffee. She shook her head. "This is fine," she said, stirring in a dollop of milk. "I know Maureen was a psychologist."

I straddled my stool and sat. "A good one. She worked with the philosophy that for most people, the search for answers is within themselves. That with patience and the right questions, the answers would come out. Her instincts were very good. Even though I'd been a cop for years, she could read people much faster than I could."

I swallowed some coffee and thought back. "Being a cop I'd learned to be very skeptical and at times tuned people out. Mo listened. You instinctively knew she was listening. You knew you had her attention."

I could look out through the bay window in the living room. The light was fading as evening settled in. Tamara sipped her coffee. Nisha gave a loud sigh, lifted her head, then worked her way up onto her front legs and looked at me. I could see the pain in her eyes, at least I thought I could. Then with much struggling, she got her hind quarters off the floor and without looking my way she went into the living room. That was to make me feel guilty.

"How did you meet?"

I took a deep breath and hesitated. I wasn't sure I was ready to go where this seemed to be headed. I got up and walked to the kitchen window and looked out. The sun was slipping below the tops of the distant trees and soon there would be nothing left of daylight. I went over and turned the kitchen light on. I checked on Nisha in the living room. In the silence, I could hear the faint sound of a siren out on the interstate.

Tamara was looking at me, smiling. Her dark eyes bright. Her mocha complexion softened in the artificial light. "Well," she said.

I grinned at her, found my stool and sat. I drank some coffee. "Well," I said, "we met at a house party the summer I graduated from high school. We had one date. After that, she brushed me off. I guess I was more intrigued with her than she was of me. At least that's what I thought at the time. Guy Jackman had joined the Marines and was going to Vietnam and I thought my number probably would come up if I didn't do something. There was a draft lottery back then. So, I enlisted figuring that enlisting would give me more options. I ended up an MP and did my in-country in a place called Phan Rang."

I paused. "Are you interested in any of this?"

"Yes," she said.

I looked at her, then shrugged. "After the Army, I went to State and got a degree in Criminal Law. Which led me to the Jefferson City Police Department. I was living in Jefferson City, and one day she called. She had called my mother, my father had died while I was in Vietnam, and my mother had given her my phone number. Anyway, she had been divorced for several years and was living in Kansas City. Her mother had died some time before and while she was back here going through her mother's things she found a post card I had sent her from Long Beach before I shipped out, way back then. That's pretty much it."

"Amazing," Tamara said. "When you ask couples how they met, sometimes the most interesting stories come out. How many years in-between?"

"Eighteen," I said. The room was getting darker. Through the front window, the streetlight was on. I stood and looked back at Tamara. "Listen, let me shower, then let's go get something to eat."

There was a silence as Tamara traced an imaginary line across the counter-top. "I thought maybe, if you had something here," she said, "we could fix it and stay in." She hesitated, her dark eyes smiling. "I have my overnight bag in my car."

I felt my stomach muscles lurch, I swallowed, sucked in a breath. It's a good thing I was leaning against the counter. A thousand thoughts burst through my mind in what had to be only seconds. "I-- Let me---" My throat felt very tight. "While you get your bag," I managed, "I'll shower and clean up, then we'll find something."

Her smile spread across her face. "Better idea," she said, her eyes twinkling. "Let me get my bag and meet you in the shower."

And that's what we did.

-35-

Later that evening Tamara stood naked in the bathroom doorway, her hair wet, her cocoa skin glistening in the humid air from her second shower of the evening. "Give me about five minutes, love," and she closed the door.

I lay back on my pillow and folded my hands behind my head. I know how proud of her body she is, but it's a pride thing issuing from staying healthy rather than from vanity. She would not tell me her age. My guess; fifty-one or fifty-two.

About fifteen minutes had passed before she came out. Other than she had wrapped a silk scarf over her hair, I saw nothing different. Feminine mystique, I thought. "Making love leaves me hungry," she said as she began to dress.

Her head was cocked to the side watching me as she twisted her arms up behind her, fastening her bra. The movement thrust her breasts out. "Hand me that blouse, Honey," she said.

I was on my side resting on my elbow, letting my gaze slip down her body, the essence of our lovemaking in the air. I remembered how she had felt, her smooth lips, how she had opened for me, how she had tasted. "I was just thinking, maybe later we could call and have something delivered."

She stood in the light of the bedside lamp, a dark v-shadow showing through her silk panties. I watched her and relished the renewed desire. The way my life had been going in the two years since Mo's death, I was sure I would always be alone. Now I wasn't sure I wanted it that way.

"I thought you were hungry?"

"Hmmm," I said. "I think that passed."

Her smile turned seductive. "Yes. I see."

There is a feline sensuality about her nakedness, and in the way she moves. But it's real, natural. A comfort about herself. She pushed the silk panties over her hips, letting them slide down her legs, then kicked them aside. "I wasn't really hungry, either," she said, and climbed onto the bed.

Cardinal Red

She straddled my legs, reached back, stuck out her chest and unfastened her bra and shook it off her shoulders.

"When I look at you, I get so damned nervous." My throat was tight and my voice sounded hoarse.

"Nervous?"

"Yes, but with practice I think I'll get over it."

The corners of her eyes crinkled as she grinned. "Even so, I see you seem to have recovered quite well."

"A nap always helps."

Braced by her hands she bent forward, her face close to mine. I couldn't help the groan that escaped my lips as her nipples touched my chest and the damp warmth of her mouth found mine and lingered. God, she tasted even sweeter than she had a few hours ago. She drew back a little and in the yellow of the lamplight I looked into those dark green eyes. She was as alive as I had known she would be. "You're beautiful," I whispered. I could smell her freshness under the essence of her soap.

"Tell me you want me again, Love," she said, her breath warm on my lips. Her lips touched mine, lightly at first, then as I slid my hands to her waist and up her back, the kiss turned to hunger. She straightened on her arms, her eyes tightly closed, her chin tilted up.

I let my hands slip to her breasts, and moved my palms in gentle circles over her nipples. "I do want you, as you can see, but this time slowly. There's no rush."

Her smile was radiant as she sat up, lifted her hips and settled onto me. She put her hands on her waist, and with her eyes shut, her mouth slightly open, she tipped her head back, and began a slow rhythmic motion.

Later, I lie on my back sucking air, letting my heart rate come back down. Tamara laid beside me, her head nestled on the crook of my shoulder, her panting breath warm on my chest. I turned my head to the wrap on her head. I could smell the almond scent of her hair treatment.

As my breath returned to normal I said, "What changed your mind about us?"

She shifted slightly, rolled against me settling a leg over mine, and lifted so we were looking at each other in the soft lamplight. "It was you, Vic. The time we've spent together over these past weeks. It's made me look at my life. Made me appreciate what I was missing. But mostly it's the way I've grown to feel about you. I realized I was letting the third act of my life slip by."

Was that what I've been doing? Letting my third act slip by? It had been a long time. I could see mystery deep in her eyes and suddenly longed to be part of it.

"Can I stay for the show?" I said.

"You can be in the show," she said, "if you'd like."

-36-

Wednesday, October 5th
Clear Sky, 65 degrees

With three people dead, one by my hand, I felt it was time to figure out what the hell was going on. So far, all I'd accomplished was not much. It had been nearly 5am when we finally fell asleep last night and nearly 10am when Tamara kissed me good morning. After she left, I showered and shaved with the feeling that my life had suddenly taken an exciting new direction. By 10:40 I was out the door. I was going to visit an old friend.

It was a bright, but cool fall afternoon and I was renewed with surprising energy. On the way across town I stopped at a fast-food restaurant and bought a large black coffee in a paper cup with a half-inch of ice in the bottom and was sipping it through the opening in the top, and trying not to dribble down the front of my new shirt. A blue, long sleeved Arrow with buttoned down collar. Pretty damned rakish even without an ascot, I thought, with my calve-length leather car coat, black denim jeans, black boots and my wraparound Oakley's. I had the top down on my BMW and the heater going full blast, and a Thelonious Monk CD playing loud enough to hear over the wind. I felt light, nearly weightless with Tamara in my thoughts. If I'd been walking I'd be skipping.

The town of Lawrence is across the county line in Cookton County a forty-minute drive down the interstate, then another ten minutes down State Highway 12, but I wasn't taking the interstate. I was driving secondary roads. Southwest out of Berring Harbor on Monroe County Road 18 to Clark Road which was weathered blacktop through rolling fields of corn the color of paper grocery bags. There were faint hints of green at the base of the corn stalk, not yet dry enough to be cut. The bean fields were the same, mostly patchworks of greens and browns and yellows. I went over the Temperance River where it touches the south end of Cedar Lake. I crossed the county line at Haskell, taking my time as the bleached asphalt twisted through and around the low hills.

At Stone Creek there's an old mill on the bank on the right. All that's left of the mill is three stone walls, the remnants of the mill house, and two stone colonnades that had supported the waterwheel, one on either side of the creek. Just across the short bridge is a small township park under a stand of oak. I pulled into the gravel parking area, stopped, stuck my sunglasses on the dash, and got out.

There were two concrete picnic tables with matching benches, a cast iron grill, and a fire pit all overrun with grass and weeds. Aluminum cans lended their intrusive charm to the neglected grounds. There's a steel flagpole that was once painted white but was now mostly rust. Next to it was a 55 gallon steel trash barrel. A stone path led past the fire-pit for thirty yards to a square cinder-block latrine painted various shades of brown and red where graffiti had been painted over. The vandals had been persistent, however.

I answered nature's call, and when I came out, a cherry red Honda Gold Wing had pulled in. A woman in black leather and black boots slipped from the rear seat and stood beside the motorcycle in exuberant conversation with the seated man. She saw me. I smiled. She smiled back, then took her helmet off and shook her long dark hair out. She looked to be in her early thirties. The man, dressed the same, removed his helmet, hung it over the handlebars and dismounted. Then they walked together to the farther table. The black leather pants fit her very well.

I leaned against my car and thought of Tamara, and thought of last night. The stillness was broken by a farm tractor going by pulling two grain wagons. The driver, a girl with a ponytail, couldn't have been over fifteen years old. A boy, about the same age, stood on the hitch behind her. I wonder what it would be like to be in love again. I found myself smiling. It could happen. I could almost feel Tamara's face pressed into my neck as she had lain against me. And feel her breath on my skin, and the brush of her hair against my cheek, and the pressure of her foot against mine. I watched after that tractor long after it disappeared over the next rise.

Finally, I sucked in a deep breath and let it out hard enough to dissipate the daydreams. Right now I was on the clock, so to speak. I'm a detective trying to find out who had Barbara Mann murdered. So I should get to detecting, not standing here on this beautiful fall day, musing. I got in, started my car, put my shades on and cruised out of the park. The dashboard clock read 12:10. I would be late. Focus, I said to myself. Stay focused. It didn't seem to help.

The sun was straight over my head when I turned onto the asphalt.

"It's alright, honey. The best moments in my life have come because I've loved you."

Stunned, I glanced toward the vacant passenger seat. "Jesus Christ!" I said to nobody. I would know Maureen's voice anywhere. Then it hit me. It's about Tamara. Mo knew. I felt my smile.

I was still grinning when I made a left onto Cookton County 7, then a right on State Highway 12 just east of the Lawrence town limits. It was 2:15 when I passed the town park where the gray hulk of a WWI tank stands guard. The weathered picnic-tables were vacant. The foliage of the maples and the elm were that hazy green they get before they begin to turn. The oaks, still their hardy green against the bright sky.

Not much had changed since the last time I was here, at least five years ago. There was a four-way stoplight that hung over the main intersection now. Bennett's Grocery was now a second-hand store. And the implement dealer had more lawn mowers than farm machinery parked on the sidewalk. Stagnant would be a good word for Lawrence, founded like thousands of communities all across the country, a day's wagon ride apart.

The Grand Hotel is an ivy covered red brick, three-story building built back in the 1920's. The green ivy crawls up the corners of the building, covers the roof of the wooden porch and frames the third story windows. Five granite steps lead to the porch along the front with its white railings and white spindles.

I parked in front, behind a ten-year-old station wagon with its tailgate down. Two bales of straw hung out over the rear bumper. I shut the motor off, hung my Oakleys over the visor and got out and stood beside the car. The stillness had a finality to it, as if the whole town had taken a deep breath and given up.

Across the street, a heavy woman with two young children came out of the second-hand store, the woman carrying a white plastic bag. She herded the two children into a dark blue Chevy parked at the curb.

I went up the steps of the Grand Hotel and pushed through the heavy doors into the small lobby. The dining room is on the right and lunchtime being over, it was quiet. The only diner, a big bear of a man, was having coffee at a table in the far corner; the table next to the doors to the kitchen, the table normally reserved for the staff during slow times, or persons of significance to the staff. Titus Closson stood and reached out his hand as I made my way through the vacant tables. "Hay, Paisan," he was smiling. "Been a long time."

It had been several years since I last saw Titus. He hadn't changed, which surprised me a little. He's my age and about my height, with silver hair in a military cut. He was wearing a blue cotton shirt, starched and crisp. Dark gray slacks, and black boots. He had a gold badge clipped to his belt on the left and he wore his gun on his right hip. The last time we'd had talked he'd been appointed a Cookton County Sheriff's Investigator but was contemplating retiring. I wondered what had changed his mind.

We shook hands. "Good to see you, Titus." I pulled a chair out, took my coat off and hung it over the back. "Thanks for taking the time, Titus."

As we sat the waitress came and topped off Titus' coffee, then looked down at me. She looked to be about thirty and about six months pregnant. Her blond hair was pulled back in an earnest pony but with wild tufts of ringlets around her ears. She had a narrow, pale face, and she looked tired.

"Black," I said, "And a glass of water." She turned and left.

"Pittaro Investigations," Titus said, smiling. "Pretty damned impressive."

"Not really. I was surprised to find you still with the Sheriff's Department."

"What else would I do?"

I smiled and shrugged. Maybe I made the mistake by retiring. "You don't seem to age, my friend. How do you do it?"

"I'll sell you the secret," he said and laughed.

"Sure. How's Ann Marie?"

"Ann Marie's fine," he said and drank some coffee. "She and Cliff 've given me a granddaughter, Kristin. Three years old and she looks just like her mother did at that age. And they live right next door. I see them every day."

"That's your secret," I said. "Young people in your life."

Titus smiled and nodded. The waitress came back with a pot of coffee in one hand, a glass of ice water in the other, and a cup dangling from one finger and a wire basket with packets of faux cream dangling from another. She set them on the table and shuffled off without looking at us. Titus leaned forward a little. "Vic, I'm sorry about Maureen. I should have kept in touch."

I nodded and poured my coffee, and looked around for a spoon. The tables were bare. No spoons. "Thanks, Titus," I said.

With two fingers I scoped an ice cube from the water glass and plopped it into my coffee. "S'pose if I ordered a piece of pie I'da had to eat it with my fingers?"

Titus smiled. "Millie's old man left her," he said softly, with two kids and one in the hopper."

"Sorry," I said. I lipped a sip of my coffee then set the cup down. "Still know everything that goes on in Lawrence, I see."

"Hard not to know."

"That's what I'm counting on."

"I have to say, when I read about the shooting I was concerned that you might have been the target."

I shook my head. "John Mann, the victim's husband, has hired me to find out who hired the killer."

"When you called you said you were interested in Mann Construction. Particularly about Robert Mann and his wife. If you're looking for a Robert Mann connection to the killing, you must know that he's seen as an up and coming politico in this part of the state. Seems improbable."

"But not impossible."

"Considering the business we're in," Titus said, looking down into his coffee cup. "I guess that's something we've learned about the human race, isn't it?"

It was a rhetorical question that didn't need an answer. Millie had come from the kitchen with a gray plastic tub of cups and glasses and was busy stacking them in an oak cabinet against the back wall. I watched her absent-mindedly for a minute or so.

"So," I said. "Tell me what you know."

Titus took a swallow of coffee and put his cup down. "Only what I've read. Has influential friends. Never went to a society function he didn't like, or take advantage of."

"I know. I've talked with him and his wife. Found them both about as friendly as car salesmen, though not as bright. But thing is, the only unusual connection I've found in this whole damn case is one between them and an L.A. pimp. And that's so tenuous it's nearly non-existent."

"Sounds like you don't have much."

"No, and Steve Tesch has even less."

"How are you and Tesch getting along?"

I looked down at my coffee and shook my head, then picked up the cup and held it with both hands. I looked at Titus through the heat of the coffee. He was smiling. "What have you heard?" I asked.

"Only that he's had a change of personality since he made Lieutenant and his promotion to Chief of Detectives."

"Personality change is putting it mildly, but I wonder how much is really change? He came from some department on the east coast. Anyway, that's Jerry Erskine's problem, not mine."

I took several sips of my coffee then put it down. "Not my problem," I repeated. "So, that's where I'm at with this. Not much, being that I'm the toughest, smartest private detective in Berring Harbor."

Titus laughed. "Yeah. That's why you came to me, my old friend."

I ignored him. "I've decided to back up and start over. Find out everything I can about anyone connected to Barbara Mann, Mann Construction, Mann Enterprises, the Brothers, and anyone remotely connected to any of the parties. Something's got to surface somewhere."

A very tall man in blue jeans, cowboy boots, and a washed out denim jacket came in with a young boy. The man had blond hair, kind of longish, and he needed a shave. The boy looked to be his son. He wore very dirty canvas shoes and his plaid cotton shirt hung out over his jeans. He wore his baseball cap on backwards. They sat at a table in the front window.

"Ever hear of the Manley Athletic Club?"

Titus grinned. "No, but someone has a sense of humor."

"The victim mentioned the name before she was shot."

"And no one's heard of this athletic club?"

"The State Licensing Board has no record. The Sheriff's investigator working the case found a website, but it's been shut down. The State Internet Crime Task Force traced the site back through the host server to a computer; get this, in the business office at the Mann Shopping Center in Bayport. They'd be all over it I'm sure, if they thought it would turn out to be a prostitution ring site like the one they busted last week. They're getting a lot of media attention out of that. Which, no doubt, will get them a big budget increase."

"Bitter?"

"Not really. Just that, Sheriff Erskine called. Asked me very genially to not interfere with Tesch's investigation. Said he'd got a call from some State Police Lieutenant. I don't believe him. Why would a State Cop be interested?"

"The Mann's probably have friends in high places," Titus said.

Millie came from behind the counter with two glasses of water and set them in front of the man and his son and stood visiting with them. Probably regulars. Maybe family. I couldn't tell. I couldn't hear over the static in my ears. "What?" I said to Titus.

"Probably political."

"Probably," I said.

"There is one guy who might know something about this Manley Athletic Club. There's nothing much that goes on in this county that Leonard Barnes doesn't know. Most of which is on the edge of the law. Finish your coffee, we'll go see him. I'll drive."

The SunDancer sat in the center of an expansive, dirt parking area that sloped down in the back, toward the Rock River. It looked to be an older one story clapboard sided building that had a weathering coat of green paint. It was a large building and sat off the ground on a raised concrete foundation. Maybe six wide steps led to the entrance.

"This guy Lenny Barnes," Titus said as we pulled in. "He and I've had some dealings in the past. It'll be fun."

We went up the steps and pushed through the front doors and into a large room where the light of day was at a minimum and probably unwelcome. Track lighting lit the bar, which was on the right side against the back wall. The wall behind the bar was mirrored and displayed a voluminous supply of liquor. There were serving stations and glowing computer terminals. The doorway to the kitchen was to the right behind the bar. And next to that, a door with a sign that said 'Office'. There was a jukebox against the wall next to the restrooms, and a scattering of tables. It was darker across the room, but I could see the stage, the dance floor and maybe forty more empty tables.

A woman bartender was behind the bar. She leaned against the inside rail, watching a game show on the television that hung from the wall over the kitchen door. We sat on stools at the center of the bar beside a serving station. A man in dirty coveralls over a t-shirt sat at the end, near a hallway, nursing a bottle of Bud, and paying no attention to the TV over his head. Other than he we were the only customers.

"Two coffees, Marcy." Titus said, as the bartender came over. She had short black hair in no particular style. "Lenny in?"

"No." She had deeper voice than I'd expected.

"We'd like to talk with him."

"He usually shows up around four."

I checked my watch. It was 3:20. "You got anything better to do?"

"I wait real good," Titus said.

Marcy went down to the end of the bar and came back with two cups and a pot of coffee. She set the cups in front of us, then poured the coffee, and walked away. She wore a green and red flannel buttoned down shirt with the sleeves rolled up. She was a big, solid woman. Round face, thick arms and she had a mustache.

Middle of the afternoon bar coffee at its best, is drinkable. At its worst it will strip paint off of a car hood. This was somewhere in between.

I sipped, and set the cup down. "Nothing like a cup of good morning brewed coffee at three in the afternoon."

"You've been serving and protecting the people your whole career," Titus said. "You should be used to it."

We were half way through our third cup when Lenny Barnes came through the door carrying a black valise in one hand, and car keys in the other. He was wearing gray slacks, black Wellington boots, a light blue cotton shirt and a blue nylon windbreaker. He stopped cold when he saw us, or rather, saw Titus. "What the fuck you want?"

"Lenny. Lenny. Why do you have to be that way?"

Lenny Barnes was in his forties, dark hair, medium height. Probably about 5'10". And maybe a hundred and eighty pounds. He came up to us, slapped the valise on the bar. "I don't want you in here. Beat it."

Titus was smiling. "Lenny. This is Detective Pittaro from Berring Harbor."

Barnes' hard stare moved to me, then settled back on Titus. He held it for a long moment. "So?" he said.

Cardinal Red

I could see his deep breathing, then he turned and looked away. "Marcy, fix me a short one and if these two assholes have a tab give it to them. They're leaving."

"Barnes," I said. "When I get a couple of questions answered, I'll leave."

Barnes had an intense glare. He pointed it at me. I'd met cops who'd had similar stares and always figured they spent a lot of time practicing. I wondered if Lenny Barnes practiced his. "Go ask them to someone who's got answers," he said.

Titus said, "Tell me about the Manley Athletic Club?"

There was a flash of recognition in Lenny Barnes' eyes, then it was gone. "No. Now beat it. I don't want you here."

I looked at Titus and shrugged. "Dead end here," I said. I took a card from my pocket and handed it to him. He took it, looked at it, then tore it in half, tossed it on the bar, took his drink from Marcy and went into his office.

We went down the steps. Titus clicked the locks open as we walked to the car. I opened my door then leaned my forearms on the car roof and looked at Titus. "I thought I detected a little hostility in there," I said, "between you and Mr. Barnes."

Titus smiled at me with his arm over the frame of the open door. "Good job detecting," he said, and got in the car.

"Lenny and I go back a ways," Titus said. We were headed back to Lawrence. "We didn't learn much, though."

"We learned that the Manley Athletic Club exists. Or, did."

"Whatever it is."

"Well, it adds to what little I know."

"Better to know a little than not."

"I guess," I said.

-37-

Wednesday Afternoon
October 5th.
Clear sky. 65 degrees

I crossed the Temperance River Bridge at five forty. Traffic was about as heavy as it gets, but most of it was going the other way. Which was the way this investigation was going.

My stomach growled, and I had to agree. I turned right onto Gerard and drove down to the water. Pinkie's Lounge was a red brick building that overlooks the river. It had started out as the neighborhood fish market back in the thirties, when this was mostly an Italian neighborhood. It had been many things over the years since, most of them legal. For the past fifteen years it's been Pinkie's, owned by Tony Anastasia. The last time I was here I got drunk after embarrassing myself with Tamara. I smiled to myself. A lot has happened between us since then.

I parked between a dirty, red, four-wheel-drive Ford pick-up and a silver Lexus and my cell buzzed. It was Tamara. I suddenly felt worthy.

"I'll be there in twenty minutes. Have you eaten?"

"No."

"Good. I'll pick something up and we'll have dinner. Bring over what you've found and we'll both go over it, maybe decide if it's a clue or not."

I turned the starter and my cell buzzed. A woman's voice said, "Vic Pittaro?"

"Yes."

"I just talked with Titus Closson. He said I should pass this on to you. If you want to know about the Manley Athletic Club, write this number down." She gave me a number that I recognized as a pre-paid cell number.

"Can I have your name?"

"Call before three tomorrow. The woman's name is Melanie Warring."

"Can I have your name?" I asked again, though I was sure I knew my caller.

"I've talked with Melanie. She may or may not be cooperative. That's up to her." There was a click and my caller was gone.

***

We were sitting on the back steps watching Nisha nose around the small pine trees looking for signs of any four-legged intruder. Next door my neighbor came out through her patio door, stopped and looked our direction. She wore jeans and a faded blue sweatshirt. Nisha spotted her. Never one to miss out on any possible attention, she stiffly crossed the lawn. The woman knelt down, nuzzled Nisha for several moments, hugged her and stood. She gave a four finger wave in our direction and I acknowledged her. She went to her garden where she was tending her roses. Nisha considered her, decided she probably wasn't going to get any more attention, and reluctantly went back to tracking an unknown interloper among the pines.

"The authorities seemed to be focused on John," Tamara said. "At least according to the news."

I shook my head.

"You don't think he had anything to do with it, do you?" Tamara asked.

"No, I don't. And I don't understand why Tesch is. He's a better investigator than that."

We were both having a Samuel Adams and drinking it from the bottle. The sun was at two o'clock. The sky was mottled with white clouds that looked like someone had stuck various sizes of cotton balls onto a blue canvas. The temperature was in the mid- seventies.

I sipped some beer. "They've gone through his personal financials, his phone records, both their cell phone records."

"Who's your neighbor?"

"Sandra Keating."

We were both quiet for some time absently watching Sandra Keating in her rose garden.

"I wonder what they've got?" Tamara asked.

"Not much, according Danny."

"He being straight with you?"

"I think so."

Again we were quiet. It was a comfortable silence, and I liked it.

"You have an admirer?" Tamara asked. "She keeps looking this way."

I must have looked confused.

"Your neighbor, Ms. Keating," Tamara said. "She keeps looking this way."

I shrugged, stared at the likeness of Mr. Adams on the bottle for a moment, then took another swallow. "Why not?"

Nisha had backed up to one of the small pines and was attempting to scratch some grass and earth up under the tree with her right hind foot. "Looks like Nisha found a clue."

"Yes. She seems a little better, today," Tamara said.

I shook my head. "No," I said.

I could feel her looking at me. "I'm so sorry, Vic."

I rolled the beer bottle in my palms then began to pick at the moisture sodden label with my thumb nail. "I had a dog when I was a boy," I said, "A Border Collie named, Zip. One day, when I was about eight or nine, he got into the neighbor's chicken yard and killed several chickens. The neighbor shot him but didn't kill him. Zip came home dragging his hind quarters and covered in blood. I remember running to the house and waking my dad, he worked nights in a machine shop, and telling him that Zip had been hurt."

I took a swallow of beer then stared at the bottle as if in it, I would find the answer to why I was sharing this with Tamara.

"He had my brother and I dig a hole out behind the tractor shed. I can remember him walking across the yard with the rifle. I've often wondered what went through my father's mind that afternoon. Now I'm finding out. It's a hard thing."

She put her hand on my forearm. "Yes," she said. "I can only imagine."

We were quiet again. Sandra Keating had gone back in her house.

"She single?"

"Who?"

"Your neighbor."

I shrugged. "Far's I know."

"Tell me about your brother."

"Dominic was two years older than me. He was killed in Vietnam."

"Oh," she said. "I'm so sorry."

I finished my beer, got up, went in, got two more from the fridge. I came back, opened them and handed Tamara one. I sat and we went back to watching Nisha sniff through the grass around the trees, occasionally stopping to look our way, making sure we hadn't abandoned her.

Tamara was wearing white shorts and a light blue, man-style short sleeved shirt with the top two buttons unbuttoned revealing a gold necklace. Contrasted nicely with her dark skin. She had slipped her black flats off and was bare footed. Her toes were painted lavender. I had never had an opinion about feet. Ugly. Pretty. I remembered how beautiful she looked last night and how she looked this morning, standing naked, backlit by the bathroom light. And, how beautiful she looked, sitting beside me on the back step of my home. I now marveled how appropriately beautiful her feet were.

We sat in silence for a long time. Nisha had worked her way down to the far pine and was working the back side of it intently. A flock of blackish purple birds, I think they're called Grackles, landed in the grass and began searching for whatever it is they eat. In moments, the birds attracted Nisha's attention, and in another moment she dropped her head, her ears went back, and she flushed the birds.

I turned and looked Tamara. She sat holding the beer bottle with two hands in her lap, her legs out, her ankles crossed. "My father left, as you know," she said, "when I was five years old so I didn't really know him. What was your father like?"

Nisha had wandered over and was circling, eyeing the grass, trying to find just the right spot to get comfortable on. "We lived on a small farm," I said. "South of Stinton. We raised Concord grapes. My father farmed during the day and worked nights in town at a machine shop. I remember he would come in from the field for lunch, then lay down for a nap before he left for work. When I was younger, maybe three or four I would lay with him on the bed. When I close my eyes and inhale slowly, I can still smell him. It was a sweet smell. The smell of the soluble oil that was used as a coolant on the high speed lathes. He had smelled that way for as long as I can remember.

On Sundays, he would give my brother and me two quarters each. One to put in the offering at church and one we could spend on candy and gum at the gas station across the road from the church."

"So you went to church as a family?"

"No. No. It was small country church near our farm. Most of the time, Dominic and I walked to church. Unless the weather was bad."

"So your mother and Father didn't go to church?"

"Mother went to mass at the Catholic church in Stinton. My father never went that I can remember."

"Seems like a strange arrangement."

"We never questioned it, Dominic and I. Mother was religious, but I think when I look back on it, my father had a deeper faith. What it was---" I shrugged. "He never talked about it." I could feel Tamara looking at me. And that was okay. "He believed the world was mostly good, I think. And the people in it, given the chance, were mostly good."

I turned to look at her. One of the things I was learning about Tamara was her interest in everything was real. Life just seemed to interest her.

I finished my beer. "Let's go fix something to eat."

Tamara sat on the living room side of the counter. I got two more bottles of Sam Adams from the refrigerator, opened them and handed one to Tamara. In the crisper, I found a sweet potato big enough for two and a bunch of asparagus. In the freezer, I got out two tuna steaks. I unwrapped the tuna, put it on a plate to thaw, then washed the sweet potato and wrapped it in foil. I washed the asparagus, then snapped the woody ends off. I discarded the ends in the kitchen trash, got the steamer from the bottom cabinet and filled the reservoir with water.

"I like a man who knows his way around the kitchen," Tamara said.

"Necessity of life," I said. "It's going to be a little while before the tuna's thawed."

"So, how do you suggest we use the time?"

"Any way you wish."

Her smile turned sensual. Her eyes sparkled. "You could take me to bed?"

"Yes, I could."

***

It was dark outside. The only light in the bedroom was what spilled from the partially open bathroom door and the weak yellow glow from the streetlight out front. I couldn't hear the rain. The only indication I had that it was raining, was the way it streaked the bedroom window. No thunder or lightning.

We lie in the quiet light, the only sound, our breathing. We had pulled the sheet high enough to cover our waist. Tamara lay on her side, against me, her face tucked against my neck. Her lashes sporadically tickled my skin. I had my arm around her shoulder. Her skin was warm and soft. She had one leg over mine. Our feet interlocked.

"You like women," she said, breaking the quiet.

"I like you."

"Yes. I know. But that's not what I mean."

"Okay." I waited.

"Roger liked to fuck, but it was mostly about him. If I was satisfied, and I rarely was, it was a bonus. I think that's true about most men. Not to say I don't enjoy the intimacy of making love. It's just that with you it seems just the opposite."

We were quiet for a long time while I thought of a response. I decided that the quiet was enough, which led me to enjoying the touch of her skin on mine, of her hair brushing my cheek, her breath on my chest.

"Where do we go from here?" I said finally.

She rose up onto her elbow and looked down at me, her dark face illuminated in the bathroom light, her eyes radiant. "I don't think we should go anywhere," she said. "Except maybe to the kitchen. I'm famished."

"Not what I ---"

She shushed me with her finger tips on my lips. "You get the sweet potato ready and make a salad. I'll make some corn bread."

She leaned over me, pressing her breasts against my skin and kissed me long and softly. She pulled back, her eyes dark and shining. And in a soft voice whispered, "I'm falling in love with you."

-38-

Friday October 7th
Wispy Cirrus Clouds
68 degrees

I met Melanie Warring in the food court of the 8th Street Mall in Jefferson City at 2pm Friday. I had arrived with time to spare, and spent forty minutes mall cruising. The 8th Street Mall was the first enclosed mall in the area, and no matter how many facelifts it had been through, it shows its age. It's anchored on the south end by Marshall's and on the north end by Walgreen's. There are three shoe stores, a pet store, a shoe repair shop, a dollar store. There's four clothing stores, three selling women's clothes and one selling men's suits. A store that sells video games, a store that sells books, and a store that sells bath products. There are kiosks selling jewelry, scarves, music cd's, and watches.

At 1:50, I had purchased a Chicago Style hot dog and coffee from Hot Dog King, paid the young man behind the register, who was very pleased to have served me, and seemed equally pleased with his career choice, and had secured a corner table where I could table watch for Melanie Warring. Which could be a trick because I had not a clue what she looked like and probably thirty people had come through the food court in the short time I'd been here. The imperative trick now however, was how to eat without drizzling ketchup, mustard, and relish down the front of me. I was wearing my gray wool slacks, white shirt without a tie, and a blue jacket and I was determined to keep them all condiment free.

At 2:05, I noticed a woman who seemed to be looking around the food court. When her gaze fell on me, she hesitated, then came my way. I put the rest of my hot dog down and wiped my mouth with the napkin.

"Vic Pittaro?"

"Yes." I said. She was a tall good-looking woman with a lot of dark brown, shoulder length hair. A black leather purse hung from her shoulder on a strap. She had a somewhat square face, with a wide mouth, and full red lips. Her deep-set eyes were dark, her brows full and dark. She wore deep blue Capri's, a light blue sleeveless blouse, black flats, and except for a wedding band, no jewelry. And she appeared to take excellent care of herself.

I put my napkin down and motioned to the opposite chair. "Sorry to be eating like this. Can I get you something?"

"No," she said. "Thank you." She had a pleasant, confident voice. I liked her.

She looked down tentatively at the chair, then slipped her purse from her shoulder and sat, her gaze on me.

"Thank you for agreeing to meet me," I said.

She seemed uneasy. Furtive. She kept moving her hands, turning the ring on her finger.

"As I said on the phone, I'm a private investigator." I took out my wallet, slipped out my license and handed it to her. She took it, studied it, and handed it back. "In the course of my investigation I ---"

"The Manley Athletic Club," she blurted.

"Yes. The name keeps turning up but until now I could find no one who knew anything about it."

"I . . . tell me about your investigation, Mr. Pittaro."

"John Mann hired me to look into the murder of his wife," I said. "Mann is of Mann Brother's Construction in Bayfield."

"That would seem to be a police matter."

"It is. They have access to many more resources than I. However, they also have more distractions, and on a daily basis."

"You said you were with the Sheriff's Department?"

"Yes, but I'm not now," I said showing my best smile. "Being retired, I'm out of the loop, as they say."

We were quiet. I could feel her studying me as I looked around. "The only reason I contacted you, is I was told you might know something about this athletic club. I can find no public records of it. It must go under another name."

A vary fat, middle-aged man and a plump woman were eating Chinese food from Styrofoam plates two tables away. Three women sat at another table having drinks. Probably store clerks on break, taking advantage of the slow mid-afternoon.

"And you think it has something to do with the murder of this man's wife?"

"I don't know that it does. It's just something that keeps coming up that I haven't been able to learn anything about."

"My sister said you and she have a mutual friend. A man named---"Titus?"

"Yes."

"Your sister," I said. "Her name is Marcy."

She nodded.

"She talked with this man, Titus. He told her I should talk with you."

"Okay," I said, smiling encouragingly.

Finally she took a deep breath and leaned slightly forward. "I was gang raped at an event called the Manley Athletic Club."

I could feel her coldly studying my face. I'd spent a career trying to find the right response to a victim's anguished revelation. "I'm sorry to hear that." I said. "Have you gone to the police?"

"No," she said.

"Do you know who these men were?"

She was looking at a spot on the table and said nothing.

"You probably should report this. If you'd like, I could connect you with the right detective to talk with."

She shook her head. "No," she said.

"Did you go to the doctor?"

Again, the head shake.

"Okay." I waited. Two tables over, the fat man and the woman had finished their meals and sat in silent repose, each looking past the other. Nothing left to say.

Melanie Warring continued turning the ring on her finger, but now she was staring at something way off to my right and at a distance, something only she could see. Maybe I should try it.

Suddenly, something struck me. 'The Manley Athletic Club is not a place. It's an event.' "Ms. Warring, where was this event?"

She was back with me now. "At a private home."

"When was this?"

"May. This past May."

"Does your husband know?"

She shook her head.

"I don't mean to sound cold about this, but you seem to be a bright intelligent woman. If you didn't know your attackers, the authorities would have had a rape kit done, maybe identified them."

She sighed a deep breath as she seemed to have come to a decision. "Mr. Pittaro," she said. "I live in Maple Oaks. I have two children. A boy and a girl, both in middle school. My husband is an investment banker at a prominent Jefferson City Bank. I have an Internet business called 'Discreet Liaison'."

An edge had come into her voice. "An adult service business." She paused, watching me.

"I entertain clients during the day while my children and husband are away, but I never entertain at my home." Her dark eyes were hard on me. "I'm a prostitute, Mr. Pittaro. A whore."

She propped her purse upright on the table in front of her, and for an instant I thought she was going to leave. "Judge me if you must, but I was raped. Gang raped. A whore can be raped, Mr. Pittaro."

"Ms. Warring, I was with the Sheriff's department for thirty-two years. A detective for much of that time," I said. "I've investigated nearly every type of crime you can imagine. I've dealt with every type of criminal and every type of victim, and I've tried not to judge. Not an easy thing to do much of the time. Now I'm retired. I'm no longer in law enforcement, but I still try not to judge."

"I'm not that altruistic," she said, matter-of-factly. "Because there's more."

"Aha, okay?"

She got her cell from a small pocket on the side of her purse and opened it. Then, with her lips set in a tight line she worked the screen with a finger, stopped and seemed to study whatever she was looking at. When she looked up she said, "Now we'll see how altruistic you really are," and handed it to me.

The video that played across the screen featured a young boy performing oral sex on an obviously adult man. There were girls with men. There was a woman with a dark skinned boy. There was another woman with a young girl. The camera moved from one scene to the next, scanning the room, very deftly avoiding the faces of the adults. There seemed to be no limit to the inventiveness of the participants.

Melanie Warring was watching me when I looked up.

"Jesus," I said.

"That's the real reason I'm talking with you. Thirteen, fourteen fifteen year old children. In the same age group as Danielle and Rob. Maybe some were older."

She was serious now. Determination in her tone. I'd seen it before. She was relating something she abhorred. Rape, her rape, her gang rape didn't touch it.

She sat back, seeming relieved and looked at me.

It took me a moment, then I took a notebook out of my shirt pocket. "Where was this?"

She shook her head. "No." she said. "And put the notebook away."

I hesitated, then slipped it back into my pocket.

"I will tell you it was somewhere south of Bayfield," she said.

"You don't know or won't say?"

Silence.

"How did you get there?"

"A client."

There was a long silence while we just looked at each other. "You're not going to tell me anything else, are you?"

"I'll tell you this," she clutched her purse to her with one hand and fumbled for the strap with the other. "I hope something comes of our conversation, but I will not go to the authorities, I will not testify. If I'm ever asked, I don't know you. I've never talked to you, I've never met you." She stood. "And I can assure you, Mr. Pittaro. I'm a very convincing liar."

With that, she turned and I watched her walk away.

-39-

Jefferson City Art Institute
Saturday October 8th
78 degrees, Bright Sky

"I found this in my computer desk in my studio," Tamara said. It was Saturday afternoon and we had met at the Jefferson City Art Institute and were having lunch in Olivia's, the museum restaurant. She was dressed appropriately in a gray suit and a white silk blouse with a lace collar and a little blue bow at her throat. I was wearing boots, blue jeans, a white pull-over shirt and a fawn sport coat.

She took a 3x5 yellow envelope from her purse and handed it to me. Our waiter, Geoffrey was what the name pin on his white shirt said, had managed to take our food and drink order with only minor disdain showing on his face, which I'm sure was meant for me. Tamara had ordered tuna with a cranberry spread on sourdough with cream cheese and alfalfa sprouts. My selection, after perusing the nouvelle menu for a time, was the ham and cheese on pumpernickel.

"I thought it was strange these would be there," Tamara said. "Since Barbara must have put it there, I thought you should see them."

I straightened the metal clips, opened the envelope and turned it over dumping the contents on the table. "These were in this envelope?"

"Yes. I thought I should show them to you."

On the table, folded to fit inside the envelope, was a blank sheet of stationary with a 'Sunshine Consultants Inc.' letterhead and a business card that read 'RD Morris Surveyors' with a phone number.

Geoffrey came with our drinks. When he had left, Tamara said, "When our sandwiches come we could cut them in half and share."

She was looking at me smiling and I liked it very much, almost as much as I liked looking at her.

"We could," I said.

She was drinking raspberry iced tea. I took a sip of my coffee.

"But only if you promise never to tell anyone I ate a sandwich with sprouts on it."

She smiled again. "I promise," she said.

I studied the piece of stationary. "So why would she leave this with you?"

Tamara shook her head.

I turned the business card over. On the back of the card, written in ink, was another phone number.

I took out my cell phone and punched in the number on the back of the card. After six rings the recorder answered. I listened, then closed my phone and looked at Tamara. "This hair ball gets stranger and stranger," I said. "It's Whitfield's office."

"Jerry Whitfield?"

I nodded. "Not your typical ambulance chaser. Tell me about him. How did you come to hire him?"

"I ran into him one day at the Cookton County courthouse when I was doing my research. I knew him, of course, when he worked for Roger. We got to talking. I told him what I'd been doing, that I had found birth certificates listing a George Hobbs as a father. I had narrowed it down to two possibilities. And, if one of them proved to be my father, then I might have siblings. He was interested. We went to the cafeteria, and over lunch we talked about what I'd found."

Geoffrey brought our food, setting the tuna with cranberry spread and alfalfa sprouts ceremonially in front of Tamara and my ham and cheese, a bit crudely I thought, in front of me.

Tamara cut her tuna in halves diagonally and looked at me with a wry smile on her face. "Sure," I said, and cut my mine down the middle.

We ate our respective halves quietly, Tamara sipping her raspberry tea, I drank my coffee. It didn't take me long to realize the tuna with the cranberry spread was the better choice; Even with the sprouts, and I said so. She smiled her 'I told you so' grin, then said, "So, tell me about Melanie Warring."

I did.

When I was through she said, "Wow. So, the Manley Athletic Club is a bunch of adult children acting out their sex fantasies?"

Geoffrey had come by with a fresh glass of tea for Tamara and refreshed my coffee from a silver server. I sipped my coffee. It didn't need any ice to cool it. Tamara's tea had a slice of lime on the lip.

I nodded.

Tamara added a packet of sugar to her tea and stirred. "You think it was Janet and Robert's home?"

"I don't know. The background in the video didn't look familiar, but I was only there once.

She watched me carefully. After a moment she said, "You think it is. You think Barbara found out about it. You think that got her killed."

"I don't know."

"You're sure there's minors in the video?"

I shrugged. "Could ruin a political career. Could ruin many politico careers, depending on who the participants are."

"God. If it is Robert and Janet's home I'm sure John Mann doesn't know."

Geoffrey came and left the check in a black leather folder. I looked at it, put a twenty and a ten inside and we left.

We walked out of Olivia's and down the wide corridor, across the entrance hall, through the heavy glass doors and down the granite steps.

In the parking lot, we stood beside Tamara's car with our arms around each other. I was looking into her face, engulfed in her perfume and thinking how good this felt.

"Vic, I'm leaving Monday morning for San Francisco. I feel I need to spend some time with Sam and the baby."

There was a snap of something like regret in my center. I recovered quickly, I thought. She took a half step back and with a sensual smile touched her fingers to my cheek. "I'll be back a week from tomorrow, Love," she said. "Try not to get too lonesome."

"I'll fight it," I said. And we kissed.

As I watched her drive away, I realized how long a week could seem. I would miss the hell out of her.

-40-

Sunday Night
October 16th
68 degrees, Raining

I was in my office on a Sunday afternoon. I had the Sunday Herald scattered across my desk and was reading Doonesbury. Behind me through the window, the sky was a solid, dreary gray and it was raining. A long, steady rain. Long, in that it had been raining for three days, and steady in that it had rained without letting up for all that time. I was getting sick of it. Plus, I missed Tamara and I missed Nisha. She would be back this afternoon. And not only was Nisha gone to never return, but I had to tell Tamara tonight, and Kitty in the morning. I was depressed.

I could have been just as depressed at home, but here I had the pretense of a place of business even if it were a Sunday. I was supposed to be investigating a murder after all. At home all I could think about was how much I missed Tamara. At the moment however, it didn't seem like it mattered much where I was.

I opened the bottom right hand desk drawer and stared down at the bottle of Meyers Rum, then decided that it wouldn't help my mood any. I pushed away from my desk, got up and went to the coffee maker and refilled my cup and carried it to the window and stared out through the rain streaked glass. A nearly empty city bus swished down Division Street, its wipers beating hard against the rain. Across the street, Liggett Park was lush, green and sodden, and empty of the usual Sunday afternoon families.

I looked at my watch. 5:36. Tamara's plane would have landed by now. When I saw her off at the airport a week ago last Wednesday, she had insisted that I not be there to meet her. She'd take a cab home. That she'd be "too tired and cruddy from the flight," her words exactly, to have me pick her up, knowing as to where we would end up. She first had to soak in the tub and rest. She would call me. I had protested unsuccessfully, but she had kissed me long and sensually, stroked my hands then turned and with her travel bag trailing went through the glass doors.

It was raining harder now and had gotten darker. The street lights were on. Cars had their lights on. Debris flowed along the curb. I stood for a long time watching the rain through the opaque window. Across the street, a bare headed man in a trench coat with the collar turned up hurried toward the bus stop on the corner across Seventh Street.

I took a deep breath and let it out with a rush. I wish I could have just let Tesch handle it. The thought made me squeamish. Christ, I'd been a homicide detective for twenty years and never quit a case. What the hell's the matter with me? Besides, I'd promised.

My cell rang at 6:38. I flipped it open feeling miraculously relieved, but I didn't recognize the number, then I recognized the voice. "Kitty?"

Her voice was hushed, as though she was cupping her hand over her phone, but there was distress in her tone. "Yes, Mr. Pittaro," she said. "Mr. Ward just called me and asked me to meet him for breakfast in the morning."

"Are you at home?"

"Yes."

"He called you at home?"

"Yes. I don't know what to do. He kind of makes my skin crawl, you know."

"What did you tell him?"

"I told him no, and he needed to quit asking."

"That was the right thing to say, Kitty." My neck and shoulder muscles were suddenly tight. I nodded to myself. "Kitty," I said. "Come in as usual in the morning. I'll take care of Bob Ward." She said thank you, and hung up.

I closed my cell phone and it rang. "Tamara, you home?" It came out sounding more like a statement than a question.

"I just got home Vic. The cab just left. But---" Her voice was shaky. "I think my house has been broken into."

"Where are you?! Inside?!"

"No. At my back door. The glass is broken out."

I felt my heart slam in my chest. "Tamara. Don't go in. Call 911!"

"Vic ---"

"Don't go in, Tamara. I'll be there in less than ten minutes. Call the police!"

It's an eighteen minute drive from my place to Tamara's house. It took me nine minutes, three blown traffic lights and many ignored stop signs. I turned onto Tower. A squad sat at the curb, it's blue light flashing in the rain, it's spot trained on the house. I jammed the BMW against the curb and sprinted across the lawn as a city officer came from the house. He was talking into a mic clipped to his lapel. A siren whooped in the distance.

Cardinal Red

He put his hand up to stop me he as he spoke. I pushed passed him. "Hey! You can't ---"

I made it through the door and through the kitchen before the cop grabbed me by the coat, grabbed my right arm with his left and jammed me against the wall with his right forearm across my throat. "Asshole? I said you can't be in here!"

He must have read something in my face. He relaxed slightly. "You know her?"

I nodded as another uniform came through the kitchen. "Tamara Phillips," I managed. I held my free arm up. "I'm retired Sheriff's Deputy."

He relaxed the pressure on my throat a little more. "My ID's in my jacket pocket," I said. "Gun on my right hip."

We looked at each other, our faces inches apart. The other uniform, a big blond guy said, "I got him, Daniels."

Daniels released my right arm and stepped back. The big cop had his hand on the butt of his gun. "You stay right there. Don't you move."

Daniels pulled my gun, then got my wallet from my jacket pocket. He studied my license carefully, studied the photo, studied me. Then he handed my wallet back. I brought my hands down and took the wallet.

"I'll keep the gun for now," Daniels said. He turned to the blond cop and nodded to the left. "In there," he said. "I called for the EMT's but she's dead."

I felt my heart stop. I couldn't breathe. Tamara! I pushed away from the wall and bolted into the livingroom. Both cops yelled stop. I froze.

Tamara lie face down in the middle of the room. Her head slightly turned to the right, her right arm out straight over her head, left arm down to the side. The hair on the back of her head was wet with blood and blood pooled under her head and had soaked into the carpet.

Tamara! Jesus Christ! Jesus Christ! Jesus Christ! Jesus Christ! Jesus Christ! Jesus Christ! Jesus Christ! Jesus Christ!

I felt hot. It came to me I was speaking aloud.

-41-

Captain Craig Welch's
Office Monday am
October 17th

It was 9:30 am. We were in Captain Welch's office in the Berring Harbor Police Headquarters building on Oxford Street. Danny Khanh was sitting beside me. Steve Tesch was there, chewing on his dead cigar. Berring Harbor Homicide Detective, Paul Lutz was there, as well as a tall young city detective I didn't know.

We had gone over the ME report, and the preliminary CSI evidence summary, learning nothing that we didn't already know. Tamara had died of blunt force trauma. The weapon used was a figurine found beside the body.

"Our crime scene techs photographed and dusted everything and identified relevant prints." Welch sat behind his desk. I could feel Steve Tesch's eyes on me.

Paul Lutz got up from his chair and walked to the window. "Smudges on the weapon. Means the perp wore gloves," he said. "Nothing else except a partial shoe print in blood near the body. The techs are working on a shoe identification now."

Welch nodded. "Per Jerry Erskine's request, the Sheriff's Department will work with us on this. They'll have full access. Evidently, the victim---"

"Tamara Phillips," I said.

Craig Welch is a big man. Bald, with a fringe of gray and dark hair and a full white mustache. He wore a white shirt and a blue cotton tie. His blue suit jacket hung on the back of his chair. He had heavy jowls and a thick soft neck that folded over the collar of his shirt. He looked at me.

"Right," he said. "Evidently, Tamara Phillips is tied into the Mann investigation."

Tesch had dug a stickmatch from his pocket and had scratched it to life with his thumbnail. Welch stopped talking and glared at him. It was like two bull walruses challenging for authority.

"Sure." Tesch said, then shook the match out, and with jaw movement, shifted the blunt cigar to the other side of his mouth.

Lutz was standing behind Welch's desk looking out the window. I had known Lutz for years. He was a stocky man with steel gray eyes that sort of squinted out of his puffy round face at you in that policeman stare. He wore a gray suit with a white shirt and a blue knit tie. The suit looked a bit too big for him but wasn't, giving him an unkempt look. He was the head of the city homicide division and had been at it a long time. Probably the best homicide detective I've known.

"What I seen," the young detective said. "The scene suggests the victim interrupted a burglary. The bedroom drawers, closets, the computer desk in the studio, all looked to have been gone through. My experience, probably one individual looking for something small to sell. Neighborhood like that, middle class. Might find jewelry. Money. Small electronics."

Paul Lutz turned from the window and looked slowly at the tall detective. "Nobody saw anything, Wills." Lutz said. His voice was normal, but he seemed tight. "That time of day, somebody should have seen something. But we'll go back over the neighborhood today. If it was a burglary…"

"You don't sound like you think it was," Tesch said.

"Connection to the Mann investigation seems curious to me."

Craig Welch cut in. "We're not making any determination about anything until the techs are through and we've looked through everything. Then you'll hear it from me."

Lutz, still watching Steve Tesch, looked my way, then back to Tesch. "Or from me," he said. "I've got work to do. That's it for now."

***

We were walking down the front steps. "That was a fucking total waste of time," I said.

The Berring Harbor Police Headquarters building, a gray stone structure now called the Public Safety Building, was built in the mid-forties in the classic Public Building architecture that today would be considered old fashioned. The granite steps were curved in a concave arch with a stone landing between the steps and sidewalk.

"We knew it would be," Danny said. "The widow of an assassinated Monroe County Attorney, all the chiefs get involved."

The rain had stopped early, before daylight. I know when it had stopped because I hadn't been to sleep yet. The sky was the same dull gray it had been for the past four days, and the air was still and heavy with moisture. Pedestrian traffic moved in and out of the building in a steady stream. Lawyers, bail bondsmen, legal secretaries moving through their day, serious, but knowing the sky would brighten and the sun would show sooner or later.

Danny stopped at a black Detective sedan nosed in to the curb in front of a no parking sign. "You on the job?" I asked.

Across the street, a work crew had closed off the handicap ramp to the public library with an orange barricade and had gotten as far as busting up the concrete before loading their tools and leaving. A woman in blue spandex slacks struggled to get a baby stroller up the six granite steps to the library doors.

"Tesch's got me on that domestic that went bad. You in your office when I get off, I'll stop."

"Yeah. Where else would I be?"

Danny opened the door of the sedan and looked at me over the car roof. "I want you to know, I'm really sorry about Tamara. You alright?"

"No," I said. And I wasn't too sure I would ever be. We looked at each other for a long moment, then I turned and walked across the street to my car.

-42-

October 17th
69 degrees
Distant Dark Clouds

I was sitting at my desk playing with my new computer. I had my boots off, my tie off, my collar opened and was having a drink. Actually, I had finished two drinks and was working on my third. I had started when I first got back from Captain Welch's office, and before I called Tamara's daughter Samantha in San Francisco to find out her flight schedule.

The computer guy had come in a week ago, and set it up, transferred my files and explained how much easier and faster this one was over the old one. After he'd gone, I found solitaire. He was right, it was faster.

Though it was only mid-afternoon, the sky had begun to get darker and the rain had begun, again. I had won five games in a row when I heard the lobby door chime, and as I had ever since Barbara's murder, I startled, and my heart thumped an extra beat.

I looked up. Danny came through the door wearing a navy trench coat, and carrying a pizza. "4:30," I said, "And all's well in the city."

"Yeah," Danny said. "Drunk husband slashes his wife. She manages to escape, bleeding all over everything. She makes it to the car behind their apartment. He's hanging on the passenger side door. As she hits the street he loses his grip on the door and hits his head on the curb. She stops, backs over him and kills him. Misdemeanor homicide in my book. Tesch's got me chasing my tail all over it. Interviewing neighbors. Checking the wife out." He put the pizza on the desk, shrugged out of his coat and opened the box. "Pour me one of those," he said.

I pointed to the other glass on the filing cabinet. He got it, set it on the desk and opened the pizza while I poured his drink. I still had some in my glass.

"Glad you're here," I said. "A guy shouldn't drink alone. Might turn into a lush."

Cardinal Red

"That's why I'm here. Crime prevention." He picked up his glass. "By the way," Danny said. "And I don't want this to sound crass after Tamara's death, but I'm sorry about Nisha."

I nodded and clicked the solitaire game off and studied the top of my desk and listened to the rain and the occasional thunder. October thunder storms are rare but not uncommon. The rest of the world doesn't stop when yours crashes.

Danny had turned his chair, sat, put his feet on the corner of the desk and picked out a triangle slice of pizza. After a while he said, "I can't figure Tesch out. You'd think he'd find something more productive for me to do, for Christ's sake." He bit off the point and chewed. After he had swallowed he said, "Especially with these two sisters being murdered."

I drank some of my drink. It was going down too well. "Tamara didn't interrupt a random burglary," I said.

"No," Danny said. "But what? A hit?"

"That makes no sense. Waiting in her house for her to come home? I don't buy it."

"So, that leaves only one thing." He ate more of his pizza, pointed at me, then at the pizza.

I shook my head. I tipped my chair back, rested my elbows on the padded arms, laced my fingers together over my chest and sat and took some heavy breaths. "Someone was looking for something and Tamara interrupted him," I said.

Danny tipped his head to the side and pursed his lips. "Uh huh. Want to go look around?"

I thought about that. Paul Lutz and his people have traipsed all through the house, as well as the CSI people. Everything has been gone over by experts and so far nothing has turned up that would indicate anything other than a burglary. Maybe Crime Scene will come up with something before they're through.

I was staring beyond Danny, though the doorway, to where Julius Santos had stood when he shot Barbara Mann. The only sound was the murmur of afternoon traffic down the wet street and the occasional growl of a city bus. "I've been trying not to be a cop," I said. "Trying to put thirty-two years behind me and let Steve Tesch handle everything. Thought I could be something else. Maybe someday that will happen, but now it's personal. Maybe my hesitation to step on Tesch's toes got Tamara killed."

I got a yellow legal pad from my desk drawer and began to make a list, reading aloud each name as I wrote it. Barbara Mann. John Mann. Julius Santos. Bobby Rico. Jamie Adams. Robert Mann. Janet Mann.

"Barbara Mann knew or knew of each, with the exception of Santos, the shooter."

We were quiet for a while. Danny had another piece of pizza and finished his drink. I reached, splashed more rum into his glass and topped mine off. "Tamara Phillips," he said.

"No," I said, tapping the pencil on the desk. The thunder had stopped and the rain on the window seemed to be lighter. I took a deep breath, said "Okay," and wrote Tamara Phillips under Janet Mann.

Danny slouched in his chair, his feet back on the corner of my desk, his elbows on the wooden arms, his fingers steepled and pressed against his lips. "Now four of the eight are dead," he said.

I inhaled and said, "I'm going to tell you a story." And I told him about my meeting with Melanie Warring and the Manley Athletic Club.

"A sex video," Danny said. "You have all the fun."

Danny was quiet for a moment, and seemed to be staring at his feet. "This Warring woman on the up-and-up?"

"Yup."

Outside, the street lights had come on. We listened to a long, low rumble of thunder that seemed to roll across the sky much longer you'd think it should. "You think Barbara Mann found out about it and threatened to expose it?"

I shrugged.

"And you think this video was taken at Robert Mann's home."

"Don't know. Just a guess."

"And you think this is all connected."

"Yup. In a way we don't know yet."

"What else?"

"I don't like Robert Mann and his wife," I said. "They're both as phony as a three dollar bill, but ---"

"But?"

"Four people killed over a sex club? It could ruin a career or two, probably. But, I think there's something more."

I took the envelope Tamara had found from the belly drawer of my desk and dumped it on my desk. "Tamara found this envelope in her studio desk. Figured Barbara Mann left it there."

Danny looked at me, then sat up and unfolded the sheet of stationary. He picked up the business card. "Okay, say she did leave it at Tamara Phillips' home. To keep her husband from finding it?"

"I don't think that's it. Tamara said that she and Barbara Mann would sometimes talk for hours in her studio. Just suppose Barbara Mann, while this talking was going on, was sitting at the computer desk, as Tamara said she did. Suppose while sitting there she was using the computer, looking into this Sunshine Consultants, and RD Morris Surveyors and when she was done she just stuffed the business card and the sheet of stationary back in the envelope and put it in the desk."

"That's an awful lot of supposing."

Danny turned the business card over. "Phone number?"

I nodded. "I checked it. A lawyer named Jerry Whitfield. Connected to both Tamara and Barbara Mann."

I got my phone out and in a moment it was answered, "Detective Schnider."

"Tommy, it's Vic Pittaro."

"Lieutenant."

"Tommy, that Tamara Phillips murder on Tower Street, could you find out who the tech was?"

"Connie Haus is the lead on the Berring Harbor CSI team. Probably her, Lieutenant."

"She wouldn't by any chance owe you a favor, would she?"

Tommy Schnider laughed. "Everyone owes me favors, Lieutenant. Even you."

"I know. I wonder if you could find out if they took the victims PC from the house. If they didn't, and I get it to you, could you work your magic?"

"Sure, Lieutenant. Someday I'm going to collect all my IOU's and retire to the Bahamas"

I looked at Danny. "Thanks Tommy. I'll let Tesch know, but if you don't mind, I'm going to hold off informing him until I find out if it means anything."

I set my phone on the desk and swiveled my chair around toward the window. It was dark in the way it gets when heavy clouds cover the evening sky. Sort of a mystic darkness. I could still see the rain in the streetlight, and I think the thunder has stopped, though I couldn't be sure with the buzzing in my ears.

I turned to Danny. "I think I'm going to go to Tamara's house in the morning and look around. You think you can get hold of that murder book again on Barbara Mann? I'd like to see e-mail and cell phone records."

After Danny left, I found the business card I wanted in my wallet and punched in the number. A woman's voice answered. "Detective Hernandes."

"Detective, this is Vic Pittaro."

"Ah, yes. The private dick from, wherever. How's that ass-hole buddy of yours."

I felt she was smiling, or maybe it was just hope. "He was fine the last time I saw him."

"I guess I shouldn't be so hard on him. Actually, we parted quite amiably."

I think I was getting the picture. "Detective," I said. "I'm looking for more on Bobby Rico, and I was wondering if you could put me in touch with someone in LAPD's Organized Crime Unit? Maybe a Captain Weismann?"

"Weismann's head of OCU. Let me make a call, I'll have someone get back to you. Where are you staying?"

"I'm not in LA. I'm in my office."

"Oh. Too bad for me. I thought, for all the help you were getting from me, you might buy me lunch."

"Too bad for me. It'll have to be the next time I'm in LA. Here's my number."

"I got it right here. I'll have someone call."

-43-

Tuesday Morning
October 18th
Sky Clear, 70 degrees

It was 7:15 in the morning. I was sitting in my car in Tamara's driveway, in front of the garage. The rain had stopped sometime after midnight. It was already seventy degrees, the sky was a crisp blue, and the sun was beaming its drying rays down on the sopping wet city. I got Tamara's hidden key from under the eve over the back door and went in. I'd been in this same scene, where a murder had taken place, probably a hundred times over the years, but this didn't feel like any of the others. It was more like Mo's wake. Where part of me didn't want to accept what was happening. I stood in the kitchen where Tamara had told me about discovering her father's grave, years after he'd left the family, and about discovering Barbara Mann, her half-sister. Where our first intimate conversation had taken place.

Just through the archway into the living room, the pool of blood had dried a fetid brown. This was going to be tough. I put my cop heart in place, steeled myself, and walked slowly around the living room. The sculpture of the headless man, the murder weapon, had been taken into evidence. I went painstakingly through the studio, and bedroom where we had made love. I saw where someone had rummaged through the dressers and closet. If whoever had killed Tamara had been looking for something, it wasn't something that Barbara or Tamara had hidden. It would have been something that had just been put somewhere. I spent the next hour going through the house. I stopped at the front foyer where I'd embarrassed myself with that kiss, and thought about all that had happened afterwards. I felt the wall slipping. It was too close.

I went outside. I walked around the yard scanning the lawn, the driveway. I circled the house looking at the ground, the windows. Had the intruder checked out the house? Looked in the windows? Made sure no one was home? I walked around the garage. In the still wet grass at the corner of the garage was a cigarette butt. From here I could see the back door, the deck, and in the kitchen through the patio windows. I went in the kitchen, found a plastic storage bag, and went back out. I squatted down. Some of the grass had been bent and hadn't straightened yet, as though someone had stood on this spot. I reversed the plastic bag, picked the sodden cigarette butt up, reversed the bag again and zipped it closed. No way to tell how long it had been here. Picking it up had pretty much disintegrated it. I went carefully over the rest of the area and found nothing more.

I stopped for lunch at a chain burger joint and got a double cheese- burger, fries and a coffee and ate in the parking lot. In the past, I would have also gotten a plain double and given it to Nisha. I felt suddenly sullen, and shook it off.

It was 2:15pm when I got to the Rosewood shopping center, a strip mall on Central Avenue in Banning Hills, an older suburb on the east side of Jefferson City. The mall was built in the early seventies, and it shows it's age. On one end, in what I once knew to be a Walgreen's is now a consignment store. I was hoping for the Walgreen's as my lunch was now sitting like a mud brick in the bottom of my stomach.

On the other end of the mall is Rosewood Liquor, the only store left of the originals. Between the two are a used book store, a coin laundry, a thrift store, a real-estate office, and numerous empty store fronts. I drove through the nearly empty parking lot.

On the south end, between the thrift store and the coin laundry, I found 6427 Central Avenue. The sign on the plate-glass window beside the door said 'Sunshine Consultants' in small, gold letters. I parked, got my beige sport jacket from the back seat, put it on and locked my car.

The room was sparse and small, even for an office. Two straight backed chairs sat against one wall, a heavy oak desk with a black desk phone with several buttons, a file cabinet against the back wall, and a door next to the file cabinet.

The woman behind the desk was forty-five, maybe forty-eight. She had a large, round, fleshy, full featured face and long dark wavy hair with a lot of gray showing. Her eyes were large and set wide beneath thick dark eyebrows, and she sported a faint but discernible mustache. There was a large, colorful knit bag on the floor beside the desk.

She was reading a magazine when I came through the door. "Can I help you?" she said in a tone that said she probably couldn't and wouldn't if she could.

I smiled my best smile and said, "I heard Andrew Jefferies, my brother-in-law from my first marriage, that was years ago now, had a consulting business around here. I was going to the liquor store next door and saw the sign on the window and got to wondering. This isn't his shop is it?"

"Never heard of anybody by that name, sorry."

"Who's shop is it? Maybe my brother-in-law's got a partner."

"I would know if there was, sir."

I nodded at the door next to the filing cabinet. "Is the owner in?"

"That's the broom closet, sir. There's know one here but me. I'm sorry sir, but I can't help you."

I smiled a contrite smile and said, "I'm sorry to have bothered you Ma'am," just as the phone rang. I turned toward the door as she punched the flashing button on the phone and answered, "RD Morris Surveyors." I opened the door, hesitated for only a second and heard her say, "I can take a message, sir. That's all I can do."

I walked to my car thinking, 'Vic Pittaro has left the building.'

-44-

October 18th
3:10 pm

I was meeting Danny at 4:00. I had a few minutes. I stopped at my office to check with Kitty. I wanted to hear from the LA OCU as soon as possible. When I walked in, Kitty handed me a message. A Detective Randall had called and left a callback number. I took the message, went into my office and called him. I guess I did owe Detective Hernandes lunch.

As I was leaving the parking lot Bob Ward came out the front doors and was walking across the lot. I stopped behind his Silver Nissan and rolled my passenger side window down. "Get in and sit, Bob."

"Hey, how they hanging old man?" Ward bent down, his arms folded over the window opening.

"Just get in, Bob."

"Ahh. Yeah, sure, Vic."

Ward pulled the door open, and got in."

"What's going on?"

"Close the door, Bob."

"Sure, Vic. What's up?"

I made a right out of the parking lot, turned left on Seventh and went down toward the river. "Got something I want to talk to you about."

"Sure, Vic. Anything I can do. You know that."

I turned left on River Road, swung into the first turnout, stopped, and turned off the ignition. I looked at Bob Ward. "Let's take a walk."

We got out. On the right was a path that led down through the trees to an overlook along the Temperance River. I locked the car and started down the path. Ward followed me. The overlook is a deck, about 8'x10', set in the side of the hill and made of heavy rough-hewn timbers weathered an ash gray. There's a waist high railing around three sides that looks over the river.

I leaned my forearms on the front railing and stared out across the river. The Temperance River, at this point, is about thirty yards across. A scattering of brown leaves flowed along the surface. I could smell the river. It was a smell I liked. About ten yards out, water eddied around a deadhead buried in the soft bottom. Ward stood beside me on my left.

"A great place to think, huh Vic? Contemplate life, so to speak?"

I turned to face him. "Yes, it is. And I'm going to tell you something." I felt my chest, and throat tighten. I closed one hand above his right elbow, my other hand round his right wrist, and squeezed.

"Wah--- Wah---?"

I tightened my grip. "I've had a lousy week so far, so don't piss me off."

"Ahhh hey." He looked at me then tried to pull his arm free and couldn't.

"Are you aware that Kitty Hynen is seventeen years old?"

His face flushed suddenly and there was fear in his eyes. "I--- I never- - - I--"

"Are you?" I twisted his wrist.

Pain flashed across his face. He tried to smile. He opened his mouth to speak, then closed it. Beads of sweat showed on his forehead. He swallowed and tried to pull loose, again.

"Answer my question."

We stood staring at each other. "Fuck you," he said. But it was a weak defiance.

I put pressure on his elbow and gave his wrist a sharp twist. "If you ever bother Kitty or any other young woman again," I formed each word very carefully. "And I find out about it," I said the words slow and concise. "I promise you I will break your motherfucking arms."

He glared at me. His face was red now, his eyes wide. "Hey! You can't---"

"And while you're at the hospital getting those shattered bones set, I will be at the county attorney's office filing charges against you for the sexual assault of a minor."

"Ahh, you're crazy! I didn't do nothing! You can't---"

I twisted him around and shoved his wrist hard enough up between his shoulder blades to get a scream out of him.

"I can, and I will." I shoved, and let him go. He stumbled forward several steps into the railing, and turned to face me, cupping his elbow with his left hand. Sweat streamed down his face.

"Fuck you." He said.

"If you think I won't--- I turned and started up the path. "You heard me," I said.

"You leaving me here?"

I stopped and turned to face him. "Great place to think," I said. "And to contemplate your life."

-45-

Tuesday Afternoon
October 18th
71 degrees

I was standing on the pier. This is the time of year when the weather can change quickly. Most of the slips were empty. The boats had been pulled, wrapped in blue shrink-wrap, and stored on wooden cradles throughout the fenced in boat yard beyond me.

I watched a ski-boat come off the river into the boat basin trailing a prohibited wake. The pilot was Mr. Midwestern Beefcake, big and broad with a mahogany tan. The squealing laughter of the two girls sitting on the transom wrapped in terry beach covers carried over the blurb of the black 190.

I heard a car door close behind me and Danny came down the ramp onto the pier. "Walk up to my car with me," he said. "I've got something for you."

"The case file on Barbara Mann."

"A complete copy. And the financial audit of Mann Brother's Construction. Oh, and Tommy Schnider said he'll have the computer dump from Tamara's computer for you later today."

"A copy? How did you manage that?"

Danny stopped with his hand on the car door handle. "I didn't. It was all on my desk when I came in this morning."

I looked at him. Danny threw up his hands and shrugged, then opened the door and handed me a manila envelope held closed with a string turned around an orange button. "And," he said, "Steve Tesch is in one ugly, foul mood."

"Fair trade," I said. And handed him the plastic bag with the remains of the cigarette butt inside. "See what you can come up with on this? I found it on the ground, on the corner of Tamara's garage."

Danny looked in the bag. "Not much left of it."

"Nope," I said.

When I got back to the office, Kitty had gone for the day. I spent the next several hours going through the copied file. There were the responding officer's reports. Tesch's initial report. Detective reports, and their notes. Interviews of John Mann, Robert and Janet Mann. Interviews of everyone in her address/phone book, including her hair dresser. Cell phone records. Copies of e-mails and URL sites off of her computer. The autopsy report, preliminary, and final CSI reports including photos of the scene in my office. Nothing seemed to strike me. When I got to the end I got up and stared out the window. It was getting dark outside. The traffic was sporadic, the streetlights were already on. I stood watching the evening settle over the city thinking it would soon be as dark as my mood. It seemed appropriate. After awhile, when I felt I was as morose as I was going to get, I went back to my desk and started the file over at the beginning. The second time through, I still hadn't found a clue.

Tommy dropped off the download he'd gotten from Tamara's computer. I went through that line by line. Nothing stood out. It was dark outside now, and I was getting hungry. I looked at my watch. It was 8:30. I put on my windbreaker, locked my office and walked west down Division and got to Abe's Deli as he was preparing to close. I bought a sandwich with Genoa, provolone, a slice of sweet onion, a large coffee from Abe, and walked back to my office.

I ate my sandwich as I flipped through the financial audit to Tommy's summary on the back page. Mann Brother's Construction, after a rough previous year was sound. The liquidity and cash flow were sufficient to meet current expenses. Though collectibles need more aggressive monitoring. On the whole, Mann Brother's Construction was a mildly profitable Limited Liability Company. It was signed by, T. Schnider.

I went through the murder book on Barbara Mann, again. I went through the print-out Tommy had gotten off Tamara's computer, again. Now I was back to the financial report. I went through it line by line, not knowing what I was even looking at or for. It was then that I found it. Checks made out to RD Morris Surveyors and Sunshine Consultants on the fifth of March for thirty-thousand dollars and twenty thousand dollars respectively, and continuing through the current date. The only change, being the dollar amounts rotated. Fifty thousand a month to a mail drop. It had all the marks of money laundering. And that could mean only one person in this muddled up mess. Bobby Rico. There was something else, but I couldn't get what it was. I went back through Barbara Mann's phone and cell-phone records and began making a list. "Bingo." Three cell-phone calls the last week of June to a number I recognized. Jerry Whitfield's office. And two more in August. The clues were coming like a snow storm. I got my phone out and called Danny Khanh, then went home.

-46-

October 19th
Wednesday am
68 degrees, Overcast
Rain Forecasted

I met Danny at 9am, in a parking lot in a small strip mall along State Highway 29. He had brought two paper cups of coffee and was eating a scone when I opened the passenger door and got in. He handed the bag over as I closed the door. In the bag was another. I got my coffee and the scone out. It was cranberry. I balanced it on my knee, then lifted the plastic cover over the drink spout and sipped. I took a bite of the scone and another sip of coffee. "What's yours?"

"Blueberry," Danny said.

I nodded and ate some more of mine.

Danny finished the last of his scone and swallowed some coffee. "Tommy Schnider said there wasn't much that could be done with that cigarette butt. Too deteriorated. He said sometimes with a filter cigarette, if the smoker was in the habit of leaving it in their mouth instead of taking it out after inhaling, they might find some usable DNA in the filter."

"Yeah, I know," I said.

"He sent it along to the State Lab. He did say it's what's called a 'cottage cigarette'. Made with untreated, organic tobacco. You come up with anything?"

I told him about my conversation with Detective Randall and my trip to Banning Hills.

"So," Danny said. "According to Los Angeles OCU this Rico has interest in two Vegas casinos plus this Sunshine Entertainment thing in LA. So, what's that mean to us?"

"It means he's fairly big time with a substantial cash flow," I said.

"You're thinking this RD Morris Surveyors, and Sunshine Consultants may be a front for money laundering."

"Maybe," I said. "I'd like you to see if the Secretary of State's office has anything on either RD

Cardinal Red

Morris Surveyors or Sunshine Consultants. Incorporation papers. Tax papers. Any official business has to be registered with the Secretary of State. Be interesting to know who the officers are, if there are any. Also be interesting to know who signed the office lease."

"The lease will be easy," Danny said. "What's the address?"

I gave it to him. He got his cell-phone from his jacket and in a moment a woman's voice came over the speaker. "City Wide Realty. This is Jen, can I help you?"

"Jen," Danny said. "Is Sherry in yet?"

"Not yet, Danny."

"When she comes in, have her call me, Jen. Thanks."

He slipped his phone back in his jacket.

I nodded my head and opened the door. "Let me know. Right now I'm going to go back to my office to think."

Kitty was at her desk when I walked in. Bob Ward's door was closed. "Bob in this morning, Kitty?"

"Yes, he is," Kitty said. "I said good morning when he came in. He didn't even look at me. Went right into his office."

I nodded with a slight smile and gave her the okay sign. Her eyes widened, then she smiled. "Thank you," she said.

I closed my door, hung my jacket on the coat tree, got my coffee mug and poured my second cup of the day. I went to the window, raised it and blocked it up with Webster's New Collegiate Dictionary. There was still a faint smell of bleach from the cleaning company.

I had a sense this hairball would come undone if I could just get hold of one end and pull. There had to be more to it than a sex club and Rico seemed to be at the center. Rico, women, Las Vegas, money, gambling, money laundering. Tesch's hesitation in his investigation. Why? And the copy of Barbara Mann's case file? Tesch must have left it on Danny's desk. Why?

I refreshed my coffee, sat at my desk and wrote out all I knew. It wasn't much. Basically, it was a list of names.

Then I wrote out what I didn't know but suspected. Rico's interest? The only thing that makes sense, laundering mob money.

I thought about that for a while.

And what about Barbara Mann's phone calls to Whitfield's office? He said he had never met her in person. I thought about that.

Whitfield said he'd left after Roger Phillips' death and moved west. L.A.? Was there a connection to Rico and Adams? I thought about that some.

Maybe I should go ask him. It didn't seem like I was learning much sitting here.

-47-

Wednesday
October 19th
68 degrees
Rain

I parked in front of the Tae Kwon Do Center, locked my car and crossed the street. Jerry Whitfield was at his desk talking on the phone when I went in. He looked up, gave me a two finger wave and mouthed 'two minutes.'

I was wearing my leather car-coat, denim jeans, and my black zip-up-the-side boots. I looked out the front windows while I waited. Across the street, a

FedEx truck stopped in front of the barber shop next to the Tae Kwon Do Center. The driver got out with a package in his hands and went into the barber shop.

"I'll get the paperwork together," Whitfield was saying, "and get it to you in the morning." He had the phone on his shoulder and tucked against his cheek while he was writing on a yellow legal pad. "Right. In the morning," he said into the phone and hung up.

"Vic Pittaro," he said and came around his desk. He was wearing olive cargo pants, a blue pull over, and leather sandals with no socks. He put out his hand.

"We need to talk," I said

He looked startled. "Sure, well --- He went back around his desk. "Sit," he said, indicating a chair against the wall.

I pulled a chair around and sat facing him across his desk. "'While back, when we had breakfast, you indicated that you never had contact with Barbara Mann. Now, according to her phone records, she made three calls to you the last of June, and two more, August 22nd and 23rd, one week before she was murdered. I want to know about those calls."

He rocked back in his chair, folded his hands across his chest. He seemed to be looking by me, out through the window. Finally he said, "Unfortunately that's attorney client privilege."

Cardinal Red 359

"Your client is dead," I said. "That negates any privilege."

Whitfield looked at me for a bit, which made me wonder what he didn't want to say. Finally, "If I said it was personal, would you believe it?"

"No," I said. I took a deep breath. "Okay, let's try this. You told me you had never heard of Jamie Adams or Bobby Rico, now I find out you're listed as the lessee on a store front office at 6427 Central Avenue in Banning Hills, whose occupants are two phony business' called Sunshine Consultants Inc. and RD Morris Surveyors. What I can't prove yet, is that you leased this office space at the behest of Bobby Rico and/or the deceased Jamie Adams."

A look of fright passed briefly across Whitfield's face before he could recover, but it stayed in his eyes as he tried to think of a response. "Well." He said, finally. "Then I guess I have nothing to say."

"Then I guess I have no alternative but to pass this information on to the Sherriff's Investigators." Which was bullshit, but he didn't have to know that.

Whitfield shrugged. "Then I guess we're through."

I watched him for a moment, nodded, and got up and walked to the door. I put my hand on the door, stopped and turned to Whitfield. "One more thing," I said. "Manley Athletic Club? Heard of it?"

He shook his head. "Nope."

I nodded and left. Old Main Street had a sudden burst of traffic, and the rain had started. I stood at the curb until the traffic cleared then crossed to my car, where I sat watching Jerry Whitfield's office wondering what just happened. It seemed that things were not as they seemed. Phone calls from Barbara Mann to Whitfield were a small thing. What it told me is if the Sheriff's investigators noticed it, and I couldn't imagine they missed it, they hadn't followed it up. What shook Westfield up was connecting him to Adams, and Rico.

So now what. The lab had the cigarette butt, which was a long shot for DNA. But that wouldn't tell what someone might have been looking for. And maybe it was a random burglary, and Tamara happened to walk into it. I told her not to go in, damn-it. No, I can't go with that. Everything is too interconnected. And why hadn't Tesch picked up on those phone calls to Whitfield?

As I was contemplating all this, a dark blue suburban came out of the narrow alley between Whitfield's office and B's Breakfast Grill. It turned right, and went by me with Jerry Whitfield at the wheel. He might be going to visit a client, or going home for dinner, or just an afternoon quickie and a nap. But, now I had something to do.

I watched my rearview mirror and when the suburban got to the end of the block I turned the wipers on, did a u-turn and I was behind him. He had assumed I'd left. "Jerry, Jerry, Jerry," I said, aloud. Never assume. The word itself says it all. To ass-u-me will make an ass-out-of-u-and me. Or at least, one of us.

It's easy to tail someone when they've no reason to think they'd be followed. We went south out of Berring Harbor over the Temperance River Bridge. The rain was coming hard now and most cars had their lights on. I turned the defroster on low to keep the windshield from fogging up. When we turned onto State Highway 29 and headed south-west I had an inkling where we were headed. By the time we went through Bayfield I was pretty sure. When we went through Sweet Water Trace I backed off a little. The wind had picked up a bit and water had begun collecting in low spots in the road. I no longer need to keep him in sight anyway. I knew where he was going.

When I got to Robert Mann's home the rain had slacked a little. I went up the red brick driveway and parked beside the blue suburban. There was a silver Audi sitting in front of the closed garage door closest to the walk. I got out and went up the fieldstone walk. I tried the door, it was open. I pushed slowly, and from somewhere inside came loud angry voices. I stepped into the foyer and eased the door shut behind me. There were, at least, two male voices and a female voice that was more a throaty screech. I knew that to be Janet Mann. I took several steps into the hall and stepped back against the oak staircase. They were in the living room, and shouting was getting louder. "You son-of-a-bitch," Janet Mann, rasped. "You've been bleeding us, and now you've the balls to come asking me for more money?!"

I moved past the oak stairway and into the hall keeping my back pressed against the wall. I could see Janet Mann, she had her back to me. Whitfield was facing her but turned slightly as if he was watching to his left. Behind him, rain streaked the French doors, and through the blurred glass I could see the green umbrella twisting in the wind. I couldn't see Robert Mann.

"You don't understand." It was Whitfield. "I have to leave. Pittaro came to see me. He knows about the sex parties."

"So he knows you're a chicken fucker. So what?!" Janet Mann, shouted.

"He knows about the connection to Rico and Adams. "They'll find out I was the one that hired Santos." Whitfield's speech was fast with fear. "They'll dump my cell phone records and find calls to your husband, and Adams, and Bobby Rico in Los Angeles and calls to Detroit."

"They'll find out about our deal with Rico," That was Robert Mann voice. "And the money." I couldn't see him, but I could hear the panic in his voice. "What are we going to do?" He would be on the right. What was there, I couldn't remember.

"What money!" Whitfield shouted. "What about money?!"

"Jesus Christ, Janet." Robert was becoming unstrung. "What the hell are we going to do?"

"I'll fix this," Janet snarled. She disappeared from my view. I looked around. Caught. Nowhere for me to go. I stepped into the open, heard a door slam, and stepped back against the wall. In a moment she was back.

"You ball-less pervert," she squawked. Then I saw the gun. I pulled my gun, held it down against my leg and stepped into the doorway as she fired. Whitfield stumbled, she saw me and wheeled bringing her gun around, her lips pulled back, snarling, her face twisted up like an iguana. I dropped, rolled right and fired as she shot. She staggered backward, I shot again, and again, until she went down against the coffee table, slumped over on her side and was still. I came up in a crouch. Robert Mann had scrunched down behind the leather sofa. "Stand up, Mann!"

He stood slowly and was backing away, one hand in the air, palm forward. His other hand shielding his face. "Don't shoot! Don't- - - Don't shoot!"

It was then I felt the pain in my left shoulder. "Face down, on the floor! Lace your hands behind your head!"

He dropped and linked his fingers on the back of his head. My heart sounded like a bass drum in my chest. The smell of cordite was strong. I was breathing normally but my breaths were deep.

I heard a moan. I shifted my gun to my left hand and watching Mann, went to Whitfield, knelt down and held my fingers against his throat. There was a pulse and blood on his left side. I dug my cell out, stood and called 911.

I felt drained. My left arm was beginning to burn, but I could still move it. I shifted my gun back to my right hand and with it down against my leg I went to Janet Mann and looked down at her, slumped over on her side. Robert Mann, his face against the carpet, was whimpering softly. I was too pumped to feel much pain. I put my gun back in my holster. A pack of cigarettes lay on the carpet between the coffee table and the sofa, where it had landed when Janet Mann fell against the table. On the pack was an image of an Indian in a headdress. I looked at Mann. The whimper had evolved into a low moan. "These your cigarettes?"

He moved his head without lifting it from the carpet. I said louder, "These your cigarettes?"

His voice was nearly a whisper. "I --- I don't smoke," he said.

I looked down at Janet Mann. "Jesus Christ," I said.

-48-

Los Angeles, California
Six Months Later

Though the sky was clear, and the snow covered mountain peaks were clearly visible, the air pockets and currents over the mountains had been unusually severe. So much so that the pilot had turned on the seat-belt light soon after we had flown over North Platte, Nebraska, and it was still on. Below us were the San Gabriel Mountains. The last time I saw these mountains, Tamara was seated beside me.

There's still a lot of anger in me, and I wonder how long it will stay? Maybe always. Tamara had been good for me, I now realize. Her life had been filled with her passions; her sculpting, her painting, and she let me into it. I'm thankful for that, and I have to admit to being in love with her.

She'd said, I remember, that she could see me living in Los Angeles. Maybe she was right. She was right about so many things. I'll have to go back for Mann's trial, and Whitfield's trial, but right now, I'm not looking forward to it. Like Mo, Tamara too was wise. "It wasn't knowing what one wanted to be in life that was important," she had said. "But knowing what one didn't want to be." Right now I didn't know what I wanted to do with the third act of my life, but I sure knew what I didn't want to do.

We banked hard right and then left and in minutes we were on the ground skimming down the concrete runway. Twenty minutes later I was standing at the luggage carousel when I heard my name. I turned and my ride had arrived, as she had promised. She held out her hand, and I took it.

"Vic Pittaro, how good of you to come all this way just to take me to dinner, even though you did owe me."

"That I did, Detective."

"Juanita, Vic."

I let myself smile, "Yes. Juanita," I said.

In another twenty minutes we were heading north on La Brea in Juanita's black Jaguar.

Cardinal Red

"So tell me about the case. You mentioned when you called that it was closed."

I told her. I told her that Robert Mann's trial was set for the first of May and that I'd have to be there to testify. That he confessed to his part in the Adams killing, though his story is that Janet, who was a sociopath, did the actual shooting. And that I imagined it true. That Jerry Whitfield and the Mann's were worried that Barbara Mann had discovered the money laundering scheme and the sex club involving Bobby Rico, and that Rico had steered Whitfield to a contact in Detroit. As of now several politicians and a Monroe County Circuit Court judge had resigned after their names were connected to the Manley Athletic Club, including Sheriff Jerry Erskine, and as of last week, Steve Tesch was now acting Sheriff until the fall elections, and I don't doubt will run for the office. I told her the worst part. About Tamara. That Janet Mann had killed Tamara when she walked in on her as she was searching the house looking for something that never was.

I told her that Janet Mann had shot me, the bullet grazing my left shoulder, and that I had killed her. And I told her that I had no clue what I wanted to do, or be, for the third act of my life. I only knew what I didn't want to do, or be. That like Mo had said, be open to the universe.

"Sounds like a plan to me," Detective Juanita Hernandes said.

The End